Ruby Ledger and the Assassination of Abraham Lincoln

Ari Skolnick

Contents

Unrecognizable Language and Inventions from the 1800

Language:

Gibface: an ugly person

Fussock: pudgy or stupid person

Cherry: Rude way of saying a woman

Vazey: stupid

Unlicked cub: a rude, uncouth young person

Flummox: a failure

Chump: a foolish or gullible person

Sweetie: first used in 1778

Gollumpous: someone who is clumsy

Blunderbus: a blundering and stupid fellow

Whoopee: an exclamation of enjoyment

Salty tone: mid-fifteenth century

Lo and behold: it can be found as early as the early 18th century

Don't count your eggs before they hatch: saying can be found as early as 1570

Cheating: first used in the 1630s

Boop on the nose: invented 3000 years ago because of cats in Egypt.

Cholesterol: discovered in 1769

Malaria: Before 1880, was known as Roman fever.

Typhoid: Before 1880, was known as enteric fever

Objects:

Doorbells: invented in 1831 and sounded like a fire alarm

Fire alarm: first created in 1852, it was a box with a telegraphic key and handle

Automobiles: the steam-powered car was invented by Nicolas Cugnot in 1769

Screwdrivers: Invented in the late 15th century

Whisks: Invented before 1850

Orange squeezer: invented in 1860

Jigsaw puzzle: invented in 1767

Lounge suit: first invented in Scotland in the 1850s-1860s

White House: built-in 1792

Clowns: first came around 2400 BC in the fifth dynasty of Egypt

Toothpaste: invented in 1824

Syrup: invented in 1609

Licorice invented in the mid-1800s

Shoe laces: invented in 1780

Prison: First invented in 1000 BC, but wasn't introduced to the United States until 1785

The Ugly Duckling: Published on November 11, 1843

Sandwiches: invented in 1762

Watches: 17th century

Metal boxes: invented in the early 1800s - 1850s

Alarm clock: invented in 1787

Paper flyers: invented between the 14th and 17th century

Pens: invented in May 1827

Bunkbeds: invented in the 16th century

Word for cafeteria: invented in the mid-1800's

Momentum: Discovered in 530 AD

Ice cream: invented in 1686 (They mostly had fruity ice
creams)

Neapolitan ice cream: invented by Louis Ferdinand
Jungius in 1839

Doughnuts: invented mid-19th century in 1847

Cow catchers: invented in 1838

Ninja: most commonly found in the 16th century, but
found as early as the 12th century.

Megaphone: invented around 1655, but the name
wasn't invented until 1878

Grades: invented in 1785

Ball gown masks: started in the 14th century

Three Little Pigs story: First published in 1840, but is believed to be much older.

Cream: invented in 9th century AD

Vaccines: invented in 1796

Dishwasher: invented in 1850

Microscope: invented in 1590

Gambling: invented in 3000 BCE

Apple cider: invented in 55 B.C.

Dice: invented in 600 B.C.E.

Jacks game: invented in 1190 B.C.

Rubber ducks: invented in the mid to late 1800s

Siren: invented in 1819

Binoculars: invented in 1823

Yoyo: can be found as early as 400 - 500 B.C.

Buttons: invented in the 14th century.

Lipstick: can be found as early as 3500 in Mesopotamia.

Grenades: invented in 1536

Birth certificate: In the United Kingdom, they were first officially issued in the early 1850s

Newspaper: 59 BCE

Stopwatch: first invented in 1695, then improved in 1776, and officially improved in 1816

Lighter fluid: invented in 1823

Playing cards: invented in the 1370s

Bombs: invented in 1221

French Fries: invented in 1775

Octagonal 50-dollar gold slugs: These were $50 gold coins that were shaped like an octagon which were used as currency before the paper bill was invented

Magnets: invented approximately 2500 years ago

Batteries: invented in 1800

Forge welding: first began around 1800 BC

First electric motor: invented in 1834

First electric circuit: invented in 1800

Iridescent paint goes back as far as the 9th century

Paint: can be found as early as 100,000 years ago

Mythology:

Vampires: discovered in the early 18th century

Unicorn: first created in the fourth century B.C.

Banshee: The first stories of them go back to the 8th century

Typhon: A mythical creature from Greek culture that was a mix of Medusa, a dragon that had a hundred legs that ruled the world.

CHAPTER ONE

My Journey Begins

Time is running out! It is 8:58 in the morning; we only have a few minutes before Mr. Lincoln is assassinated. We all took in a lungful of air as we pushed through the crowd of giants and began to look for the perpetrator with our silver shaky detectors. We only have ten minutes to find them. We head upstairs toward the right end of the balcony. That's when the first announcer said, "Ladies and gentlemen, please rise for the early morning announcements."

"Our republic of people is..."

I can practically hear the ticks of the clock counting down; we only had a matter of minutes My miniature body began to quiver because it was already nine o'clock; there were only eight minutes before his death. Mr. Lincoln launches into his speech.

I was suspiring repeatedly as if I had just run up a mountain trying to grasp puffs of air. As I look up again, I see the assassin. I veer myself towards Willie and Lulu and whisper, "Go get the police and meet me in the front. I'll get the assassinator."

I trudge right behind the perpetrator, squirming through the tight pathway between each person, unraveling my silver shaky detector from the pocket I had sewn into my dress, and shook it behind them. Yes, it works; I found them!

I hastily stuck my little shaky hand into my pocket, felt around the silky cloth, and acquired my pen. Then, I wrap my arms around the perpetrator's waist because that is how I could reach while saying, "Доброе утро! Как вы? Я таквзволнован, наблюдая за этим важным событием, кто будет избран!"

Which means: "Good morning! How are you? I'm extremely excited to watch this momentous event of who will be elected..."

They recoil in disgust, trying to peel me off of them, and shove me to the floor as they respond, "Почему бы тебене бежать сейчас." Which means: "Why don't you run along?"

It is 9:07 a.m., and only one minute remains before they try to make their move. I stand on the filthy ground and run to the edge of the balcony to watch.

Finally, as predicted, at 9:08, they place their colossal right hand in their pea-sized bag, obtain the pen gun, point it at Abraham Lincoln, and shoot it...

Now, you may be wondering how I found myself in this situation. To understand this, let's go back to June 15, 1859, when my journey first began. But first, let me introduce myself and my family so you can understand my life's dynamic.

My name is Rebecca Annarose Ledger, but I go by Ruby because my cheeks were rosy red when I was a baby. I was born on May 18, 1850. Today is June 15, 1859; I am nine years old and a member of the prominent Ledger family. When I grow older, I want to be a detective/inventor! I have lengthy, cocoa, flattened hair with a few waves at the ends, glistening violet eyes similar to the color of a lavender bush, and am about as tall as a mid-sized emperor penguin; I know I'm diminutive, but what can I do? Honestly, I don't care. I always say, "I might be tiny, but I am mighty!"

My family is incredibly affluent; our primary land is over 10,000 acres, but I will get into that a little later. We live outside Boston, Massachusetts, and are in the railroad business along with the Vanderbilts. My parents are always mightily stuck up, saying things like "You need to be a girl" or "Only men can be inventors and detectives; you need to focus on learning how to cook, clean, dance, and do needlepoint for a man."

Honestly, it constantly feels as if I'm alone. This is partly because I am the family's owl (even though technically owls aren't that intelligent, they are associated with it). I am constantly inventing new gadgets, like my closed candle, moovo, silver shaky detector, and so many more (don't worry, I'll explain those later)! I always carry my mini tool set just in case I have a new idea to bring to life, and my journal has a blue and purple rose on the cover and my name engraved on the spine.

I am the youngest in my family. I have an older sister named Clara and a brother, Charles. Clara is eleven. Her face looks like a fennec fox, but who am I to say that? Also, she is incredibly tall for her age. She stands like a giraffe and is more than a head taller than me, but I guess that doesn't mean very much, considering I look like "A little six-year-old." Or at least that is what she says ad nauseam. She has baby-doe eyes, caramel hair, a stick body, and a baboon butt's face due to all the makeup she wears.

Now, onto my brother Charles. He is a thirteen-year-old boy as tall as a mountain. I know my family is made up of giants, except for me, of course. Charles has muddy eyes, soft chestnut hair, and a pretty smile. He sort of has a nice-looking face, but don't tell him I said that.

My whole family has to be perfect all the time. With my gorgeous violet eyes, miniature body, and chocolate hair, I look like the most beautiful ugly duckling ever. I love The Ugly Duckling story. It came out 16 years ago and is definitely one of my favorite childhood books because I relate to it so much. Although Mother, Father, and the rest of the world say I am a beautiful child, I am the one who stands out from the crowd.

This is probably because I am the most intelligent pupil. However, this doesn't take much compared to my siblings, considering my sister thinks the first president was some random person named Isaiah Greenwich, and my brother has about the same intelligence as me. However, my vocabulary is more potent. Now that I think about it, maybe that's why I am treated so differently from my siblings because my parents view me as a threat...

Clara loves makeup, cooking, styling her hair, and all of the "typical girl activities," Honestly, I think it's revolting. My mother always has to do my hair because I don't care. She always says, "To be a young lady, you must look like one first."

I think it is a bunch of bogus, but what can I do? Charles loves horses and this new thing called "automobiles." I believe that they work by some sort of steam engine, like trains.

Honestly, I enjoy being a sleuth; I think it is filled with awe! But my parents think it is a bunch of garbage and that "I need to be a girl." I don't understand why they can't appreciate me for me, but I guess you can't choose your family. I am always the first in my daily life to go out and find trouble to solve mysteries with my pet capuchin monkey, Coconut (but I call her Coco for short). I named her that because her coloring looks like a coconut, and I was three when I met and named her.

When I was little, my family traveled to the tropics. This is where we found Coco. She was severely injured, and I begged my parents to let me take her home and care for her. Finally, after days of imploring them, they said YES!

She was only an infant then, and I know you're not supposed to take in monkeys, but I did what I had to do to save her. Now she is my best friend. I can even understand what she is saying because I decided to teach her sign language to communicate as she was healing. I already spoke sign language because all wealthy kids are taught it to exclude the poor. I know this is the most gormless reason ever, but I put it to good use.

Once I successfully taught her sign language, I started associating it with words; for example, every time I would say something, I would sign it, and as time went on, she learned what it meant–the same for when she spoke to me. So, basically, I can talk monkey. It's amazing! I know I'm odd, but I wouldn't say I like that word; instead, I consider myself unique.

Now, returning to what I was saying before, I always feel lonely in this world; even my nanny doesn't understand me. Her name is Gertrude Josephine Williams. She is a large, morbidly obese woman who always thinks she is better than everyone else. I call her Gibface Gerty between you and me because she has always been a callous bully who eats like a dog! She practically swallowed a whole chicken once and left nothing but the carcass. What a fussock!

My academic study includes math, science, language arts, and history. We are homeschooled because our parents wanted to separate us from the other students in our town since we are among the wealthiest. However, we interact with other kids by walking in the park.

We must take five languages, physical education, and art in school, like music or painting. I have the most fabulous teacher. His name is Mr. Henry Jones. He is a six-foot, two-inch tall male with blue eyes and many muscles, and he is the only person who truly understands me. He has taught me everything I know, from academics to identifying suspicious activity as a detective. He told me that he used to be one many years ago, but he is only 42, so I guess it wasn't that many years ago...

You might be wondering what languages I know. I speak English, Russian, French, Italian, German, Polish, Swedish, Latin, and Dutch. Mr. Henry taught me more than the required five. He says he wants me to be able to communicate with important people all over the world. But he is especially adamant that I learn Latin. I don't know why, though. Mother and father say learning languages is essential, and you know what, for the first and only time ever, I actually agree with them. I'd say my favorite language is Russian because it sounds funny.

My parents began teaching me all these languages before I was taught English. Now that I think about it, I never actually introduced them. My mother's name is Margaret Ledger. She is a five-foot-eight-inch tall female with brown eyes and a slender figure. She is gorgeous. Even though I don't want to be anything like her personality-wise, I do hope to be as beautiful as her one day. She is considered one of the most beautiful people in America, or at least that is what Father says. Father's name is George Robert Ledger. He is a tall, six-foot-three-inch male with brown eyes, light brown hair, and many muscles.

So now you have met my family. Oh wait, I almost forgot: we have a dog named Prince. My vazey sister called him that because he is her "little prince." He is a tiny chihuahua. My parents only thought it was fair that if I had a monkey, she should get a dog, and Charles has a cat named Pigeon since he is a gray and white tabby. I know, exceedingly original... but the dog. Well, I think it is a naked mole rat with hair if you ask me... It is too yappy and doesn't know when to be quiet. Ooh, like Clara... Honestly, the only thing in the house that lives with us that I love is Coco. I think she is more of a person than my family, but maybe it's because they constantly chastise me.

The last thing you need to know is my house, basically, the giant castle I live in. I am grateful for everything, but my family is posh, rich, and "perfect!" It is just highly irritating, but here we go. My house is almost as big as the Vanderbilt house. The only reason it couldn't be bigger was that the construction team working on it felt that my cheap parents weren't paying them enough, so they quit halfway through the job. This left my parents with a house half-complete. Serves them right.

Our house has thirty bedrooms, twenty-five bathrooms, forty fireplaces, and over seven acres of land. That land is the only part that makes our house bigger than the Vanderbilts'. We call our house the Richmond house; subsequently, everybody knows about it. On the inside, there are rooms that we are not allowed to go into because they must be in portrait-perfect condition at all times. I still go to them anyway because I don't care.

Actually, one time it was raining, and I was in a gosh mood at my mom, who stole my magnifying glass that I spent two weeks building, and my invisible ink, which I begged Charles to get my parents to buy for him so he could give it to me, and then burned them right in front of me saying "I need to be a girl."

What a cherry! It was roaringly unfair. So, to get revenge, I rolled around in the mud in my fresh, pristine clothing, then ran inside and wiped myself off on the new furniture. She practically had a hemorrhage; it was hilarious.

Moving on... Inside my house are so many rooms for all the "friends" that my family keeps having over, and a swimming pool. Which I know is very uncommon, but our parents wanted to make sure we could swim so that if we ever fell into a body of water, we would survive. I enjoy swimming. It feels nice, and I am my family's best swimmer. Clara hates the water; it's as if she is a witch like the ones from the Salem Witch Trials. I imagine her touching the water and screaming, "I'm melting, I'm MELTING!" Because of all the makeup she wears. Ha ha... I love my sense of humor. Sorry, I'm practically always alone, so someone ought to laugh at my jokes.

Going back to what I was saying before. My family has a horse barn in the back of the house, but only Charles can ride. I think it's unfair, but what can I do? I'm nine, so it's not like I can change my parents' feelings. I mean, it is, of course, "only a boy's sport."

We have a sports field, a court, a bunch of kitchens, running water, many baths, basically everything you can think of. This is not just in this house; my parents own homes all over the North. They own four. I think. I don't know what they use the others for because we never go to them, or at least I can't remember the last time we did, but that's unimportant.

So, this is my life, a crazy daily adventure of my parents telling me that "I am not girl enough," my sister being a vazey person, and my brother being a complete dingo. What can I say? Welcome to the Ledger house!

CHAPTER TWO

My First Mission

The clock struck five on Monday afternoon. The sun glowed through the windows, leaving streaks of gold light on the west side of the lounge area, where I was a starfish on the couch with my crinkly dress and untidy hair, trying to construct my cameras to spy on people. I was about to hide them around the house when my mother stomped in.

"Rebecca Annarose Ledger, what in god's forsaken name are you doing?!"

"Mother, I'm playing with my new cloth doll set that you gave me. What does it look like I'm doing?" I snarled in a sarcastic tone, with my back facing her, just wanting to be left alone. "Also, Mother, my name is Ruby! Please understand it for once. You are the person who named me after all...."

"Alright, get up! You will not howl at me and give me your attitude; it is disrespectful, and I will not take it! We have guests coming over tonight, and I want you to be friendly and gracious to them. I don't need them thinking we raised a child as...." She pulled my feet off the head of the sofa and pushed me around to face her in the eyes.

"As what, mother?" I whispered.

"Nevermind. Rebecca, go upstairs and change. I will do your hair again, and if you mess up your outfit, I will lock you in your room for two weeks without any studies."

I hated her calling me Rebecca, but before I could say anything, she stomped out of the room like an angry Typhon slamming its tail on its prey. My eyes watered like when you cut an onion. I hated her! Sometimes, I wished she would go on one of her business trips and never return.

I proceeded to head upstairs to my room. On the way there, I strolled past Clara's room, where my mother gently professed, "You are my perfect little angel; I wish your sister were more like you..."

I wanted to storm into the room and say something, but I didn't want to risk being grounded for two weeks, so I kept my mouth shut and sauntered to my room to wait for Mother to arrive.

Once she did, her hands were filled with many creams and a comb. She sat me down on the bed and slowly ripped the braided pigtails from my hair. After that, she unscrewed the first cream and wiped it in my hair like my life depended on it. It felt incredibly uncomfortable, so I kept squirming around until I turned towards her, glared her in the eye, and asked, "Do I really need all this hair product? Can you please just brush my hair and tie it?"

She completely ignored me, faced me back towards the mirror, and continued with the following hair cream. After she put in what felt like fifty million different creams, she finally started brushing. It was excruciating!

So, I hollered, "Are you trying to make me go bald? Can you please be gentler on my head?"

She took a deep breath, swirled me around, looked me in the eyes, grabbed my arms above my elbows, and calmly verbalized, "Beauty is pain, and I am trying my best to ensure you don't mess up your hair again. You choose to play harshly; then I must do this."

I squinted in anger as tears filled my eyes from the pain, "Mother, please try to be gentler, I beg you!"

She paused momentarily, sighed, then continued, but this time, she listened and tried her best to be gentle. Once she created a half-braided, half-up ponytail, she tied off my hair with a large purple ribbon to tie it together and to match my eyes. Subsequently, she handed me a light purple dress (it was almost always a purple dress) to match the ribbon for the evening and watched me dress myself to make sure I didn't change into something else. She knew that once I got the dress on, I couldn't get it off without assistance. I guess she was a little brighter than I thought...

Suddenly, my ears spiked with pain as my tiny hands blasted over them to cover them from the blaring noise caused by the vazey doorbell. I instantly knew the visitors were here. My father got the doorbell installed a few years ago. As of today, my family is the only one with a doorbell and fire alarm.

Once the alarm went off, I instructed Coco to stay in my room and then dragged the chair from under my vanity to the outside of the door, stood on it, and latched the lock shut so she could not escape. I was required to lock her in there because when most people find out, I have a pet monkey, they either freeze, shake, or yell, which is eccentric because I know at least two families in our neighborhood with pet birds and sloths, yet somehow, a monkey is odd. I think it is absolutely preposterous! I don't even care about my family's friends, but as my father always says, "As long as you live in my house, you will abide by my rules."

It made me want to stomp and throw my hands around! But what could I do? I slowly crept out down the stairs with my ugly doll in my hands, which my mother had sewed for me by its head, and trudged down the stairs. I only carried it with me to make my mother happy, but mostly, so I wouldn't get grounded again.

I marched to the door to greet my mother's friend Mattie Taylor, a housewife with four children. Mattie was an average chubby woman with flax-seed-colored hair and copper eyes. I liked her, though; every time she came over, she was always friendly with me, so I was friendly with her. I showed her to the family room, where my parents squished the sofas with other friends. Then, I headed back to the door to repeat the process. I went in circles about twelve times until I could finally join the rest of my family and their friends. By this point, I was ravenous and desperately wanted to eat; I prowled to my mother and asked, "Mother, may we please eat now? I am famished."

"Give us some time, Rebecca. The world does not revolve around you."

I wanted to tell her off very badly, but I didn't. Instead, I squeezed my tongue with my teeth and sat next to Mattie because she was the only one I liked at the party. Well, there was always Mr. Edward Williams, but I have always felt that there was something off about him. He was a stubby man with black hair that was always combed back. I always joked that he looked like the unempowering George Washington.

Mattie then questioned me about the so-called "beautiful" dolls that my mother gave me. I honestly thought they looked like Vicki M., the creepy doll that supposedly crawls into sleeping children's beds at night and murders them in their sleep. I used to beg my mother for one so I could try to analyze it to determine why it did that. But of course, she yelled, "NO!" Because it was too unsettling. Honestly, I don't fault her for that. It is pretty terrifying...

Moving on, I looked back at Mattie, knowing that based on the fact that the little hairs on the back of my neck were standing up, my mother was staring at me like a hawk and lied, "Yes, I love my doll! I sleep with them every night, and playing with them is my favorite daily activity."

After those words came out, my chest curled in, and I threw up in my mouth a little. I felt terrible for lying to Mattie, but I did what I must to not get grounded. I looked right at my mother, and she had a slight smirk. She never allowed me to lie before, but now... Oh! I can lie. As this realization appeared as an expression on my face, my mother pulled me aside, "Thank you, but whatever maniacal plan you are thinking about right now, get it out of your mind, Rebecca. Remember, if you don't cooperate, you will be grounded for a month."

Wait a second; she couldn't be serious, a month! I thought she said two weeks before. You know what? I wasn't going to question her because it was a risky game. So, I replied, "Yes, Mother, I know."

After that, we all went to the dinner table and sat down. The table was filled with vegetables and a steaming hot goose covered in this special sauce. There was also beef, ham, turkey, cheese, milk, potatoes, and a wide variety of bread. It made me feel like we were kings and queens.

My father proceeded to make a toast. He banged his small spoon on his wine glass and started to give this whole sappy speech about us and how excited he was for everyone to be there. He even mentioned something nice about me. I was shocked, so I smiled, and to make him feel better because I was by far the youngest, smallest, and cutest person in the room, I shouted, "I love you, Daddy!"

Everyone gleefully cheered, "Aww, isn't she the most precious little girl!" Which caused me to put on a fake smile.

Then, we started the feast. About halfway through dinner, I noticed somebody was missing from the table, but I didn't remember who. This was probably because it was about ten o'clock at night, and I was exhausted.

I got up from the table, went to my mother, and asked, "May I please be excused to the living room so I won't leave and be rude, but at the same time, I can go to sleep." She agreed.

After everybody left, I was fast asleep when my father picked me up and took me upstairs. He and Mother put me in my sleepwear and kissed me goodnight. Just at that moment, I quietly woke up without him realizing it; his faint voice whispered, "Thank you for that cute moment at the dinner table." I smiled and instantly fell back asleep.

The following morning, my nanny came into my room at seven sharp, slamming pots and pans together. I jumped out of my bed and screeched. "What is wrong with you? Why couldn't you tap me or even say my name? You don't have to be such a–" I snarled at her.

She cut me off, glanced at me, and asked, "Such a what?"

You know what? This was not the time for me to get in trouble; it was only seven in the morning, and just like the sky was barely awake, so was I. I didn't want to bother her, hoping she would let me go outside for free time today. So, I retorted with a smile, "Such a lovely, beautiful person, of course."

She looked revolted, handed me my dress, and mouthed, "Breakfast will be ready in twenty minutes."

Then she dared to grab my hair, drag me to the vanity, and sit me down. I uttered, "What are you doing? That hurts!"

She explained how she had to do my hair today since my mother went to the market. I wouldn't say I liked that idea, but I chose not to say anything because I didn't want to get in trouble. After I got ready, I went downstairs to eat my breakfast.

I handed Coco her steaming plate and looked at Clara, who was casually applying makeup at the table. She was horrible at makeup, so I told her, "You look like a clown."

Charles laughed, but she came over and pushed my head into my plate of food. I guess I deserved it. Then my mother walked in. She held a bag of hay and exclaimed the horses had eaten sixty pounds of food in one day. I was questioning it because I know they always eat about forty pounds, so where did the other twenty pounds go? I didn't think much of it because my classes start in ten minutes, and I must prepare my supplies.

I entered the school room to greet Mr. Henry Jones. As I took my seat, I took out my books and papers, "Hello, Mr. Henry. How are you?"

He always had a smile on his face when he saw me. It was only when my siblings walked in that he was frowning. That's how I knew I was his favorite student. Also, I am the only one allowed to call him by his first name, while my siblings must call him Mr. Jones. I approached him with the spy cameras I was building to ask him for help. Clara then eyed me up and down and hollered, "Why can't you ever be a girl? Nobody cares about your stupid spy cameras. You're not even smart enough to make them, you little six-year-old."

I tried to pounce on her and punch her, but Mr. Henry grabbed me back and spoke in Russian, so she couldn't understand, "It's not worth it. She doesn't understand your intelligence."

I chuckled, then asked him to take a quick look at them. He told me there wasn't enough silver chloride on the copper, and they needed to be smaller. He also told me to move the pictures together with a pulling system that quickly pulls them in and out of a photograph roll. This way, it creates a moving picture. I wonder what that would be called? Maybe a moovo, like a moving photo combined! After that, he offered to help me build them. I was ecstatic!

Then, we began today's lessons. Before lunch, we learned about the countries of Europe and quadratic equations, then had a test on them. My vazey sister couldn't figure out her multiplication tables and got an F. Now, that's what I call karma.

When we went to lunch, my mother didn't seem to care that she got an F and that I got an A. She stated, "Girls only need to learn culinary arts and how to care for their men."

I thought it was very foolish of her. After lunch, we went back to learning in the afternoon. We learned about the ancient hanging gardens of Babylon and had to write a two-page essay on Nebuchadnezzar. I understood the material incredibly well and ended early. It was exceedingly straightforward. Clara struggled, but she never was and never will be brilliant, and Charles, well, he got it, but he is also four years older than me, so...

Since I finished early enough, Mr. Henry helped me complete my spy cameras. When class ended, there were two hours until dinner. Like always, I stayed with Mr. Henry and spoke to him. He is my favorite adult! He is the only one who truly understands me, other than Coco, of course, but she is not an adult. I don't understand how I was born into a family of wankers. After talking to him for about thirty minutes, we ran around the house and hung the cameras with nails everywhere. We finished very quickly, and then Mr. Henry went home. I was always sad to see him leave, but I knew he would return tomorrow.

Once he left, I was summoned to the kitchen. When I walked in, my mother was teaching my sister to bake. She turned around and demanded that I learn, so Mother grabbed me by my arms and skidded over to the nearest stool, which she kicked with her foot over to the counter. "Put me down! Put me down! Please, Mother!" I yelled as I did not enjoy being held since it reminded me how tiny I was.

I was kneading dough within five minutes of standing at the kitchen entrance. I thought I would hate it, but I didn't. Surprisingly, I enjoyed punching the dough as if it were my family's faces. What a delight! When we were done kneading, I had to put it in a pan when my father came storming in.

"Hello, Father. What causes you to be colossally angered?"

Shouting at the top of his lungs, as he puffed up his shoulders in the air while holding one of my smashed spy cameras, he shrieked, "You, Rebecca, what the hell is this?"

I was furious that he had smashed it, but I had kept a straight face. I can't believe he would do that! You know what, I could. He always did stuff like this. "For starters, how do you know that is mine? For all you know, it could be Charles'."

Father's face turned red like a beetroot, just like Clara's horrible clown makeup lips. "Rebecca, I know it was you. You are the only one in this house who cares about this spy's stupidity. Why can't you ever be like your sister or mother?"

I had a blank look and responded, "You're right, it is mine, but you know what? I love who I am; I know I am brilliant, and you should be lucky to have a daughter like me. I only put them up in the house for a security system to keep all of YOU safe, and you shouldn't be mad at me! You should be grateful! All I was doing was trying to help you!"

He stormed out of the room, kicking the little chair that I had previously stood on into the corner, and stopped speaking to me for three days. I knew I had done the right thing, but I never understood why he couldn't accept me for me. Whatever, I had other things on my mind.

Today was a solo day with Mr. Henry and me. It was bright and sunny, about seventy degrees. It was perfect for a sports day in school. First, I had swimming lessons, then ballet, and finally, he secretly taught me to ride horses. This has happened for years because riding horses is apparently a "boys-only" sport. I don't really care, though; I am better at it than the rest of my family. He holds on for dear life every time Charles gets on his horse. He doesn't have a brave bone in his body.

Mr. Henry says having more skills than needed is always good so you can conquer any challenge. Later that evening, I asked him to watch the moovo pictures. We decided to go to all the cameras and check the footage. We went to the darkest room in the house. Then, we collected the hot mercury and poured it onto the film imprinted on a silver-plated copper plate. This only took a few minutes for the photographs to develop. This process is known as daguerreotypes.

As we were scrolling through the moovo pictures, there was just a bunch of garbage, like my father consoling his work team, Charles hugging my parents, my sister playing with her dolls, and a bunch more rubbish like that. Until we found something that looked out of the ordinary: an unrecognizable man headed away from the barn with hay bags. I noticed this started the same night Mother said the horses ate twenty pounds more than usual. I could tell because each day, the moovo photo rolls go through approximately four rolls, so you divide the number of rolls by four to get the number of days.

I turned towards Mr. Henry and expressed, "I think this man is stealing our hay! My mother told me a few days ago that the horses had supposedly eaten twenty pounds more hay than they normally do, and I knew that couldn't be right."

Mr. Henry's face squeezed into a look of curiosity, "Are you ready for your first spy mission?"

My eyes widened as far as they could go. Filled with excitement, as my chest puffed in and out, barely keeping my breath in, I shouted, "YES! THIS IS THE BEST DAY OF MY LIFE!"

He quickly shot his hand over my mouth, making sure nobody would hear us. We had to be inconspicuous about it. We placed the cameras back where they were supposed to go, and I returned to the house. We made a plan for that night and set a trap so that whoever entered the barn would be captured.

When I returned, I asked my mother if we could have turkey for dinner. This was because, in the past, when we had turkey, it made all of us very sleepy. I think there is some chemical in it, but I'm unsure because there hasn't been any research yet.

She only agreed if I helped, so I put on a fake smile and more or less helped. I made sure to make the gravy extra lumpy because, based on past experiences, the lumpier the gravy, the faster we were knocked out. As dinner came, I pretended to put up with my family's shenanigans and be nice so they wouldn't watch me. I told them I was exhausted and wanted to go to sleep early. They agreed, and I went "off to bed."

I waited for my family to go to sleep. Then, I snuck out and met Mr. Henry outside of the barn. He brought me a cute little outfit that matched the night. Then, the suspicious, secretive man came. As he was leaving, I got too excited and set the trap off, but it was too soon, so the only thing I could think of was to chase him. He saw me and opened the horses' pens to be a distraction. Mr. Henry chased after him, and I followed but slipped in the mud and hit my head on one of the horse fences. Luckily, Mr. Henry managed to capture him and take him to the town square for punishment.

The following morning, I woke up with my parents huddling around me, looking at me as if I were some ugly creature they had just found. My father looked angrier than ever before and started yelling, "You let the horses out, you little dunce! And you are all filthied up. That is it! You are going to Miss Holmes' Academy, a preparatory school for girls, so you can learn to be a girl."

My eyebrows scrunched together as my lips pursed back. They didn't even ask to see if I was alright. I wouldn't take it anymore, so I yelled, "NO! I will not be going to Miss Holmes' Academy! For starters, you didn't even ask if I was okay. And you know what? I helped stop the guy stealing our hay to save you money, but you only care about your vazey horses."

Father's eyes reeks of annoyance as Mother patted him on the back and then stuck her pointer finger out in my direction, "You stupid girl, for once, stop making up stories. I know you intentionally let them out to destroy our lives, and we won't take it anymore. Tomorrow morning, you are off to Miss Holmes' academy, and no more Mr. Henry!"

I was about to burst into a flame! I got off the ground and walked back into the house, where my mother hosed me off and forced me to wear this embarrassing purple, green, and orange dress. I knew it was my last day of classes with Mr. Henry. This was the worst moment of my life. The only person who ever understood me and my needs, I could no longer see.

When I first walked in, I declared I was sorry, with tears streaming down my face. It was all my fault that I couldn't see him anymore. He wiped away my tears, "Oh Ruby, none of it is your fault. It was your first mission, and you succeeded. The man is now in custody, and you saved your family's hay supply. Don't worry, child. I will find a way to teach you again at Miss Holmes' Academy. I promise you will not lose me."

Tears filled my eyes as I smiled and hugged him. We did mathematics, geography, and English and finished the day with the history of spies and detectives. It was one of the best classes I had ever had. I wish it hadn't had to end, but unfortunately, my parents called me to dinner.

I walked in with a frown, barely touching my food. My parents had put Brussels sprouts that weren't even in season on my plate, knowing I was not too fond of unseasonal sprouts. They said I had to finish my vegetables before leaving the table. So, I had two options. Option A: I could sit here staring at them and be here all night. Or option B: I could shovel them down my throat and leave so I can be away from my family as long as possible. I chose option B. I scarfed them down, holding my nose. After dinner, I grabbed Coco and went to my room to pack. My mother was already waiting there.

I chose to stay quiet because I didn't want to speak to her for sending me away to the world's worst place, an academy to learn to "be a girl." What a waste of education and life. The only thing she could tell me was, "It will be okay, Rebecca;" then she shook her head, "Ruby, I mean Ruby, it will be alright. This is the best girl's school in the country, and maybe you can finally let go of this stupid dream of being a boy."

I stared at her as if she was a foul spider. After she had packed all my clothes, she kissed my head, told me goodnight, and then turned off my closed candle. This was a candle that was encased in glass and filled with gas. Then, you put lighter fluids in a small capsule and a sparker on the side of it. To put the small candle fire out, you just cut off the oxygen to burn it out. To turn it back on again, you flip a little knob connected to the sparker and lighter fluid. It was one of my inventions that is now used all over the house.

The following morning, I woke up, and my mother was there to prepare me to leave. After she gave me my outfit and did my hair, I went downstairs. I grabbed a piece of bread and went outside to leave. Clara was standing there, looking sad, but not really. Charles was also there. He actually looked upset. As I walked to the horses to get to the railway, Charles grabbed my arm and said the most astonishing thing I have ever heard come from his lips: "I think your inventions are—" he paused, taking a few minutes to collect his thoughts, "nifty."

I smiled at him and proceeded to the horse carriages. At least I was allowed to take Coco with me. I don't know what I would have done if I wasn't. Mother and Father allowed her to come with me because they didn't learn how or want to care for or communicate with her. Only I did.

Miss Holmes' Academy was in Washington, D.C., so the fastest method of travel was by train. I hopped in the carriage, and after thirty minutes of traveling, we arrived at the train station. After 300 long minutes of the train speeding at eighty miles per hour, we finally arrived in this gray, cloudy, humid terrain. I knew I was going to hate it here. I hopped off the train, and my father introduced me to Miss Holmes. She was a tall British woman from London, England, like Mother. She had three sons with her. One was about five years old, another was about three years older than me, and the last was a few years younger. Then my father left, and I was all alone. Or at least it felt that way.

When we arrived at the academy, it looked similar to a castle I had read about in my storybooks. Beautiful cherry blossom trees covered the campus, with the American flag with all 33 stars for each state. There was also Great Britain's flag, probably because of Miss Holmes. There was a nice bridge that led onto the other side of campus. The structure was disappointing because it wasn't a drawbridge like I've read in my fairytales.

I noticed boys wandering around and asked Miss Holmes about them. She said, "The academy is coed, but all your classes and interactions will be with girls. There should be no contact with the boys."

I looked at her funny and thought that was the stupidest thing ever. She continued, "Additionally, you will be divided into grades depending on your birth year. Ruby, you are our youngest female pupil here since you were born in 1850, but we made an exception for you because I am close to your relatives. All the other girls in your year were born in 1849."

I wasn't paying too much attention to what she was saying, but to the fact that all the students were wearing uniforms. The girls wore white long-sleeved undershirts with navy dresses, and the boys wore white shirts and navy pants. "Miss Holmes, are we required to wear those uniforms?" I questioned unenthusiastically.

She hastily responded, "Yes, all students must wear the uniform, including Coconut. We sent your uniforms to your room already."

I sighed in exhaustion, frustration, and whatever other feeling of annoyance I could think of. However, at the same time, I wasn't angry because that would mean that all the students would look like each other, and nobody would make fun of me for my rich-looking attire. Additionally, Coco had to suffer with me as well.

Then she took me to a small room with two beds, no closed candles, a dresser, and a window. This place felt like a prison already. I met the girl who was my roommate. Her name was Lulu Hughes. She was taller than me but was average height for a ten-year-old; she had big blue eyes and red hair. She was the first girl I had ever met with fire hair. It was pretty interesting. I introduced myself, and she thought it was fun I had a monkey, but Coco didn't seem to like or trust her for some undetermined reason...

Miss Holmes proclaimed, "Goodnight, ladies, Rebecca."

I corrected her and commented, "Ruby."

She had an irritated look in her eye but continued, "Alright, Ruby, goodnight. Tomorrow, we have breakfast at eight in the morning sharp. Then, we start classes at 8:30 a.m. and last until 6:00 p.m. We also have a break in between for lunch. Your classes will include culinary arts, sewing, makeup and hair, poetry, needlework, dancing, and pottery."

I was shocked to find that there were awfully many boring classes, and they started incredibly early and ended very late! This wasn't fair. But what could I do? This was my miserable "life" now. Then, I had an intriguing thought about how I would escape, so I started laughing.

Lulu asked, "What's so funny."

I replied, "I will find a way to escape this place. Want to help?"

She agreed, and then I knew we'd be best friends.

CHAPTER THREE

Miss Holmes' Academy

A blasting ringing sound filled the room, causing Coco to fall off her railing and land on my face. This led me to jump out of bed and screech: "Ow! Coco, that hurt."

It was seven in the morning when my alarm clock went off. I was not in the slightest ready for today. Lulu began to giggle at me. Honestly, I don't blame her. I started laughing as well. Finally, Lulu exclaimed, "Are you excited about your first day of school."

I barely lifted my head off my pillow as my arms came together from the starfish position they were in and gave her a grimaced look. "No, I just want to be at home getting ready for my lesson with Mr. Henry."

She looked sorry for me. We both knew it was going to be a very long day. After getting dressed, we both headed downstairs. The other girls started laughing at me. At first, I didn't understand why until one yelled at me, "Haha, bed head, bed head."

Was this the best insult they could come up with? Oh god, save me. These girls are not intelligent. I'm just glad I have Lulu. So, with dreary eyes, I answered, "I may have messy hair, but honestly, I would rather be an intellectual genius than a vazey girl with perfect hair."

Miss Holmes glared at us and screamed, "That's enough, ladies! And, Ruby, I will be happy to do your hair in the mornings if you stop by my office before breakfast."

I smiled and wondered why she was being especially nice to me. I mean, I didn't care how my hair looked, but the fact that she did make me feel warm inside. I still thought about how this was not the place for me. The only thing on my mind was that I wanted to find a way to escape. After breakfast, we were required to go on a morning walk. I wasn't too pleased. Miss Holmes put us in pairs with our roommates, and we were off. About halfway through the trip, I looked at Lulu and said, "Hey, do you want to wander off on our own."

She was a bit hesitant, inching on and off her left foot because she didn't want to get in trouble. I shrugged be-cause I understood and muttered, "Come on, please! You know your way around this school. You've been here for a few weeks."

She finally agreed, and we left. After ten minutes of strolling, I saw this dark, black door with a half-circle window on top and a silver handle. We decided to go through it, and it led us to the back dining hall right where Mr. Henry was sitting. My eyes widened as I ran up to him and hugged him as hard as possible. I introduced Lulu to him and asked, "How are you here? I know it has only been a single day, but I've missed you so much!"

His small smile was all I needed to see to return the big one on my face as he replied softly, "I came to teach here so that I can keep my eye on you and your naughtiness."

I giggled. Lulu suggested we return to the group before anyone noticed we were missing. So, I concurred.

After we met with the group, Miss Holmes led us to the classroom for the day's first class. It was hair and makeup. What a lovely class... Before we walked in, Miss Holmes quietly confronted us, "I noticed the two of you walked out of the group, and we expect that you don't do that again. I hope you enjoyed your little journey."

Then, I walked into class. I noticed that all students were in the same year. This is the first time I have ever seen this. Usually, a classroom will be filled with 8 - 13-year-olds, but I guess this school is different...

During class, we were given lipstick, face cream, and a bunch of other garbage. This class felt like a century. I was definitely over it when the second professor, Elya Nidyevon, our makeup teacher, announced, "Pick up your lipstick."

Professor Nidyevon was tall with muscles, white hair, green eyes, and the ugliest brick-colored lipstick. It was very surprising to me that the professor was a woman, considering that men are usually the ones who teach. However, Miss Holmes believes that both women and men can teach if they are passionate about it, which I completely agree with!

I sat in class with my arms crossed, yawning and staring into the distance, thinking about the next time I saw Mr. Henry. Finally, Lulu hollered, "Come on, Ruby, it's not that bad. The faster you do this, the faster the class will be over."

I shrugged; I guess she was right. So, I reached for the tiny mirror in a little box and started the cream application to my face. Now I understand why Clara always looks like a clown; makeup was hard! I was horrible at makeup. What made it even worse was that Professor Nidyevon called me to the front of the class and had me stand on a little podium to show everyone what not to do. They all laughed. I couldn't blame them...

After fifty grueling minutes, the class was finally over. Before I left, I skid over to Professor Nidyevon's desk, leaned on it, and asked if I could keep the makeup. Her face lit up, "Of course! I'm glad you enjoyed it."

With a very monotone voice, I answered, "Oh yes, definitely." But, of course, she didn't know I was keeping the products to add to my spy gear collection. What a fool... I quickly returned to my room to drop the make-up off and headed to my next class. It was culinary arts.

When I arrived, I saw Mr. Henry waiting patiently for me. I wanted to run up to him and say, "Let's blow this joint," but I didn't. I wanted to see what he was teaching. Luckily, he taught us how to make a dragon out of a cantaloupe. It was amazing! Finally, something that's fun! I was the only girl able to construct the perfect dragon. I got a hundred. Serves the other girls right.

After class, I waited for the other girls to leave before I approached Mr. Henry, "Mr. Henry, is Miss Holmes going to be cross with you since you did not actually teach a culinary seminar, but rather a carving one?" He uttered, "No, Miss Holmes and I go back many years. When I was younger, I worked together with her in England. We were in love at one point, but it ended shortly after she had our son together and then had an affair with another man."

My eyes shot out of my head, "Wait, you had a son with her? Was he the oldest of the three boys?"

"Ruby, he was–"

"Does he know?" I howled, cutting him off abruptly.

"Ruby, let me finish, and then I will let you ask your questions, alright? You must have patience, little one."

I held my head down, looking anywhere else in the room but him, "Yes, Mr. Henry."

"Yes, he was the oldest child, and no, he doesn't know because the other man raised him. My son is named Theodore. I found out she was having an affair with another man, so I left. Unfortunately, she took Theo away from me and moved to America. Although I met my beautiful wife before I left, our romance ended quickly. So, I came to America and learned that Miss Holmes became headmistress at this academy. She told me she would only stay here for a few years before she moved back because of her husband. Now let's move on, alright?"

I stared into his soul because I had so many more questions, but before I asked, I realized Miss Holmes was leaning against the wall with her arms crossed behind me, "Ruby, I know it is hard for you here, but Professor Nidyevon told me you asked for the makeup, and I am proud of you for giving it a chance."

I jumped because she scared me. Where did she come from? She was not there two seconds ago; at least, I don't think she was. She is like a ninja! "Thank you, Miss Holmes; I just have one question. If you're married, why don't you go by Mrs. Holmes."

"Ruby, I go by Miss Holmes because the school is named after my family. But good question."

I was not exactly expecting that answer, but I guess that makes sense. Moving on, I had to go to my next class before lunch. I rapidly collected all my belongings and left the room. Leaving the ex-lovers together.

On my way there, the Acker sisters, Mary, Emma, and Caroline, supposedly the prettiest girls in our year, were staring at something on the ground; I was intrigued. They were triplets, which was very rare, but they weren't identical, even though they did look similar with their caramel hair and ocean eyes.

When I walked over, I saw the carcass of a bloody mouse lying upside down with its little feet hanging in the wind. The school was old, so I didn't think it was odd, but what intrigued me was that they were staring at it because they didn't seem like the kind of girls who would be seen near a dead animal. They seem more of the "Ahhh, scary mouse" type. It was as if they had something to do with it.

I faced the poor mouse and noticed little holes in it as if someone had stabbed the poor creature. I didn't question them but decided to go on the case. Shortly after, a bell rang, meaning the next class was about to begin, so the sisters dragged me into the schoolroom for the next lesson. It was sewing. I couldn't think about anything else besides the poor mouse. I sat on the wooden stool in the class, bouncing my leg up and down, glancing around the room as if the answer to the poor creature's death was written on the walls.

Then a muffled sound came from my left ear, "Lulu, can you please get Ruby's attention? She needs to learn this."

Lulu nodded, came before me, and snapped me out of my trance, "Are you alright, Ruby?"

I blinked hastily, "Oh yes. Sorry, I just got distracted."

The professor walked over, "Distracted? Ruby, did you hear anything I said?"

I stared at her solemnly and shook my head. She sighed, "What on earth could be more fascinating than sewing?" There are literally so many things, but I did not say that out loud. "Ruby, please pay attention. I do not want to fail you."

I nodded, and she continued with the lesson. She was teaching us how to attach buttons with pins to clothing. After I finished doing a minimal job on my piece of cloth, I continued to sit there patiently for the class to be over, rummaging through my thoughts about the mouse. That is when I noticed Mary had buttons on her dress with little red spots that did not look like they were supposed to be there. I scrunched my eyebrows and pursed my lips as I went right up to her and confronted her in front of the class, stating, "Did you kill that poor mouse."

She flinched. This was the first time her attitude changed toward me, marking the beginning of our rebellion against each other. "No, of course not! How could you think I would hurt such a small and innocent creature?"

I shook my head. She was clearly lying, so I rounded my fist and punched her in her right eye. I was now thinking that maybe I shouldn't have become physical, but I did what I had to.

Because of this, she flew backward, and the teacher approached me as quickly as possible. She grabbed me backward, scolded me, and then sent me to Miss Holmes's office. When I arrived, her office was this little brown room with multiple windows, a cute little blue-clothed chair, and an oak desk.

In a soft voice, "Ruby, why did you punch her? We do not tolerate violence in our school."

I explained what happened, and Miss Holmes asked me to show her where the mouse was. I took her to the death spot, but it was gone. There wasn't even blood on the floor. Miss Holmes became tense with rage and told me I had to go without lunch. "Miss Holmes, I don't care about petty lunch! I promise it was there, and Mary killed it!"

"Ruby, we do not like false accusations at our school. Please go to your room."

It was not fair! I knew she stabbed it. She had little red drips on the sides of her buttons and wouldn't get away with it. I may look like a six-year-old because I'm tiny, but I am mighty, and she just messed with the wrong person.

After the time when we would normally have lunch ended, we had a thirty-minute break. I was already in my room trying to invent a new device out of boredom. It was a pair of shoes that I attached springs to the bottom of them to make me bounce since I was not allowed to jump on the bed. I think I will call them my moon shoes.

When the break started, Lulu came into the room to study. She handed me a Reuben sandwich, a bowl of insects, and two apples that she had swiped from the dining hall and the unique pantry dedicated to Coco's special dietary restrictions for Coco and me to eat, so I thanked her. I even offered to allow her to be the first one to try my moon shoes. She giggled, kept rubbing her palms together, and politely declined. I think she was a little nervous.

I offered to invite her to Mr. Henry's office for my daily lesson on real subjects like math, science, English, and history. She agreed, and we both left.

Then, the Acker sisters strolled in, causing me to gag in disgust. "What do you want, Mary? I know you killed that poor mouse, and you will not get away with it!"

"Aww, poor six-year-old Ruby thinks she is better than us. Just wait; I will destroy you." Mary harshly grunted.

"I'm not six, you strumpet! I am nine and will annihilate you if it is the last thing I do! Annihilate means destroy because your vazey mind probably can't comprehend basic words."

Mr. Henry was clearly pretending to be grading students' work as he tried very hard to shove his laughter down his throat.

Then Coco sprung onto Mary's chest and secretly took her pin out of her dress without her knowledge. Mary screamed, trying to shove Coco off of her, and unfortunately, she was successful. Coco crashed to the floor, and she and her sisters paced out of the room with their elbows staggered high and grumpy expressions on their faces because they knew I was right. "Coco, are you okay?" I helped her up from the floor.

"Yes, Ruby, I'm fine. I got the pin that killed that mouse from Mary here." Coco handed me the bloody pin.

Although I felt bad for her, my face lit up, "Coco, you're a genius!"

Lulu eyed us up and down with an odd look and said, "I'm sorry, Ruby. Can you understand her?"

"Yes, I can; I taught her sign language and then used the language to mimic our vocal expression. I know everything she is saying."

Lulu's face was aghast, "Wow, that is incredible! Can you teach me?"

"Sure, Lulu, I would happily try to teach you, but it is difficult... Well, for others, I mean. I have been speaking to Coconut for six years now. But I could definitely try. It would be my pleasure."

Unfortunately, I did not have enough time to talk to Mr. Henry, so I headed off to my next class with the pin in a napkin because I didn't want to get my fingerprints on it. I learned about fingerprints because when I was about three, I was finger painting in the den of my house on the walls. Mother was incredibly furious. When I did it, I noticed that there was a small print left on my fingers, so I decided to learn more about them. I went to every family member (including Coco) and examined their prints; they were so different. I even went as far as to ask strangers (Mother and Father's friends) who would come to the house to look at their hands. Mother and Father thought it was very odd and constantly apologized to me, but that is not new or different. They still do.

Later on in life, I asked Mr. Henry about them, and he told me that the organization he worked for used them. However, he says he wants me to keep it secretive because not many people know about their identification methods. The following class was pottery; how boring. It was in this large room full of sculptures next to the walls of all sorts of clay masterpieces ranging from Greek gods and goddesses to small castles, and a kiln right in the center. I headed to my seat, and the professor instructed us to make a cup.

Towards the end of the class, I was covered in clay; it even stained my face. Surprisingly, it wasn't as bad as I thought it would be. It was kind of fun. I guess that is why Miss Holmes tells me I should always try something before deciding I don't like it. I guess she was right.

I realized if you press your finger down into the clay, your fingerprint appears. So, I pushed it up against the pin, and the culprit's fingerprint appeared. I took another piece of clay and handed it to Coco to press against Mary's right pointer finger since I figured she probably would not let me get close enough to her to get it. Also, even though I am tiny, Coco is much smaller and can sneak around a lot easier. I determined that based on the lines' shape and angle, I knew it was her right pointer. I approached Mary and sighed with the biggest fake smile in the world, "I'm sorry for how I treated you earlier. Can you please forgive me?"

She gave me a stern look, "Of course, see, I told you I'd win."

I then hugged her. As this happened, Coco went up from behind, pushed her pointer fingers into the clay, and went back out. I returned to my seat and matched it with the pin fingerprint. Whoopee! I got the evidence and knew she was done for it, but I had to wait until I could get it to Miss Holmes.

Fortunately, this class ended, but I had three left... This felt like the longest day ever. I dragged my feet to each of the next lackluster courses; finally, it was dinner time. I disregarded the rules and went right up to Miss Holmes at the faculty table in front of the dining hall. She was stabbing the piece of lettuce on her plate with her fork by the time I reached her. When she noticed me, she gave me the look of a kid-you-need-to-follow-the-rules-and-sit-down. She breathed, "Not again, Ruby, we are past this, and I need you to move on. Additionally, you need to go sit with your classmates. You are not supposed to be up here."

I scoffed and scrunched my eyebrows, raising my shoulders, "To all due respect, Miss Holmes, I won't go sit down because I need you to listen! Please. I have Mary's pin and the clay fingerprints to prove she was the culprit. Please believe me."

She sighed, faced Mr. Henry, and then asked me to hand over everything so that she could consider it as evidence. Then she told me to eat my dinner. As I returned to my seat next to Lulu, I accidentally bumped into one of the servers and spilled the liver out of her hands in frustration, making a ruckus. Miss Holmes grasped her hand in her face and shook her head. I whispered, "Sorry," as everyone turned towards me, but I ignored them, hopeful that Miss Holmes would help me. I helped clean up the mess and then sat, watching Lulu giggle.

After dinner, we had an hour of free time. So, I decided to go to Mr. Henry's office because when I bumped into him earlier, he exclaimed that he would teach me about the value of money. He gave me an in-depth synopsis of the history of money and even how salt used to be a type of monetary value.

The following day, during breakfast, I went to Miss Holmes and asked her about the pin, which kept me up all night thinking about it. She could only say, "It was an event in the past, and we will move on. I have spoken to Mary, and she will not do it again."

My eyebrows heated in fury as my arms and legs tensed, with my hands clenched. I wanted to yell at her about how unfair that was, that she killed a living creature, and how unladylike that was, but I chose not to. What could I do? Because clearly, Miss Holmes didn't care. I guess she wasn't the person I thought she was...

Many days passed, and small events like this began to happen all the time. Whenever I caught the Acker sisters red-handed, I would get in trouble with Miss Holmes. She never believed me, and then I always proved her wrong. This went on for weeks of constant pranks. It was now almost Christmas time. Snow covered the lush grass fields; it was a peaceful and beautiful time. I thought these childish pranks of the Ackers were over, but unfortunately, I was wrong.

Last night, Mary and her dingos, whom she calls sisters, took her stupid pranks too far. She. Put. A. Live. Snake. In. My. Bed.

Luckily, I noticed it slithering around before it could bite me. So, I built a hook with the wood planks from the fireplace on the floor and pieces of metal and glass in my spy kit to move the snakes to their rooms. But then I thought, what if I play mind games on them? So, the following morning, during breakfast, I told them, "Thank you for the lovely gift in my bed last night. You might want to check your sleeper sheet before you go to sleep tonight," and then crept away with Lulu to my first class with my lips curled upwards in a wicked fashion.

"Ruby, what did you do with that snake? I know you didn't put it in their rooms," Lulu said.

"You're correct; I just wanted them to believe I did. For two reasons: First, every time they walk into their room, they are nervous. Second, they tell Miss Holmes, and then she would confront me and go to their room to find absolutely nothing." I belched.

Lulu's mouth curled outwards as she cheerfully voiced, "Ruby, I've said it before, and I will repeat it again. You are a genius!"

"I know. Now, let's go before we get in trouble."

After blasting the doors to the charcoal walls of Professor Nidyevon's class, we were scolded for being a few minutes late, which, honestly, I didn't care too much about. Today, she was teaching baking. We learned how to jumble the floury, sugary, and sweet ingredients to make the tasty concoction known as cake. I got flour everywhere, including my clothes and face.

The construction of the scrumptious dessert fractured my mind with anecdotes of my past from the night before I was kicked out of my house. My eyes overflowed with globules of saltwater. Professor Nidyevon noticed and came over to ask if I was okay. I thought I was, but I felt this deep anguish in my heart for whatever reason. Then my mind filled with the darkest, dankest thought that I could have ever thought of, "I think I might miss my family."

Wow, I never thought I'd have any emotion toward the horrible cult members known as my parents. Professor Nidyevonhad a confused look in her eyes and uttered, "Oh, Ruby, it's okay. Come here. Why don't you go to Mr. Henry's room? I know you have a strong connection with him since he was your teacher before you joined this school."

Mary and her snake sisters laughed at me, "Aww, look, baby Wuby has a wiking towards her teachew."

I squinted my eyes in anger, and my fists clenched, but I stopped myself before I attacked. I stood up and ignored her, so I didn't give her the benefit of satisfaction. I went to his office and knocked on his door. When he opened it, a flash of instant relief washed over me. He guided me to the chair as I entered, "Mr. Henry, why do I miss them? I have never liked them and always stayed away from them as much as possible."

"Well, Ruby, you may not like them, but they are still your family, and believe it or not, you love them somewhere on the inside."

My eyebrows crushed down as I gazed at him with filth, but I realized I did. No matter how much they made my heart throb, I still do. I could only respond softly with my head down, "Mr. Henry, I should probably return to class now."

"Bye, Ruby."

When I got back, the class was over, and Lulu was waiting patiently for me with her legs crossed like a "t" and her back hunched over her notebook on the bench outside of Professor Nidyevon's class. Upon hearing the meager pounding against the floor due to my footsteps, her head snapped at me as her happiness shined through her soul to see me. She quickly lifted her body from the chair to run over to me. I beamed as I saw how happy she was to see me.

We only had that one class today. I'm not entirely sure why, but I think it is to get ready for the annual bake-off tomorrow. Next Friday is officially Christmas, and I go back home tomorrow, Saturday morning. Lulu is coming home with me because her family went to Louisiana, so mine invited her to come back with us. I hope that goes well and my parents don't embarrass me.

Lulu and I left; we returned to our room filled with drawings of Mr. Henry and me. I knew it was the Acker sisters, but I didn't want to give them the satisfaction. So, I decided to get back at them and ensure they would never mess with me again.

Throughout the past few weeks, they had pulled foolish pranks, and this was going to be their last. Lulu and I spent the rest of the day formulating the most maniacal plan we could think of in the time that we had without going too far as to get expelled.

For the annual bake-off, each student must work in groups of two or three and bring their ingredients. We have practiced this in the baking class throughout the year, and now it is finally here, but we knew that it was more important to get them back than to get a good grade at this bake-off. So, we decided to sneak into the kitchen where our multicolored, juicy, fruity ingredients were lounging on the table and replaced them with crushed little beasties that love to creep and crawl around to make the judges think they did it.

So that each and every bite out of the judges' mouths would be revolting, we knew this would be their last prank, considering Miss Holmes mentioned that if there were any pranks, the student would be suspended and have detention for three months when we returned for the spring semester. We knew the consequences if we got caught, but they were well worth it. Also, when the Acker's parents visited last month, they said they would take them out of school if they played any more pranks.

The following morning, the annual bake-off had begun. As the clock passed the 12 five times, it was time for judging. Lulu and I were quivering and tapping our shoes on the hard timber floor, hoping our plan would work. Cake after cake, the judges licked their lips and smiled so big in satisfaction that you could see their milky teeth. Our turn was next. I started to fingerspell to Lulu, "This will work, don't worry."

We both took a deep breath and introduced our creation to the judges. Then they took a snap at our insect gateau and spat it out all of the Ackers. Our shoulders were pinned back as our eyes flared. Bullseye! I was not expecting that, but it was a nice touch. The judges turned towards us and verbalized, "Are these bugs?"

Lulu started speaking while pretending to play dumb: "I don't know. All of our ingredients were here last night, EWW. Those are legs in your teeth," she said this as she began to gag a little, as did I.

Then we both stared at the Ackers. Miss Holmes called all of us to the office because we were all in trouble. "Mary, Emma, Caroline, what have you done? I know it was you, and I said no pranks today. Yesterday, Mary, you laughed at Ruby, and it was not okay. Because of this, the three of you are suspended. I will be sending a letter with you home tomorrow morning. You may leave."

They crossed their arms in fury as their lips pursed and their brows flattened. Mary tried to rebut it, "But Miss Holmes, we didn't do–"

"Save it, child. You may leave."

They slowly stared for a few seconds before exiting, "Miss Holmes, our parents are going to take us out of the school."

Miss Holmes nodded slowly, "You should have thought of that before you played this prank. You have to understand there are consequences to all of your actions, and this was too far. I will not ask you twice. You may leave now."

They held their heads down and left as Miss Holmes' speech replayed in my head repeatedly. I had little remorse, and they got what they deserved. Then Miss Holmes turned towards us and asked, "Ruby and Lulu, are you two okay? I am incredibly sorry they did that to you. But I must ask, did you have anything to do with this prank?"

Lulu looked at me but kept silent. The room was so quiet that you could hear an ant cheer. Miss Holmes picked up our uncomfortability, "I'm sorry, I didn't mean to accuse you. You may leave now."

It was our time. We did it! We went back to our room to pack. "Ruby, do you feel kind of bad for them?" Lulu enquired with a solemn tone.

"No, why would I? They have been messing around with us for months, and I'm sick of it. Besides, in this world, I need to show I am a leader, and I won't ever let anyone take advantage of me or mess with me just because I am small and a girl. You know, I might be tiny, but I am mighty!"

Lulu knew I was right, or at least I hoped she did. We both finished our packing duties. That night, I asked Mr. Henry if he was coming. He expressed, "No, Ruby, I am staying here, but I will see you in two weeks, don't worry."

Of course, I was worried he wasn't coming because then my parents would chastise me again, but it was time for bed, and I couldn't fight him. He was an adult, after all. On the way back to the dorms, I ran into a boy. I apologized and introduced myself. His name was William Wallace Lincoln, but he goes by Willie. He was a medium-sized boy my age, with medium-length brown hair and blue eyes. He was very friendly, so I invited him into our dorm. Even though it wasn't allowed, I didn't care.

Lulu, Willie, and I immediately became friends. He lives in Washington D.C. but is originally from Springfield, Illinois, and goes to the boys' Miss Holmes Academy preparatory school, where they teach essential subjects like math, science, English, and history. I still learn it through Mr. Henry, though.

However, for the break, Willie was going to Boston to visit his aunt and uncle and would be on the same train as me. Since Miss Holmes is British, we get a winter break to celebrate Christmas because, in England, they have celebrated Christmas since 597 AD, while Americans still have yet to declare it a holiday.

Will was staying with close family in the Grover Manor. It appears that his relatives who live there were the second most affluent family in Boston. My family is friends with them, so I got excited. After a few hours of talking, it was almost midnight. The faculty was starting to come around to ensure the students were in their rooms, so he left.

The following morning, Miss Holmes took us to the train station together and exclaimed, "See all of you in two weeks after the break. I hope you have an enjoyable time!"

Then she trotted away. We spent the entire train ride messing around. Finally, after five hours, we arrived, and my whole family was waiting for Lulu and me. It was such a surprise. I bet they hoped I had stopped my "boy interests;" I hadn't. The first thing Mother said when she saw me was, "Oh, you look lovely, Ruby, with your combed hair and beautiful dress."

She didn't know that Miss Holmes helped me get ready that morning. I proceeded to introduce them to Willie. My family was glad to see I had made friends.

CHAPTER FOUR

Winter Break

Lulu and I raced to my room when we got to my home. Unfortunately, when I walked in, my spy gear was gone. All my time building and inventing my gadgets went down well. I went straight to my father because I knew he was sick of my devices, "Where did all my gadgets go?"

He didn't hesitate or even look at me when he responded, "We gave it all to your brother; we figured that the past few months at Miss Holmes Academy had changed you. That you would be done with all of this funny boy business and start acting like a girl."

When he was done speaking, my heart felt heavy, and I could feel a pit forming in my stomach. Lulu and I sped out of Father's room as quickly as we could, and then slammed Charles' door open and shouted, "Give me my spy gadgets back! I know you're not using them!"

He barely glanced at me, not giving me a second thought, and pointed to a large brown box in the corner beside his dresser. I went to open it, only to find all my gadgets broken. My eyes filled with tears, and my throat closed. It felt like my heart shattered.

Lulu watched the little tear droplets roll down my cheek and shrieked, "What is wrong with you? Why would you break her gadgets?"

After a few minutes, he shrugged, "I'm sorry, Ruby, I didn't think you would want them after you went to the Academy. Besides, they didn't even work anyways, so I don't know why you're upset."

I gave him a grimace and wanted to pounce on him, but then I remembered that if I showed him weakness, he could just make fun of me more. So, I decided the best method would be to ignore him.

Lulu helped me move the box to my room. Once we entered the narrow doorway, I heard a loud kerplunk repeatedly from my window. I hustled over to see little pebbles scratching the glass. It was Willie; a smile shined across my face! I guided him up the tree to my room and then let him climb in, "Hello, Ruby." He paused briefly, scanning my puffy face. What's wrong? Are you alright?"

I finally found the words to whisper, "No, I am not alright! My irritating father gave all my spy gadgets to my vazey brother, who broke them. I spent years inventing them, and now they are broken." A gadget I held crashed to the floor as I stared into the abyss of broken tools.

He put his arm around my shoulder and hugged me, "Do you remember how to build them?"

I barely looked him in the eyes and commented, "Well, yes, but it will take days if I try to rebuild all of them myself."

Willie and Lulu smiled at each other and then, in unison, stated, "Let us help you. We will rebuild them together."

A small grin grew on my face. I have the best friends. I handed each of them a screwdriver, and we got to work. Finally, after about two hours, my collection was complete. I guess after determining how to build them the first time, it is very easy to recreate them a second. Since I had to rebuild them, I analyzed them, and they became even better! Then, Mother walked into the room. "Oh, Ruby, I didn't know you had Willie over. Well, he is always welcome."

I was nervous she would say something about us working, but I didn't want to bring it up, so I shoved the materials under my dress and answered, "Thank you, Mother."

She glanced around the room as if she were a naughtiness scanner, noticed the tools sticking out from under my dress, and gasped, "Rebecca, are you and Lulu playing with tools? This is unacceptable! I thought we sent you to

Miss Holmes' Academy to become a girl and not to play with foolish boy toys."

I guess I was mistaken. She proceeded to pick me off of the tools and then take them away. Lulu and Willie stared at each other out of shock as she had said that in front of them.

I didn't want to say anything because I realized I loved it at Miss Holmes Academy; it was like my home, and I didn't want her to bring me back to this place of solace. So, I gazed in her direction and spouted, "I'm sorry, Mother." She nodded and left the room.

"Sorry, you had to see that. This is my typical day of not being 'girly' enough."

Lulu turned towards me with clenched fists and hollered, "Woah! Does she always talk to you like that?..." She paused for a few seconds, "Also, what was that? I thought you would respond, but nothing."

I got up from the floor and went to my bed, where I hid another whole box of tools under my bed. "Lulu, you think this is the first time stuff like this has happened? Coco and I switched out these tools with my broken ones as she focused on you. Please, I think much further ahead than she does."

All three of us started to laugh. After assembling my "new" gadgets, we went to the horse pen. I noticed some old horses and some new ones. Charles was there practicing with his long-black-bearded teacher; I asked him what had happened after the August horse incident. He said, "We could only find a few of the horses that had escaped, so Mom and Dad bought new ones. Now leave me alone, you little twit. I'm busy."

I rolled my eyes. I guess that made sense. I still didn't feel bad for what happened. The three of us returned to one of the living rooms. Willie asked me what had happened, and at that moment, I realized I had never even told Lulu what had happened and why my parents had sent me to Miss Holmes' Academy. I took a deep breath, and my eyebrows scrunched, "One afternoon in early August, my mother had come into the house and told us that the horses had eaten twenty pounds more hay than normally. At first, I didn't think much of it. Then, a few days later, I built my first moovo cameras, which you can see around the house. I caught some guy trying to steal our hay. So, that night, I set up with Mr. Henry to catch the guy. During the process, I let the horses out and hit my head. The following morning, I woke up with my family hovering over me, furious at what they saw. I tried to explain what had happened, but they didn't care. Also, Mr. Henry ended up catching the thief. So, that is what happened and why I was sent to the Academy."

Willie looked crazed as he backed up in horror. "That's not fair. You were trying to help your family, and they didn't even care!"

I shrugged, "I know, and at first I was cross with my family, but then I realized I prefer it at the Academy than here anyway. I still get the education I need. I have both of you as friends, and everything turned out great! Honestly, I am glad my parents sent me there, and I still stand by my actions."

Lulu hesitated, but then a smile flashed onto her face, and she slumped her posture. By now, it was almost dinner time. Willie left for home. It was just Lulu and me. We went to Mother and asked if she needed help in the kitchen. I wanted to use my invention of the faster working whisk, which I created at Miss Holmes Academy, to make the class more manageable. It worked with a gear, a pulley, and a handle.

My mother noticed it, furrowed her eyebrows, held her right pointer finger at me, and stated, "You may help me, but I do not want your invention in the kitchen. I don't know where it has been and honestly do not care to find out."

My face went pale as if I had seen a ghost as I tried to prevent the fire in my eyes from bursting out. My mother was the type of person who did not care about my feelings. What could I do? I jumped on the stool, and Lulu stood beside me as we kneaded the dough. After we were done, Mother put the dough in the oven so we would not burn ourselves, and then she expressed, "I'm glad they are teaching you something important instead of this detective nonsense."

I rolled my eyes to the side and watched Coco do a little monkey dance to make me smile before we left. After dinner, we went to the shed in the backyard to throw a ball at each other and catch it. It was just a way of ending a long day before we went to bed.

We rose at the first light break in the sky the following morning and went to the garden. We had breakfast of eggs, toast, and freshly squeezed orange juice. It tasted like happiness. Lulu and I had pressed them earlier that morning after a new cargo box of oranges came the night before. I always loved squeezing my oranges, especially with my father's new squeezer from the inventor Lewis S. Chester. It let me get my anger out from the day before.

After my family and I finished breakfast, Willie came over for a visit. He always made me smile when I saw him. Then the Clara creature saw him, strolled up to me, and yakked, "Aww, look at the ugly love creature things with…" she thought for a minute, rubbed my hair back and forth, and continued, "Hair. Yes, that makes sense."

My mouth gaped open at her stupidity. Lulu and I tried to hold back our laughter in a gulp. Lulu finally saw how vazey my sister was. So, I rolled my eyes and replied, "Love creature things… for starters, we are just friends. I'm only nine, and you are a ludicrous koala without the ability to comprehend simple verbiage."

A look of confusion enveloped her, "Thank you, I love koalas! Wait..."

Her best response to me was, "Well, at least I don't look like a freak with your weird purple eyes. I mean, who has purple eyes!"

I sighed and tapped her on her right shoulder, "I do. Also, not that you would understand anyway, but the reason I have violet eyes is that there is a lack of melanin, also known as a type of pigment, in my eyes, so when the light reflects off of the red blood vessels, it makes them look like they are purple. It's the same as people with blue, green, or brown eyes. Mine are just prettier."

I could see that the expression on her face was lacking as she tried to come up with a response to insult me, but she wasn't smart enough to. So, she walked away. It wasn't even that bad of an insult. Honestly, I think Frankenstein had more brains than her, but it doesn't take too much.

All three of us burst out laughing. Then Willie questioned, "Why a koala?"

It made sense to ask that. I mean, it wasn't necessarily common knowledge. I retorted, "As of today, koalas are supposedly the stupid animals in the animal kingdom. This is because they have a smooth brain. The size of the brain doesn't matter, but how wrinkly it is. This helps optimize the brain matter inside it. Meaning, more neurons make thinking more efficient. That is what helps determine intelligence. Mr. Henry taught me this at the Academy."

This is how I learned all my knowledge, not only from Mr. Henry but also from books. Which is why is is important to be well-read like me. Later that day, we were lying in the house's den when Mother and Father called for me. I walked into the office, and they had a look on their faces that I had never seen before. It looked like they were a mix of happy, mad, and possibly... constipated. All at once. Maybe they were relieved...

They asked me to sit down. I thought maybe this was a trap because they had never really been this calm around me before. It took me about a century to slide over to the chair they were pointing at. Mother was the first to make a sound, "Rebecca, we are extremely proud of you for trying at the Academy," *my face was still; they had never told me they were proud before. Who are these people, and what have they done with my parents,* "We honestly thought you would fail," *Ahh, there they are,* "and we want you to continue there for at least the rest of the year."

I gave them the sarcastic look of "Thank you so much for thinking I would fail," but I didn't say that because that wouldn't be clever since they were actually being nice to me for a change. Instead, I uttered, "I would love to continue at Miss Holmes' Academy. It feels like my second home."

They then said if I continued with this trend of "girliness," they would re-enroll me for next year. I was immensely excited, but I had to ensure my siblings wouldn't torment me so that I wouldn't get in trouble.

I left the room with a feeling of delight. My parents had never told me they were proud of me before. It felt refreshing and relieving all at once, like when I got to read while lying upside down in my bed.

When I returned to the room, Willie and Lulu laid on my bed, happy for me, as they saw the smile on my face. Then we returned to the giant jigsaw puzzle we were doing. We were finished after seven hours, two thousand pieces, and many colors later. Activities like this occurred for the next week. Whether we were building a gadget, putting together a jigsaw puzzle, or reading books, it was finally Christmas Eve.

We celebrated Christmas in my family because Mother was from London, and it was her family tradition. Christmas Eve in my family was "special." Or at least that's what Mother says. We were always required to wear the same red, navy, and green outfit. It was this big poofy dress for the girls—Mother even made Lulu wear one—and for the boys, it was a nice lounge suit. Then we gathered at the dinner table and said the best part of our year. I chirped, "I am incredibly grateful to be attending Miss Holmes' Academy."

Clara blurted, "My favorite part of the year was when Ruby came back from the spaces beyond us," just to suck up to our parents.

Then she pulled me aside and commented, "Now that's how you do a real experience."

I rolled my eyes, "Experience, don't you mean speech? Also, that didn't make sense because I'm not dead."

After that, it was Charles' turn. He murmured his favorite part was watching me get sent to the Academy. Then my parents went, Coco went, and finally, it was Lulu's turn. Lulu mumbled, "Well, I don't know exactly what to say because I have never celebrated Christmas since I'm Jewish, but I am extremely grateful for this year. For starters, when I met Ruby, Coco, and Willie. I am also grateful for you to invite me into your lovely home, Mr. and Mrs. Ledger, and to be happy and healthy."

"Lulu, I didn't know you were Jewish. That's so fresh!" I thundered.

My family agreed we love Jews (especially because Mr. Henry is also Jewish)! We loved all religions. It doesn't matter what you look like on the outside or what religion you celebrate; what matters is who you are on the inside. Because she mentioned this, everyone thought she was the star of the table. I was glad she communicated that. It made me feel warm inside that I have her as my friend. Though I didn't consider her my friend by this point, I thought of her more as my sister.

After dinner, we were escorted to the Christmas tree and gathered around it for the Christmas Eve gift opening. I got a new doll and makeup kit. Oh, how excited I was; NOT. I said, "Thank you," even though I was not too fond of it, it is always good to be gracious. Then, we moved on to the next gift. Like always, Clara got makeup, and Charles got these incredible magnifying glasses and hourglasses. I clenched my fists, staring at his gift like it was the most beautiful thing I had ever seen.

Before bedtime, I snuck into his room and asked if I could have them to add to my collection. I brought my little knife to trade with him. He responded, "I like the hourglass, but you can have the magnifying glass. I mean, it is pointless. It only makes things bigger, which is very boring. Also, you can just have it. I don't want any of your odd-looking belongings." He held up the knife with two fingers and a revolted look.

I was glad he was okay with it. I slowly crept back into my room and added it to my collection of tools. It was seven in the morning when my mother walked in to wake Lulu and me up. "Good morning, Mother. How may I assist you?"

She ignored my question and roared, "Where is Charles' magnifying glass?" As she ripped away my belongings from their rightful place.

I gave her a look of confusion. "I know you have it. Rebecca, your father, went to your brother's room this morning to use it for his work, and Charles mentioned it was here. So, where is it? It is not for girls!"

I had a blank expression, "Charles gave it to me yesterday. I didn't take it from him."

She growled, "Well, your brother says you stole it, so I am asking you nicely, and I will not ask you again, child. Where is it?"

My eyebrows furrowed, and my shoulders tensed. Of course, she believed him over me. She always does. It wasn't fair; I knew something like this would happen, so last night, I switched out the piece of glass with a much cheaper piece that looked almost identical but didn't work as well as the expensive one. I crawled under my bed, got it from the tool kit, and handed it to her. She picked me up and put me in the chair. She began brushing my hair furiously. It was excruciatingly painful, but she stopped right before I told her to.

She turned me around and exclaimed, "Don't you ever take your brother's gifts away from him. Is that clear? Now be downstairs in five minutes before I destroy all your presents."

All I could think about was how I would get Charles back. I didn't care about my gifts, so I gulped, "Crystal."

Before breakfast, Lulu said, "Ruby, what will you do?"

At first, I lied, "I'm not going to do anything," but Lulu knew me immensely well.

She knew I was lying and responded, "Come on, your Ruby Ledger, the naughtiest bully-fighter I have ever met. What are we going to do?"

I thought about it briefly and proclaimed, "Let's wait until after Christmas; also, we can ask Willie if he can help us." I smirked.

She concurred, and we slowly went downstairs. Breakfast was silent. I stared at Charles, and he looked frightened as he knew I would get him back. After breakfast, we went to the tree and opened presents. After about thirty minutes, we were done. Mother and Father whispered in the corner while staring and pointing at me. I wanted to know what they were whispering about, so I had Coco secretly climb onto the bookshelf behind them and listen.

Then they walked over to me, held Coco by the scruff of her neck, and whispered, "It is quite rude to eavesdrop, Ruby." They dropped her in front of me. "We have one last gift for you, but you may only have it if you are good for the rest of the day."

I thought it was probably another doll. My mother has given me four dolls, six face care packages, some sweets, a sewing kit, and plants. Even though I was grateful, I only enjoyed the sweets. So, I wasn't too excited, but at the same time, I was intrigued, "Okay, I'll be good."

I was trying incredibly hard not to be rude after what had happened earlier because I didn't want my parents to rescind my enrollment for next year at Miss Holmes Academy.

For the rest of the day, Lulu, Clara, and I were required to sing Christmas carols for all of my parent's friends, even though they didn't celebrate Christmas, so it makes no sense to me why we had to do it...

We must have gone to thirty different houses. After five hours of singing, we finally walked to the last house. Luckily enough, we knew it was the Grover manor. We just hoped Willie would open the door. He did. My eyes lit up; maybe it was from the light coming from the windows, but I still beamed. This was when we met his family's cousins for the first time. Usually, when Mother and Father would invite them over, it was just the parents, so it was the first time I met their kids. His second cousins were named Belle and Everett. They were nice. We sang to them for about twenty minutes.

Willie then invited Lulu and me into their house. It was gorgeous. It was filled with gold, beautiful paintings, and sculptures. The ceilings must have been twenty-five feet tall. The house has twenty-five bedrooms, twenty bathrooms, sixteen living rooms, and many offices and plants. Even though our house was larger, theirs was definitely nicer. His second aunt was very kind. She invited us for some bread and juice. I couldn't believe mothers could be that nice. Sometimes, I wish my mother was like this. Finally, after a few hours of relaxing together, it was time for us to return to my house. We said our goodbyes and left.

That night, we had one more tradition before we could go to sleep. It was time for the annual family board game competition. This year was the game Backgammon. Typically, I wouldn't say I liked this competition because we always play in teams. Since there were only five members in my family, I was always alone with Coco, which worked for me because she was my only friend, and we typically won anyway.

This year was different, though. I had Lulu, but my mother and father let Coco play with us as a team of three. We won by a landslide, but this meant that Mother, Father, Charles, and Clara all had fiery faces. They hate it when I win because it makes them feel stupid. Also, they are very competitive. It was okay, though. I won fairly, unlike team CC—which stood for Charles and Clara—who always cheat. If you're going to cheat, do it well enough to the point where you don't get caught and actually benefit from it. They always laugh their maniacal laughs, switching pieces in front of others. Overall, they are horrible cheaters.

When the game concluded, Mother and Father sent us to bed. As we were getting ready, my parents walked in with a gift in their hands, wrapped in blue and silver paper with a large silver ribbon on top. Lulu sat at the vanity brushing her hair, pretending to pay no attention to what my parents gave me.

Mother spoke first, "Rebecca... I mean, Ruby, even though today started horribly because you stole your brother's magnifying glass and then had Coco spy on us... I will say it turned out pretty well."

My father tuned in and continued, "You did all the caroling without a complaint and didn't cheat like you always do. So, we have this gift for you."

I glanced at them with a look of unfairness because I never cheat. They don't understand that I have a brain, but what could I do? I took the box out of their hands and uttered, "Thank you."

Then I opened it. It was a beautiful key necklace with a blue and purple rose, a white stem, a white diamond border, a little shield that had three little triangles on it, a fingerprint on the back that matched my thumbprint, and wings with white diamonds on the edges of them. The key's bow resembled a little with a rhombus-shaped middle connecting the two dragons. This middle also had little branches connected to each side of the rhombus-shaped center with a bar on top of the rhombus.

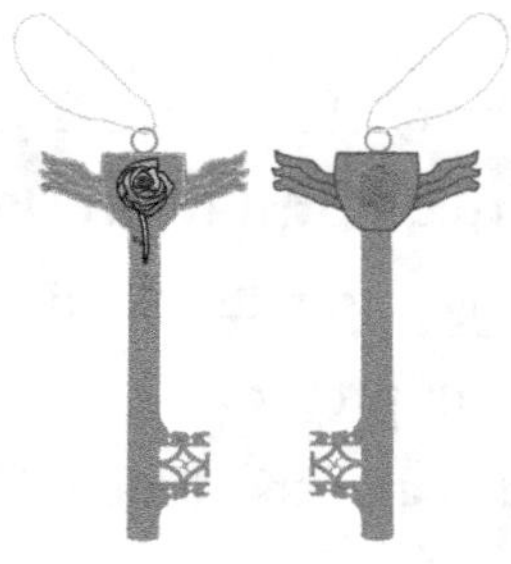

I had never received any gift as unique as this one. I smiled from ear to ear, hugged Mother, and yelled, "Thank you again! But where does this key go?"

Mother paused, not knowing what to do with my hug. She slowly patted me on the back and answered, "We don't know. Mr. Henry gave it to us when you were a baby."

I ripped myself off of them and examined the key. Then, I didn't understand what they meant by that, but I didn't question them. All I could do was hug them. They had never received a real hug from me before, and they didn't know how to respond other than tapping me on the back. Then they left.

Lulu looked at my necklace and muttered, "Why would Mr. Henry give that to you?"

My eyes squinted at the necklace, "I don't know... When we get back to school, I will ask him."

A few days passed since Christmas, and it was finally the morning we had to return to the Academy. Since the automobile wasn't big enough for Willie, Lulu, Father, and I, Willie met us at our horse stable, and we rode the horses to the railway. We hopped on a silver train lined with a gold streak and spent the next five hours traveling. When we arrived, it was a very gloomy and rainy day. I said goodbye to Father, and Lulu thanked him for letting her stay with us.

Then, Miss Holmes, who carried an umbrella, escorted us to the school. Once we arrived, she noticed my necklace and spouted, "Wow, Ruby, you have such a beautiful necklace. Did your mother give it to you?"

I wondered why she cared about it. I mean, I had worn beautiful jewelry before, and she never said anything, so why now? I didn't want to be impolite, so I answered, "Yes, my parents gave this necklace to me. They mentioned that Mr. Henry gave this to me as a baby."

She had an odd look in her eye. That was the weirdest interaction I have ever had with her, but I ignored it. She continued, "Classes begin again tomorrow. Go to dinner and get a good night's rest."

After dinner, I went to Mr. Henry's office, and Miss Holmes was there. She was talking to him about my necklace and how I needed never to lose it; if I played my cards right, I could use it to change the world. Then, I accidentally stepped on one of the floorboards, and it creaked.

Her head cracked in my direction as she gently approached me, muffling, "Hello, Ruby, shouldn't you be going to bed now?"

I communicated, "Yes, I just wanted to say hello to Mr. Henry. I haven't seen him in a while."

She answered, "Carry on. Henry, we will discuss this matter later." She kept her gaze on me as she exited down the hallway.

I went in and hugged him, "Mr. Henry, Why is my necklace highly important? Why is everyone having a cow about it? And why did you get it for me as a baby?"

He calmly retorted, "Woah, woah! No hello?"

I giggled as his large chair enveloped me into the cushion, "Sorry... It is good to see you, Mr. Henry."

"It is good to see you too. Little one, I gave you this necklace when you were a baby because it means something. Its meaning isn't important right now, and when you're older, you will understand. I only hope you know that everything I have given to you is special. Especially this necklace because it unlocks..." Then he stopped.

I stopped him and shouted, "Unlocks what?"

He responded with, "Nothing, never mind. It is important because I gave it to you. Don't ever lose it, Ruby! Because you only have one, and that's it!"

I knew he was hiding something by his tone of voice and uneasy movements, but I didn't question it. I had never seen him care about something more in my life. I could only say, "I won't, I promise." Then he hugged me and sent me to my dormitory.

If this necklace was exceedingly important and couldn't be lost, why would he give it to a child? I mean, children lose things all the time. Although, of course, I don't, but even so.

The following two weeks went as boring as usual. Then I saw them, the Acker sisters. Lulu pulled me to the side and whispered in my ear, "I thought we got rid of them."

I screeched, "Yes, me too!" She covered my mouth tightly, hoping they didn't hear what I said, as did I.

They came right up to us, and the leader of the warthogs hollered, "I knew you two got us in trouble, and this semester will be hell for you."

Lulu had a nervous look in her eyes while I rolled my eyes. "We're not scared of you!"

Mary shook her head and sneered. While the other two gagged in rebellion. "Well, you should be, you little twirp." Then she walked off. It was weird, though; why didn't she do anything?

The following morning, I lifted my body from the clutches of my blanket, and my necklace was missing. I scrambled around everywhere, skipping breakfast and the beginning of my first class. I began hyperventilating, so I sat on the rigid floor of my bedroom, grasping my arms around my legs with my head tucked between my knees in a pool of tears. Miss Holmes walked into my room and asked before she noticed I was having a panic attack, 'Why aren't you in class?"

She got down to my level to comfort me as I told her I had lost the necklace. Her eyebrows shot up as she froze with fear but tried to stay calm. Then she sent me to the end of my first class, hoping I wouldn't notice her hyperventilating and pacing back and forth like she was on a track.

I wiped away all my tears and put on a straight face before I walked in. As I entered, I immediately saw that the serpent had my necklace on her neck. I should have known before! I confronted her and screamed, "That is mine, you a foul-smelling cherry!" Then I pounced on her. Although I was tiny, I had enough momentum to knock her to the ground, and she tried to fight me off as I tried to grab the necklace.

Professor Nidyevon rushed over, grabbed me by my arms, and ripped me from the serpent's clutches. "Ladies, what is going on?" She managed to get me to my feet and pulled me to the side, "Ruby, stop fighting me!" She was more red than ever. She even said some words in Russian that I didn't recognize. "Ruby, you cannot just pounce on someone like that. It is not lady-like and is against our school code. We do not hit peo-ple!" She shrieked as she held me still in place, staring into my soul, preventing me from pouncing again.

"Mary stole my necklace! It was probably when I was sleeping last night, and it was around her neck. Look!"

Professor Nidyevon sighed and rolled her eyes, "I don't care if she stole your monkey, child! You do not hit people!"

My nose scrunched, and my eyebrows curved as I watched Mary stick her revolting tongue out at me, "Professor Nidyevon, I promise I did not take her little necklace. She is just infuriated because she did not get a good grade on her test from the last class, and now she is taking it out on me. It is not fair!"

I rolled my eyes, "You stupid, vazey, cherry! We didn't have a last class. If you are going to lie, at least do it properly. This is the first class since the break ended, and I missed nearly the first half of this one. Professor Nidyevon even has a note..." My face became flame-red, and my eyes began to bulge out of my head, "Professor Nidyevon, please help me with this!"

Mary still tried to deny my claim as embarrassment flushed her cheeks.

"That is enough, ladies. The both of you will go immediately to Miss Holmes' office."

Mary's eyes fell out of her skull, "What? But I didn't do anything; she was the one who pounced on me!"

Professor Nidyevon shook her head, "Kid, Ruby is right. If you are going to lie, do it well and make sure the lie can be backed up. Ruby did have a note, and this is your first class of the day. Now, I would appreciate it if you didn't fight me on this because not only did you lie, but I know Ruby, and even though she has some... issues. She wouldn't accuse you of taking something that is hers if you didn't do it. She may have many flaws and may not be able to be a proper young lady or–"

"Okay! I think she gets it!"

"My point is, I believe her. So, I am sending both of you to Miss Holmes' office with this note explaining why you are there. Now leave!" She said, handing us a small note with the tiniest cursive writing I have ever seen. It was practically illegible to read.

Mary crossed her arms as if she wasn't the one causing the trouble. I would have stuck my tongue back out at her, but I am more mature, so before we left, in the words of Shakespeare, I put my right thumb behind my top front teeth and flicked it out at her. Of course, she was too simple to recognize my more mature and subtle version of sticking my tongue out. At least I knew the meaning, and that is all that matters.

When we walked in, Miss Holmes grabbed the note from my hand, then saw the necklace on Mary's neck, and her voice dropped four notches as she enquired, "Mary, what are you doing? Give Ruby back her necklace, or you will be expelled."

For the first time, she was on my side. Why did she care?

Mary proceeded to say, "But Miss Holmes, it is my necklace. She was the one who attacked me for it." Miss Holmes was displeased.

"Mary, I do not appreciate being lied to. Professor Nidyevon claims here that this is Ruby's necklace, and she only pounced on you to get it back. One thing about this child that I entirely love is that she stands and fights for what is right. Even though she fights for what is right in an inappropriate way, and she is an unusually tiny child, so picking on people bigger than her isn't an intelligent decision, but–"

"Once again, I think we get it!"

Miss Holmes looked a bit irritated, "She always stands up for what she believes in. I completely respect her for that." She turned towards me, "Now, Ruby, we will discuss my policy on hitting others after I am done with Mary," she faced Mary again, "But Mary, I demand you to give me her necklace now!"

She told Mary to take the necklace off, and she did. Then she lifted my right finger and matched the print together.

After that, she told Mary, "If you ever touch her necklace again, you and your sisters will be expelled. Am I understood?"

Mary gulped, nodded, and left.

My pupils became small as my eyes widened when I enquired, "How did you know there was a fingerprint on the back of it and that it was mine." She didn't reply; she just stood there solemnly before sending me back to class.

I always kept the necklace attached to my neck and hidden under my clothes. I couldn't stop thinking of that moment but never brought it up again. Luckily, as the next few weeks passed, the last week in February approached. Instead of having culinary class today, Mr. Henry directed us to the great hall, where Miss Holmes gathered all the first-year students.

As we arrived in batches for the first time, I was able to grasp how many other students were in my year. The females were on the right of the hall, sitting delicately and chattering quietly, and the boys on the left were throwing paper balls at each other while shouting. There appeared to have been about 50 students of each gender.

"First years, please take your seats and be quiet." Miss Holmes announced, standing in the front of the hall while she stood on a podium. "We have some very important information to go over today. Next week, we will be visiting the White House and meeting the president. I expect each and every one of you to be on your best behavior." She glanced over the audience until she found me and then winked.

I straightened my posture and moved my hands to my sides. Of course, she targeted me. I don't blame her, but I wouldn't do anything so foolish at the president's house. I'm not that thick. As I glanced around the room, the other girls didn't seem to care and weren't paying that much attention, "Uh uh, okay, Miss Holmes," they mumbled.

I rolled my eyes and shook my head. The only other girl who seemed interested was Lulu, which wasn't surprising. I faced the boys, and they seemed to be a little intrigued, with Willie being the most. "Ruby," Lulu whispered, "This will be extraordinary. Don't you think?"

I nodded; she knew me so well.

CHAPTER FIVE

The White House

The following day was going per usual until the Acker sisters approached us. I clenched my fists, crossed my arms, and hollered, "What do you want?"

"Oh, nothing precious, Ruby. I love your hair, necklace, and style, and you're amazing!"

Then she grasped me in her tight grip. This is the weirdest thing I have ever seen in my entire life. What is she doing? Then, with her amber teeth stretching outwards, she yelled, "Hey, best friend! Later today, can we go and relax in your room?"

I thought it was a trick and wanted to say, "There is no chance you will even get a foot into my room."

But Lulu pulled my right arm to the side as she softly covered her hands to my ears and whispered, "Come on, Ruby, they are being nice. Maybe they changed."

My eyes squinted, and my eyebrows fell as far down as they could go, and I acknowledged, "I don't think so, but fine, but if she ruins anything, I will be very cross."

Lulu shrugged her shoulders and chirped, "That's fair."

So, we agreed and planned for the Ackers to come after dinner. Before they arrived, I rushed into our room and hid all my gadgets because I knew they would try to break them. Although I had already gotten permission to hide them in my room before, I didn't want them to know.

Twenty minutes later, they strolled into our room like they owned the place and brought the sponge pudding we had made earlier that day. They said, "Here, Ruby and Lulu, this is a peace offering," with giant smiles that stretched from ear to ear.

I didn't believe this could be happening. They even brought some for Coco. I thought they might have poisoned it, so I chucked it into the garbage bin. They stepped back with hesitation but continued to smile and acknowledge it with, "I understand that you don't trust us, but you can. We didn't poison it."

After they mentioned that, they noticed a closed candle on my nightstand. They were suspicious about why there was one in our room because they didn't have one in their room, even though there were closed candles all over the Academy, thanks to me, of course. They weren't in school for a few weeks, so their room wasn't occupied.

After two hours of them trying to interact with us, we yawned and stretched; it was time for bed. Or at least that's what we told them. Before they skipped off, Mary offered to do my hair in the morning. Lulu convinced me I should. I only agreed because of Lulu, and then they were gone.

The following morning, I got up, dressed, and went to their room. I sat down, and she whispered, "Close your eyes. It will all be over soon."

I refused to close them fully, and she pulled out a pair of scissors from her musty drawer. Before she could cut my hair, I turned around and grabbed them. I knew she had an ulterior motive, and I was done with it. I left and was on my way to Miss Holmes' office, but then realized I shouldn't tell her about what just happened because then I could mess with the Serpent sisters for the rest of the semester, which would be much more fun. Now that I think about it, I have never had an arch nemesis before. Ooh, this was going to be fun!

A few days passed, and the prank wars began again. We started small by changing each other's toothpaste. Then we went large and started sneaking into each other's rooms at night and putting syrup on the walls so bugs would come. We deeply loathe each other. The day before we left to go to the white house, we went to class, but something was off.

Miss Nidyevon explained, "Today's lesson will be differ-ent. We will not be doing hair and makeup, but we will be learning about the history of the White House to prepare you for tomorrow's trip. Professor Jones will be teaching all of you today."

Finally, an exciting class! Mr. Henry casually strolled in and sat down in front of the students. He said, "The United States' first president was George Washington. Washington was president for eight years and then stepped down, beginning the two-term presidential amendment."

He explained that the White House was built as a symbol of American democracy. It was not meant to be a palace but more of an office that presidential leaders could reside in with their families for four to eight years.

My eyes were wide open, my muscles relaxed, and my pearly teeth shined through my lips as he went on to talk about the Declaration of Independence. He told us there might even be a map on the back of it. I knew I had to fact-check that for myself. It probably isn't there, but you never know... As these rapid thoughts ran through my head, I veered my head around the room, and the other girls in my class fell asleep. They didn't understand history because they were all airheads. Lulu was the only other person who seemed intrigued, but that didn't surprise me.

If I was going to pick the lock of the box that holds the Declaration of Independence, then I need to create some type of method to do that. I could use my melting stick to loosen the bolts if the declaration is encased in class, but I need another method as a backup. I decided I wanted to make a device that I could control and would crawl around, see the inside of things, clip, melt, and have a micro moovo inside of it. So, I went straight to the little room behind the spiral staircase that led to the upper floors. At the beginning of the year, Miss Holmes showed me this little room for any time I wanted to work on a project and have my own free time. Inside, she put a little forge welding machine, many tools of all shapes and sizes, and many other little broken or extra pieces she had. I also had one of my extra toolboxes in there.

I think I knew what I wanted to build, so I pulled out all of my magnets, a few batteries, a small sheet of aluminum, my small forge welding machine that I created after watching the process of how a forge welder works, my little switches, the circuits, my micro motor I invented a few months ago after I watched Father take apart one of the big motors from his train engine, and my broken steel pieces I had stolen from my when Father took me to the railway center a few months ago. Then I got to work.

I spent the next few hours on my stomach, building a little bug-shaped device. It was so cute! When I was done, it had an aluminum exterior with a little engine on the inside, and I could control it with a little magnetic controller I built. The controller has multiple types of magnets that can "talk" to the little bug and tell it what to do. I included a mini moovo inside of it, a little "hand" that the bug can use to pick locks or clip something; I even put this little heat-sensitive capturer inside of it. I built one a few years ago after Mr. Henry taught me about a man named William Herschel, who learned how different objects can sense different levels of heat when he looked through his telescope about 59 years ago.

After finishing building the device, I chose to paint it. The little device kind of looked like a cute spider. I wanted to make it look more realistic, so I brought out my painting supplies and painted it with blue and purple iridescent paint. It was so pretty!

Now, it was testing time. I called Lulu and Willie into the little room. It was a bit squished, but we all managed to fit in. Then I released the little bug, and it roamed around. I tested all of its features, and they worked very well. I was incredibly proud. I think out of all the inventions I have created, this was my favorite.

"Ruby, can you please make me one? This is amazing!" Lulu beamed as she hopped up and down from excitement.

"Yes, me too!"

"Of course, I can make the both of you one. What colors do you want? I can make any color or color combination."

"Um... I would like to have pink and light yellow if that is possible." Lulu asked calmly but with a high-pitched voice.

"May I please have blue and red?" He paused for a few moments to admire my work. "Ruby, what do you think you will name it?" Willie continued, as we all were very enthused.

I held my head to the floor for a few minutes, "I think I might call it a special pocket intelligence device for enhancing ratiocinative. Also known as SPIDER. I was possibly thinking of the name Robota because, in Czech, it means to labor since it would be doing all the labor and hard work for me, but I think that is too brutal, so I will call it my SPIDER."

"Wait, why Czech? I didn't know you could speak Czech."

"I am learning a few words because in class with Mr. Henry, we are doing a small unit on the Czech culture and language."

"That's interesting!"

Then we all giggled.

The following morning, we left to go to the capital. I grabbed my scalpel to get the Declaration out of the box, the melting stick I created to loosen bolts, just in case the Declaration was encased in glass, and my gloves so no one could pinpoint me. I stuffed them in my pocket, which I had sewed in the undergarment under my dress to carry objects. When we headed outside, Miss Holmes assigned the Acker sisters with Lulu and me in the horse carriage to "Hopefully get along."

I thought this was very foolish of her, and Lulu and I were furious. We tried to change the seating arrangement but were unfortunately unsuccessful. Luckily, the trip was only about twenty minutes. We knew we didn't want to talk to the Ackers, so Lulu and I finger-spoke the entire time.

About halfway through the trip, Caroline snapped the silence and blurted, "When we were in your room a few weeks ago, we saw a painting of what I think is your family. I understand why they sent you away now. You were the odd one out. No wonder your family doesn't love you."

That was it! I stood out of my seat, reached for her arms, and shouted at the top of my lungs, "Don't you ever talk about my family, you cherry! I may not look like them very much, but I don't hate them either. They are my family, and nobody insults them except me! And you know what? I may be different and get on their nerves, but at least my parents visit me every so often. Unlike yours, who don't come at all, except for that one time they yelled at you for the entirety of their visit! So, don't talk about my relationship with my family, you serpent!"

Lulu pulled me back from her grasp. The other sisters started to shed the waterworks as I sat back down, rolled my eyes, and crossed my arms. Then Lulu embraced me. I couldn't believe that Caroline had told me that, and maybe I shouldn't have said what I just did, but she deserved it!

The last eight minutes of the ride were in silence. After we arrived, we jumped out of the carriage and headed in line. We ensured to be in the front because the Serpent sisters weren't knowledgeable and viewed the front as the "Answer the question zone."

We waited patiently for about twenty minutes, and then the boys' Academy arrived. They lined us up next to each other, and luckily, Willie was at the front with us. Miss Holmes screamed, "Ladies and gentlemen, we are about to go inside, and I expect each and every one of you to be on your best behavior." Then, we started on the trail.

The trail was covered in beautiful flowers: cherry blossoms, tulips, magnolias, and wisterias. It was stunningly beautiful. It looked like we were in a dream. When we got to the entrance, many guards wore plain white and navy clothing. Two walked up to us and split us into groups between the girls and boys. But first, every student had to be patted down to ensure we weren't hiding anything. I got a little nervous because of all the gadgets I had brought, but I knew my plan wouldn't fail. All students got a pass and were free to go. Our tour guide approached the girls' school. I think he was in the army, considering he had an army badge on his arm, "I will be your tour guide today. My name is Lester. You may call me Mr. Lester."

It was pretty interesting how they had massive guns and were very friendly. I didn't think much of it. We began climbing the large staircase to the entrance. When we first walked in, there were a few tables on the sides of the walls and paintings of previous presidents hanging on top. We first headed into the blue room. I finally understood why it was called the "blue room" because the carpeting was blue. It made a lot of sense. Looking around, I noticed wooden tables and chairs with blue cloth padding. I asked Mr. Lester, "Why did they make everything in this room blue? I understand this is the blue room, but what made them choose this color? Was it because blue is the color that calms people down, or is it because it is supposedly stimulating to the eye and indicates freedom, intuition, imagination, and freedom? Or was it something else? And if so, what was the real reason behind it?"

The Acker sisters gave me a dirty look with their faces red from all the crying they did. They are such cry babies. Mr. Lester responded, "Wow, little one, I am impressed. You are the first girl I have met in many years who has asked such an intellectually stimulating question. What is your name, young child?"

I responded, "Ruby."

He continued, "Well, Ruby, I don't know the answer. I have never thought about it in that way. I will surely find out for you if you would like."

I smiled and nodded, knowing I had just stumped a middle-aged adult. The other girls looked at me with disgust and astonishment. So, I hollered, "Yes, I would love that very much! Thank you."

He smiled, and we continued on the tour. The next room we went to was full of paintings. It was beautiful.

This reminded me of home with all of the extravagant and beautiful portraits. The first painting he took us to was the Lighter Relieving a Steamboat Aground. It looked like a small wooden platform used as a boat with seven people riding it. The guard told us this painting was illustrated thirteen years ago by George Caleb Bingham. It was interesting...

Following the portrait room, we went into many other spaces. Then we entered quite an interesting room you'd think they wouldn't show to the public. It's pretty foolish that they let the public see this room due to the weaponry, such as guns, knives, swords, etc... in it.

Mr. Lester explained, "These guns don't work. They are fake; we show this room to people to say that if anyone ever breaks into the house and tries to steal one, the white house will know because they are printed heavily."

Oh okay! See, that makes a lot more sense now. That is brilliant, but if they tell this to the public, the enemy won't waste their time looking for this room. We went to the garden for lunch after finishing this room. Miss Holmes brought sandwiches. We had the choice of picking ham, corned beef, or cow tongue. I was not fond of cow tongue and didn't enjoy pork, so I decided on corned beef. It was delicious.

After lunch was over, the students played while Lulu, Willie, and I roamed the gardens. Mr. Lester casually shuffled over to me and said, "The blue room is blue because they liked the color, but I am happy to tell you that because they liked your response so much, your answer is what we will start telling people now."

I couldn't believe it; they would use my response at the White House. I didn't want to annoy him, so I played it off well with a shrug and smile and stated, "Thank you."

We then went to the Andrew Jackson horse statue. Mr. Lester explained that "Jackson was a general during the Mexican-American war battle."

I abruptly snapped his sentence in half, "I'm not trying to be rude, but he wasn't a general during the Mexican-American war, but he was during the War of 1812, otherwise known as the Battle of New Orleans. No offense."

Miss Holmes glared at me, considering I had just cut him off, but I continued by saying, "Also, sorry for interrupting you."

Lester retorted, "I don't know if that is accurate, but based on the brilliance you have presented before, I can imagine that your response is correct. After he was president, the southern and western people felt they needed to honor him because, in their opinions, he was considered 'one of the best presidents there has ever been.'"

Lulu's eyes glittered, "Well, what do you think?"

Mr. Lester responded, "I think he was an outstanding president. I started guarding duties when he first became president and have been here ever since."

I thought that was an appropriate response. After that, we moved back inside the White House. We split into two groups, one for the girls and one for the boys. The boys went with another tour guide to the writing room while another tour guide took the girls to the kitchen. Mr. Lester sat us around the big table and said, "You will be learning to make Washington pie."

Washington pie, oh, come on! This isn't fair. Even visiting such a historical and critical place, we have to bake. I wanted to escape, but Miss Holmes knew me and decided to sit beside me, "It's okay, Ruby, you will be fine. This will be fun. Just think about it like a chemistry experiment. Not many pupils like yourself get to go to the white house and bake Washington pie while inside."

With no response, I side-eyed her. We were handed eggs, sugar, baking powder, flour, raspberry jam, and powdered sugar. I told Miss Holmes I wanted to wash my hands, and she watched me slowly walk over to the sink next to Mr. Lester. I whispered to him, "Is there any way you could get me out of here so I could learn something actually important?"

He smiled but shook his head. I had to go back to my seat. At this point, I knew I didn't have a choice. We spent the next hour and a half baking. Then we were required to eat it. I wasn't too pleased because I only wanted to meet the president and look behind the Declaration of Independence to see if there was a map. But I decided I might as well try to enjoy it if I couldn't do anything about it.

I ate the pie, even though it seemed like it was more of a cake than a pie. It looked like a yellow circular cake with jam in the middle and more cake on top. When we were done, we rejoined the other group. I asked Willie what he did, hoping I wouldn't regret it. I did. He explained how he went and learned about the different writings sent over from other countries. Some of which were from the Queen of England. I wanted to see that! So, I raised my hand. "Yes, Ruby."

"Will we be seeing the writing room?" I questioned quietly.

Mr. Lester shook his head and laughed a little, "That room is only for young men to see as only men can read."

I gave him a grimace look of stupidity. It astonished me that even in the mid-nineteenth century, they didn't let a girl see writing because we supposedly "can't" read. Well, maybe the other girls can't read, but I can!

We headed to the next room, the official president's office. It had a few flags hanging from the walls, multiple chairs, and a big desk right in the middle. The only thing we didn't see was the president. I was disappointed, but we still had a few rooms left.

Once we left his office, we went through this dark hallway with no windows. It felt like we had walked into an abyss. However, once we arrived in the presidential conferencing room, silence filled it. There was a large table in the middle with many seats surrounding it and a few candle holders on the walls. Mr. Lester explained that this is where the secret meetings are held between the president and his officials. I looked over to the right and saw a small metal door. "Mr. Lester, where does that door go?"

He could only respond, "Sorry, Ruby, that is confidential."

What could have been in such a small room with no light and a metal door? They must be hiding something. That intrigued my curiosity. What if it's something dangerous? Oh, I have to get in there when everyone else is gone. After we left the room, I asked to use the restroom. Miss Holmes agreed and sent Lulu to ensure I wasn't doing anything foolish. I decided I wasn't returning to that room so soon because I wanted to go alone and didn't want to get Lulu in trouble. I knew Miss Holmes would have checked there, so I waited. I started walking down the abyss again until I reached the light.

In the meantime, I decided to find the Declaration of Independence. I faced Lulu, and she mentioned, "I think I know where it is because I came here about a year ago with my father, and they typically don't like to mess with an eighty-three-year-old document. Follow me."

I followed her into the room, and there it was encased in glass for all eyes to see. A sign beside it explained how it was supposed to be moved to Philadelphia, but the train didn't arrive on time, so it would be transported tonight. I went up to it and noticed the screws on the back.

Lulu gave me a dirty look, "What are you doing? Are you mad? You could destroy it!"

"No, I won't. I just want to see the map. The faster you help me, the faster this will go," I retorted sternly.

She sighed, shook her head, and concurred. I let my little SPIDER loose, and it managed to get it off within five minutes. I guess I didn't need my melting stick after all... I took out my gloves and picked it up. We looked at the back of the Declaration, put it back in the container, then latched the glass back down and left it how it was. Then we went to find the group.

Once we left the room, we began running. Then, the worst thing imaginable happened. I ran into the president, James Buchanan, and was knocked over. He had light hair, light eyes, and a pin on his chest that read CAD. Lulu held her mouth open and started laughing, but her face went straight once she saw who it was. The president looked down at me and lifted me back onto my feet. I apologized as much as I could.

He smiled, "It is alright, little girl. It didn't hurt. Are you alright? Based on your uniform, I assume you're a part of Miss Holmes Academy."

Lulu and I both nodded, and he continued, "I admire her Academy. But what were you two doing in the room with the Declaration?"

I didn't want Lulu to be in trouble, and I didn't want to lie to him; I uttered, "My teacher said there is a rumor about there being a map on the back of it. I wanted to see if it was true."

He smiled and squeezed his eyes, clearly profoundly astonished, "What is your name, little girl?"

"Ruby, Ruby Ledger."

"Ruby, you are the girl who came up with why the blue room is blue. Am I correct?"

I beamed, "Yes, Mr. President."

He snorted, "You know, Ruby, you are the first young girl I have ever met who is as intelligent as a boy."

I was pretty insulted because girls can be just as intelligent as boys, if not more. While at the same time, I didn't know if that was good or bad coming from him, so I nodded.

"Ruby, I will take you and your friend back to where your group I don't blame you for looking at the back of the Declaration. I did as well when I first came into the office. Do you want this to be our little secret?"

Lulu and my eyes widened as we faced each other, then snapped our bodies towards the president, and I whispered, "If you don't mind..."

When we returned to the group, Miss Holmes didn't look pleased. She turned towards President Buchanan, "I'm very sorry for these two girls. I should have known they would get into trouble. Ruby, the little one, has been a troublemaker since arriving. I will make sure they both get the proper punishment."

As she presented this, President Buchanan had a disagreeable expression, "Actually, on the contrary, they didn't get into any trouble at all. They are precious and brilliant little angels, especially the little one, Ruby. In all my years of service, I have only once met an older woman as clever as your little six-year-old, but I will say Ruby is the first with a pet monkey."

Miss Holmes gasped in shock, considering Lulu and I are typically the ones to get in trouble. As he said this, I gave him an intense look because I'm not six and exclaimed, "Actually, I'm not six. I'm almost ten, and I might be tiny, but I am mighty!"

He apologized for mistaking me for six, "I like your statement of 'I might be tiny, but I am mighty.' It's cute. Well, it was an honor meeting both of you. Specifically, you, Ruby, Bye."

Wow! He just said it was an honor. Oh, whoopee, this is one of the best moments of my life. Miss Holmes congratulated us, and we continued the tour until we had forty-five minutes left. During this time, we had free time to go back and look at the rest of the architecture they hadn't gone over. Miss Holmes pulled me aside, "Ruby, I trust you to go off on your own since I know Mr. Henry gave you a report to write up. Please do not do something foolish, and let me regret this. Here is a watch and a map so you don't get lost."

I don't do stupid things that make her feel regretful! Okay, maybe sometimes I do, but not always! I nodded and went off. I knew I wanted to return to the room I was in before with the small metal door. So, I retraced my steps until I found the dark abyss they call a hallway. When I reached the end of it, I checked to ensure no one was in there, and I entered. I went to the small door, and it was locked. Coco was excellent at picking locks as she unlocked the door in under twelve seconds. I timed it.

When I snuck into the room, I looked around. It was a midsize room, enough for three people to fit inside. There was a table with a burnt-out candle and a large metal box on the left side. I had never seen such a secure-looking metal box before. Maybe they were just invented. That's when I heard footsteps. Someone was coming. As I looked around, I saw an open board in the wall and decided to crawl into it.

We managed to fit inside with barely any space to spare; I was delighted to be petite at this moment. However, I accidentally dropped my SPIDER before entering. I had to let it crawl to the ceiling so they wouldn't see it; otherwise, I might have been caught.

Then they walked in. I heard their voices. It sounded like the president and a colleague. They began talking about me.

President Buchanan said, "Marshall, there is this little girl I met earlier with and a witty character just like Millie Jones. Her name is Ruby Ledger. She is a tiny genius who seems to know a lot about the world, and if she is anything like Henry or Millie Jones, we will have an issue."

Henry Jones? Like my teacher, why were they talking about him? I signed to Coco. She told me to stay quiet.

Marshall continued, "She is just a little girl, and Millie Jones has no children. I don't think you should be concerned about her. We can ignore her if she doesn't get into this box or get the scroll. She won't foil this plan."

As they were opening the box, President Buchanan paused for a second and vocalized, "There was only one other key that was made to open this box. Even the organization's keys don't work on this box, which is why I stole it, so they made a second, but I didn't notice it on the girl."

Marshall didn't seem to care and grabbed the key from Buchanan's hand, opened the box, and took out a book.

After a few minutes, they closed it, entered the other room, and locked the door. Coco patted my shoulder, "Since this has to do with Mr. Henry, what if it also has to do with you? He talked about you a lot and said something about a key, so what if your key opens the box? The one Miss Holmes and Mr. Henry are cautious of you not losing."

I agreed to try it, considering I couldn't think of another option. I must find out what was inside and what Mr.

Henry has to do with it. I must find out their plan. Now, I knew it was clear to try to examine and pick this lock. So, I quietly crept up to the box so that Buchanan wouldn't hear me and peeked at it.

CHAPTER SIX

The Key of Assassination

The box looked rusted and beaten up from possibly being shipped overseas, but it didn't look that old. An engraving wrapped around the side of the box; it was Latin and read "Filiae nostrae dulcissimae Ruby. Invenies omnia quae debes in hac capsadetectiva esse, sicut pater tuus et I. Te amamus et dulces cerasas genas."

This meant "To our sweetest daughter Ruby. You will find all you need in this box to be a detective, like your father and I. We love you and your sweet cherry cheeks." Since it had my name on it, I decided to write it down on the side of my dress because I didn't have paper.

Mr. Henry may be able to explain it. Perhaps he knew why my parents wrote this box for me. I didn't understand. My parents don't know Latin; at least, I don't think they do; also, they couldn't be detectives. They constantly degraded my talents and excitement, so how could this come from my parents? Also, in the past, they have constantly repeated, "Latin is a language of the dead, and it is useless for the present day to learn."

I thought this was incredibly foolish because although English is a Germanic language, Latin is the basis of many world languages. It also helps you identify the meaning of words due to their prefixes and suffixes of them. When Mr. Henry was teaching it at home, he was conscientious about ensuring they didn't find out. But at the same time, he wanted me to be fluent in Latin. Maybe it was just a coincidence, or this box belonged to me. Well, there was only one way to find out: to see if the box opened with my key.

I removed my necklace between my shirt and dress and put it next to the keyhole. I deeply breathed and silently whispered, "I hope this works."

I inserted the key, and it was a perfect fit. I watched Coco in shock and turned the key. I slowly unlatched the latches on the sides of the box for extra protection. I didn't want them to hear me because I knew they would make a loud noise. I proceeded to open the box. It felt as if I was a real detective, which I am. The lid was heavy, and it took some help from Coco to open it entirely. Once I did, I was astonished.

It was my box, filled with many random gadgets and tools, and there were a bunch of photos of me in it, but from when I was a baby. I must have been under two since I don't have any memories from before then. Considering memories start to develop at around age three, maybe a little younger, perhaps a little older...

I knew these pictures were of me because my parents have identical ones on their desks at home. I couldn't believe it! Why would a random box with my name on it, my key that fits perfectly, and a bunch of tools and pictures of me be located in the White House? What are these people up to? I decided to look through more of the box. The first gadget that caught my attention was this pocket-sized, odd-looking gadget that looked like it could kill someone without a trace. It is made of metal and has a knife, a magnifying glass, some vials of liquid, and many little tools like screwdrivers, lock picks, and more. I think I will call it the pocket spy. Then I stuffed it into my pocket. After safely placing it there, Coco signed, "Earlier, they took out a book. It must belong to you! What do you think they were doing with it?"

I quickly signed back, "I don't know, but I agree it's mine, and if it's in here, it must be important!"

We slowly closed the box to see what President Buchanan and Marshall discussed. I put the box just as it was before and went to the door to listen in on their conversation. My SPIDER had a mini-sized megaphone connected to its stomach that I pulled out to listen through the wall.

Then, I guided SPIDER to crawl under the little crack to get some evidence.

"Abraham Lincoln, the crummy Republican, is up against us in the running. He is a low-life who wants to make everything equal for all enslaved people. I view the opposite. I want to ensure the South knows rich people will always win." Buchanan mentioned to Marshall in a toned voice.

With an exhausted attitude, Marshall replied, "So, did you receive the plan?"

"Yes, I did. The only thing not clarified in the letter is that Lincoln will be at the Wigwam. This is where it will all take place," Buchanan uttered as Marshall smiled.

What was going on? I had to find out!

"What if the Jones find out?" Marshall whispered under his breath.

"Don't worry, they won't, and we will be unstoppable for the next race."

My eyes widened as far as they could go as I turned toward Coco. I was very anxious but wanted to find out what was happening, so I decided to sneak out of this room to find the scroll after they left. I hoped that SPIDER was able to detect it. Unfortunately, heading to the metal door, I stepped on a creak in the floor. They heard me and walked over as fast as they could. Fortunately, I was quick enough, so they didn't see me.

Once they entered, they saw a piece of Coco's fur on the ground and picked it up. "The girl, she has a pet monkey. Do you think she heard us?" Buchanan exclaimed concernedly.

"Well, she doesn't appear to be in here right now, so maybe she came in here and couldn't open the box. I wouldn't worry too much about her. She is useless." Marshall explained.

Buchanan didn't say anything but had a look of worry on his face. Then they left. I waited about three minutes and crept out again. I checked to ensure there was nobody in the other room before I went to find the note.

Coco stood by to watch to ensure nobody was coming while I crawled out of the room. I picked SPIDER up and checked the drawing inside of it. It appeared that Buchanan's scroll was located inside his desk. I used my pocket spy to help pick the desk's lock. When I got it open, I found a long scroll. In the colors of the words, the scroll stated:

(blue/lime,   blue/red) (blue/orange,   blue, pink/lime) **(blue/yellow)** (blue/purple/yellow/white) **(blue, blue/pink, blue/pink)** (blue/lime, yellow) **(pink/white, purple, lime)** (blue/yellow, pink/blue, pink, blue/pink, brown, orange) **(blue/brown, purple, blue/lime, pink/blue, blue/pink, red)** (pink, lime) **(brown,**

blue/red) (pink/white, purple, lime) (orange, blue/lime, blue/red, pink/pink, lime, blue/red, pink/white, brown, blue/lime, blue/red) (orange, lime, blue/red, pink/white, lime, blue/purple) (pink, pink/lime) (blue/red, brown, blue/red, lime)

[...]

(blue/brown, brown, blue/red, orange, lime, blue/purple, lime, blue/pink, pink/lime)

(lime)

I don't understand. "Coco, what do you think these colors mean? It must be some sort of code."

I decided it would be best to capture it with my mini moovo and tell the SPIDER to draw it when I return to the academy. This way, I could decode it when I returned to the Academy. But, first, I had to find Miss Holmes. Time is of the essence.

I put the SPIDER in my pocket under my dress, went through the big room, the dark abyss, and finally, I could sneak back to my group. That's when President Buchanan walked up to my teacher. I knew he was going to ask about me.

"Good afternoon, Miss Holmes. I wondered if the little one, Ruby, had left your group?" He said, standing on one leg lopsided, watching Miss Holmes' slow movements as she veered her attention towards him, then me.

Miss Holmes retorted as his eyebrows scrunched, and their voice fell a little limp. She looked like she was about to lie, "Yes, but only to the restroom. I took her there myself."

I jumped back a little to her lied response. Why was she protecting me? Unless she knew something, I didn't. He gave her a look of affirmation and walked off. Miss Holmes approached my level and asked, "How was your adventure? Did you find anything interesting?"

I didn't want to lie to her, but I didn't know what she was hiding. Maybe she knew and would try to confront me later on. I just don't know. "Miss Holmes, I had a great time. I didn't find anything too interesting, but it was nice."

She looked disapproved and shook her head, "So, you didn't go and find out what was behind the metal door?"

I felt terrible for lying, so I decided it would be best to tell her the half-truth, also something I like to call a white lie. "Yes, I did, but I didn't find anything interesting. There was this box, but it seemed boring, so I left."

"Alright, Ruby, well, I'm glad you had fun. We are about to return to the Academy, so find Lulu and head to the horses."

I nodded and left. I think she knew I was lying. But I couldn't let her know what I saw. So, I left and went to the horses to meet with Lulu and Willie. We jumped into the carriage, and we were off. I sat quietly for the first half of the trip, but they both knew I was hiding something. They tried to ask me about it, but I shut them down instantly, "I will tell you when we get back home. Willie, meet us in our dorm room at 10:15 tonight. I will share everything."

We passed the flowery blossoms of the earliest Spring and lovely, luscious fields before we arrived at the Academy. When we did, we were required to go to dinner. However, first, we strolled around the campus so we didn't have to leave each other just yet so I could give them a short summary of what to expect in our longer conversation later. We were separated as we approached the dining hall since boys and girls weren't allowed to eat or be together. We entered, but unfortunately, the only open places to sit were next to the serpent sisters, Mary, Emma, and Caroline.

"Oh look, the little gnat exists," Emma grunted with a sharp look of evil.

"Hello, the gollumpus, the inept, and the blunderbuss. How was your visit?" They stopped smirking and snared at me like the serpents they were.

"It was fine. I see you are still a small, bubble-headed six-year-old. Did the outcast known as yourself find it interesting? Because I didn't." Mary loudly snarled.

With a straight face, I retorted instantly, "Yes, I did. But, maybe you didn't find it interesting because you don't understand the simplicity of presidential history and how it affects our country." I softly spoke, and a small smile jumped onto my face.

She huffed and puffed like the big bad wolf from the three little pigs and walked away. Dinner was over, and we were supposed to return to our dorms, but I had to stop first to see Mr. Henry, so I told Lulu, "I need to get something from Mr. Henry, and I will meet you in our room later."

She walked off, and I headed to his office. When I entered, Miss Holmes had her left leg hanging over the desk while discussing something. At first, I was nervous she would send me away, but she didn't; when she saw me enter, she stood from her stooped position and walked right out the door without a response or looking at me. I approached Mr. Henry, and he enquired, "How was your trip? I heard you found the metal door. Did you find anything inside?"

I looked suspiciously at him as I carefully took a step back, "How did you know I went in?"

He chuckled, "Ruby, I know you, and I know you went in. So, what did you find?"

I shrugged, "I found this metal box. It read 'Filiae nostrae dulcissimae Ruby. Invenies omnia quae debes in haccapsadetectiva esse, sicut pater tuus et I. Te amamus et dulces cerasas genas engraved on it. Also, I could open it with the key you gave me."

"Well, Ruby, that is very interesting," he said in a light, calm voice before turning to collect his notes into an orderly pile.

"You know what else is interesting? The president walked in but didn't see me. He spoke about you, another woman, and a girl with the key. Which I presume to be mine. What did you have to do with it? Why did my key work? Why was my name engraved on the box? Also, why was the box full of gadgets." I slowly took out my new pocket spy, showed him, and said, "The president has a plan about something happening at a place known as the Wigwam–"

Mr. Henry raised his hands to stop my speech abruptly and shouted, "Ruby, slow down, alright?" He turns his head towards every other corner of the room. He is not making eye contact, as if he is trying to find something else to trigger a different discussion, as if he is hiding something. "Oh, I see you have a pocket knife."

"Pocket knife? How do you know what this thing is? And why do you seem to know about this? What is going on, and why did he say your name?" I questioned, starting to become agitated.

"Ruby, take a deep breath and relax. I know this is a lot to take in. Now for the pocket knife, I also have one of those; see..." He pulled it out of his pants and continued, "For the president, I used to know him long before you were born, but don't worry because I know everything."

"What about the Wigwam and–"

"Ruby, stop. Everything is okay. Alright? You have to trust me. Now, I will teach you how to use your pocket knife, and everything will be fine...."

Why did it feel like he was hiding something? I just knew it. He was a bit standoff-ish, his tone was a notch lower than usual, and his eye contact was everywhere except me. Although he seemed a bit off, whether it was him or Miss Holmes, I had to trust him. He was all I had here. So, I took a deep breath, and he taught me how to use the pocket knife for the next ten minutes.

Honestly, I think the name Pocket Spy makes more sense, but that's not its actual name. It was almost 10:10 at night, and I had to meet up with Lulu and Willie. As I left, Miss Holmes stood outside the door as if she waited the entire time—which she probably did—with a slight look of worry. I could tell because her posture was more tense, and her face drooped. She returned to Mr. Henry's office. I turned to ask many more questions but decided it would be for the best if I didn't; There was no time.

When I returned to the dormitories, Willie was already there. After I entered, sat on my bed, and puffed some air out, Willie noticed my pocket spy and asked, "What is that, Ruby?"

I debated whether I wanted to tell him, considering it felt like everyone was constantly hiding something from me. But ultimately, I needed to trust him because he would do anything for me as I would for him. Also, he was the only friend I had that Coco actually liked. She always kept away from Lulu for reasons unknown.

I explained it to him because he was one of my best friends. Afterward, I told them what happened at the white house earlier that day and showed them the script that I had the SPIDER recreate the message on a big scroll. Lulu pursed her lips with shock as her eyes jolted out of her head, "Well, Ruby, we have to figure it out before it's too late. You're the smartest person I have ever met, and what if it is something bad? It must be important if it takes all this trouble to decode it."

Then we heard squeaks and pitter-patter from the floor outside. The noise kept growing louder and louder, and we knew that if Willie didn't leave now, we would all be in trouble. So, he quickly gathered his things, climbed outside, and lowered his head just enough so it was out of view of anyone inside. If we had moved one second later, we would have been caught because our door slammed open, and can you guess who it was? The Serpent Sisters.

"Hello, serpents." I turned to the side and mouthed silently, "Oops, did I say that out loud?" Then turned back to face them with an irritating tone of voice, "I mean Ackers. What do you want?"

"Well, little six-year-old, we heard a boy in here, and you know the rules. NO BOYS ALLOWED! So, we have to report you." Mary enunciated and squinted with enrage.

I scanned the room, pulled up the comforters on the beds, and checked under the dresser, "I don't see any boys. Maybe it was the hallucinations you seemed to get from your stupid bonnet squeezing your head too tight. It must be suffocating you."

Mary pushed me down, and my pocket spy fell out of my dress and slid under the dresser. Then she looked around and found nothing as if I hadn't done so, not even two seconds ago.

"See, Mary, there is nobody in here. Now get out before I call Miss Holmes!" Lulu shouted, throwing her pointer finger towards the door.

They gave us the dirtiest look, scanned the room as if she would find something else, shrugged, and sighed deeply before walking off. We smiled, facing each other, and then began laughing. We waited a few minutes to make sure they were gone, then slammed our door shut, locking it from the inside. We went to the window to see if Willie was gone, and he was just under the tree waiting for us.

Then, a black rat snake slithered from the tree next to him onto his shoulder.

My eyes widened as far as they could go, and my voice became stuttered, "Willie, whatever you do, don't move!" I gulped, and he got a scared look in his eye and obeyed.

Luckily, it didn't bite him, but unfortunately, it climbed up the window and slithered into our room. Lulu watched it and was about to scream. I ran over to her and shoved my hand over her mouth. Then continued, "Lulu, shh. We can't. Say. Anything! If you scream, you will wake everyone up, Miss Holmes will come, and we are not allowed to open the window. We will both be in trouble."

I moved my hand from her mouth as her voice shook with fear, and she closed her eyes momentarily, trying to hold her attitude together. "But it's a snake..."

I didn't hesitate to say, "It's okay." We will get my new pocket spy and defeat it. Could you help me?" She barely nodded with bated breath, trying not to scream.

The snake slithered under our long mirror where a pile of clothes was and stayed there for warmth. We helped Willie climb back inside and then rapidly ran to the dresser and tried to get the pocket spy out, but there was no luck. We tried moving the dresser, which probably weighed four hundred pounds. I even created a pulley system out of our clothes, but nothing. It wouldn't move because we weren't strong enough, and our clothes were about to tear.

Coco curiously mentioned, "Maybe I can fit under the dresser. I am tiny."

I smacked my forehead with my right hand, "How did we not think about that before?"

We shook our heads, tried it, and luckily we were successful. She got it out in a matter of seconds and then handed it to me. I pressed the little button with a web shape on it. It shot out a collapsable net, bolting the snake to the ground so it couldn't move. Then I shot it with the dissolvable tranquilizer dart, which looked like a clear, repugnant-smelling liquid, and it passed out. I slowly walked over to it and tapped it with the edge of my shoe to ensure it was asleep because I didn't want to kill it or be killed by it. I picked it up and threw it out the window when it was out cold. Willie said, "Maybe it is best to return to my dorm." We all nodded in unison, collected all of our supplies, and cleaned everything before going to sleep.

The next day, when we woke, we threw on our undergarments and uniforms. Then I grabbed a big purple bow for Miss Holmes to do my hair because I always went to Miss Holmes to do my hair before breakfast. She didn't mind it and seemed happy as she had no daughters and always wanted one. So, I'd like to say I was a good substitute. We went to breakfast, classes, and lunch. Finally, we had a free period of about twenty minutes. During this time, Lulu and I went to find Willie. When we finally did, fifteen minutes passed. We decided to meet again tonight because we needed to devise a plan to decode the message.

After dinner, we met near the theater when we heard a creak from a broken wood panel. Our heads snapped towards the creak, and the serpent sisters were there. Of course, they had to hear our conversation from earlier.

As I walked up to them, they ran faster than I had ever seen before. We chased them, but unfortunately, with my little legs, I wasn't fast enough to catch up. They went straight to Miss Holmes' office and snitched on us. Miss

Holmes exited out of the doorway way with a salty look, and her arms crossed over each other, without removing eye contact, especially from me. "All six of you to my office! Right! Now!"

"All six of us, but Miss Holmes, we weren't the ones sneaking out. They were!" Mary yelled with a snarky tone and pointed towards us three with her jelly-like fingers.

"Yes, all six of you, since you also snuck out after hours." Miss Holmes responded with a disappointed voice. I smirked at her. At least if I am getting in trouble, they are too.

When we entered, Miss Holmes scolded us to sit down. She sat in her headmaster's position and stated, "Detention for all of you will be going around the school for the next week, starting tomorrow morning, and turning all the lights on and off before sunrise and after sunset." We all dropped our mouths. We had to wake up early enough for class; this wasn't fair.

She continued, "You may be excused."

Caroline's mouth opened as her uvula fell back, "This is extremely unfair!"

Then Miss Holmes, who was pleasantly sitting with one leg on top of the other, grasped some air and calmly stated, "All of you may leave except for you, Ruby."

I gulped, "Why me? What did I do that they didn't do?"

Miss Holmes shook her head and sighed, "Ruby, sit down. I know you are courageous, but I need you to understand that you are our smallest and youngest pupil and could have gotten seriously hurt. Everything that happens at this school and around it is for a reason, and when you are older, you will see why. You have to trust me, alright?"

My eyebrows and nose scrunched as I crossed my arms and fell back into the chair. It wasn't fair that she singled me out, but what could I do? "Yes, Miss Holmes, I trust you. I'm sorry, but I need people to understand that nobody can't mess with me, even though I am small. I hate always being made fun of because I look like a tiny munchkin of a person, and I want to be heard. I was only sneaking around to meet with my friends, and I promise it won't happen again. It's wrong that you have the vazey rule of 'there may not be any boy-girl interactions.' I may be tiny, but I am mighty, and nobody can take that away from me or tell me otherwise!"

Miss Holmes's lips curled up to the sides as she responded with a gleam, "I understand you are friends with young Willie. I hope you cherish your relationship with each other. I'm sorry that you can't be together during the day, but I will work on trying to allow you to see him. I know how much he means to you. Oh, little one, you are just like your mother," and then she dismissed me.

As I sauntered through the halls and loafed down the corridor, I replayed, "You are just like your mother" in my head. For the millionth time, I was nothing like my mother. My mother was a selfish, foolish, feigned cherry.

I didn't even look like her. Why would she say that? I am beautiful like she is, but my features are different.

I decided to shrug it off and then caught up with Lulu and Willie. I claimed, "Tomorrow night when we turn off the lights, we will meet up and discuss our plan of attack." They agreed, and we headed back to our dorms to sleep.

The following morning, we woke up at five to turn on all the lights. It was torture waking up early. They spent two hours going around the Academy, turning every light on. After that, I went to Miss Holmes' office to do my hair. She braided the top, put it into a half ponytail, and put a purple bow. Instead of returning to my room, I decided to see if Mr. Henry was awake. I entered his office, and he was preparing for the day. I figured I could get an hour and a half of his lessons and then meet with Lulu and Willie later. He agreed. During the lesson, we learned about mathematics. This was when I became fully aware that the numbers I looked at were colorful, even though Mr. Henry didn't use colored ink. I always knew I had this genetic defect, but maybe the culprit who wrote this did as well. What if the colors aren't colors? What if they're numbers? I can't focus on this right now, though. I have to wait until tonight.

After that, he brought out a bunch of exciting gadgets. He taught me about the upcoming election with a politician named Abraham Lincoln. Apparently, he is supposed to be a very influential member of society.

By the end of the lesson, I was wide awake and intrigued. I wanted to learn more, but there needed to be more time. I had to go to breakfast. The day went as usual until his culinary class. Instead of being a typical culinary class, he taught us the proper incisions for removing a grape on the inside of a melon. I quickly figured out he was trying to teach me the perfect incision to make if I ever were to get shot. Or at least that's what I got out of the lesson. It was exceedingly informative. Finally, we finished one of the most boring days except for the grape surgery, and nightfall came. After everyone went to sleep, Lulu, Willie, and I went to turn off all the lights.

We decided to start on the west side of campus in a place called the droid, a dark wooden cabin that used to hold the agriculture classes. Nobody, especially the serpent sisters, goes there because people are too nervous, considering I created the rumor that there were ghosts that are shadows with no faces that attack you and take your beauty. You know they are there when you hear the sound of a beetle click. The cabin is covered in beetles. Honestly, I can't believe people bought that, but it worked out well for me because I wanted a secret location where Willie, Lulu, and I could go during the day without getting caught.

CHAPTER SEVEN

Decoding the Rebellion

When we arrived, we looked around to make sure nobody was there. We sat down in a circle and lit some candles because it was pitch black outside.

"So, what are we going to do to solve this?" Lulu said.

I grinned and whispered, "I might have figured something out. I'm about to tell you something nobody else knows about me." Lulu and Willie scrunched their eyebrows in confusion. "I was born with something known as synesthesia. It means that I can see numbers as colors." Lulu scootched back further. She seemed to be a bit distraught. "I fully learned what it is called today when I went to the library after class and checked out a book about it.

I always knew I could see numbers as colors, and others couldn't, but it wasn't until today that I chose to research it. I remembered that when I was in his office, he took out a book from the metal box I found my pocket spy in, and it was the same book. So, he could decode it because he probably doesn't have synesthesia. Each number has a different color, with zero being white, one blue, two pink, three orange, four red, five lime, six yellow, seven green, eight purple, and nine being brown. So, what if each color isn't a color, it's a number, and the colors with the slashes through them are double-digit numbers like 12 or 25."

Willie and Lulu smiled, and we fully decrypted it into numbers. We also bolded the numbers to split between the words, just like in the message. The results were

__(15,14)__ (13,1,25) __(16)__ (1860) __(1,12,12)__ (15,6) __(20,8,5)__ (16,21,2,12,9,3) __(19,8,15,21,12,4)__ (2,5) (9,14) __(20,8,5)__ (3,15,14,22 5 14 20 9 15 14) __(3 5 14 20 5 18)__ (2,25) __(14,9,14,5)__ (19,14) __(20,8,5)__ (13,15,18,14,9,14,7)

[...]

__(19 9 14 3 5 18 5 12 25)__

(5).

I grinned, "The largest number on here is 25. What if this is the alphabet? The only ones that are further than that are 30, 1860, and 980. Those could be addresses or times."

We figured this because the slashes for those colors were together, and there was no comma. We had to decode it into English before confirming that those numbers were times or addresses. The decoded message said this:

On May 16, 1860, all of the public should be in the convention center by nine in the morning. We will make our move at exactly 9:08. This is when Lincoln always gets to the part of his speech when the trombone starts. Between the crowd cheering and the trombone, it will be the perfect amount of noise to block out the poison dart gunshot. Luckily enough for us, the Jones family made this dart gun look like a pen, and once it's shot, it goes straight into the bloodstream without a trace; therefore, nobody would notice it can kill someone.

I have already scoped out the convention center. It looks like a box with multiple stories for people to sit. We will go to the top right opening to make our shot. It is the perfect place because there is a staircase right next to it and nobody will know. The day before the event, we will go to the convention center and block off that entrance; nobody goes there. When everyone arrives at the convention center, we will be dressed as convention usher workers, handing out flyers that look like the American flag. They say, 'For President Abram Lincoln, For Vice President Hannibal Hamlin. So, we won't be noticed. After everyone enters the room, we will close the doors and lock people in to ensure Lincoln doesn't escape. Then, I will go around to the back of the theater, climb the stairs, and go to the shooting location while you grab the horses for the great escape. Once we arrive, we will wait for the crowd to go wild before we make our move, which should be precisely at 9:08. Once I shoot him, it should take approximately 30 seconds to take effect. I will rush down the stairs and head to the horse carriage during that time.

Then we will leave.

Sincerely,

E.

Lulu's eyes lit up as she dropped her water flask and howled, "Ruby. You are a genius!"

Oh wow! I couldn't believe I figured it out. Well, I could, but I thought it would be significantly more complex. This makes much more sense!

Willie's face drooped, and his eyes narrowed to the floor, so I asked him, "What's upsetting you, Willie?"

He tried to hide the tears streaming down his face by using his hand to wipe them away, "There is something I need to tell both of you. The all-mighty Abraham Lincoln, you know as a political figure, is my father. That's what upsets me!"

All of our faces became solemn. I galloped over to him, gave him the world's biggest hug, and laid my head on his shoulder. "Don't worry, Willie. I will make sure nothing happens to your father. All we need to do is devise a plan to warn him before it happens!"

"Well, how are we going to do that?" Exclaimed Willie.

"I remember last week I was reading the newspaper, and I read somewhere that he will be in Middlebury, Vermont, at the President's Convention this weekend. We can find him there. This weekend is a long one because of the teacher meetings. We have four days to leave and return without Miss Holmes or our parents finding out. Remember that machine I built that sends messages?" I questioned, removing my head from his shoulder.

"Yeah, of course." Lulu and Willie communicated unanimously.

"Did you guys explain what it did to your parents when I gave you one to give them?" I questioned.

"Yes, we did."

"Brilliant, I am going to send messages through there and a letter—just in case they don't get it—to our parents, saying that I am sleeping at your house this weekend, Lulu, Willie is coming to my house this weekend, and you are also coming to my house this weekend."

"Wait! Ruby, what if Miss Holmes writes to our parents."

"Umm.... Let's cross that bridge if we come to it. Okay? We will sneak on the first train out on Friday morning. It is about a half-day trip. We will have only a few hours to tell Mr. Lincoln, and then we have to head back; therefore, we must not delay anything. When we arrive, many adults will surround us, and if anyone asks you, 'Children, where are your parents?' You must respond, 'Oh, I must have lost them in the crowd. Never mind, I see them right there. Mother, father! And then run in the direction you supposedly saw them in. Okay?

This event takes place in the Sheldon Hampton Theater. Children may not enter without any adult supervision. I went there once when I was younger. I remember a stairwell in the back that leads to the stage, but you must go through the front to get there. Once we make it back there, there may be people guarding him. I need you two to distract them while I talk to your dad, Willie."

"Wait, why do you get to talk to him and not us, specifically Willie?" Lulu enquired with a slight attitude as she bit the stubs of her fingernails off.

"Well, Lulu, I know the plan the best, considering I was the one who came up with it, remember? Also, I might figure something else out in the near future that you guys didn't see."

She rolled her eyes, "I guess that's fair."

My face scrunched at her reaction as I slightly shook my head, not to let her know I was annoyed. "After I tell him the plan, I will try to get him to return with us to the Academy."

"Why?" Willie stated with a soft voice.

"Because he might know Mr. Henry. When the president spoke, he mentioned Mr. Henry. Maybe your dad also knows him."

"Okay," Lulu sighed, "this better work. I don't want detention again."

We all chuckled. Then we got up, finished de-lighting everything, and returned to our rooms for the night. It didn't take long for us to fall asleep.

Miss Holmes walked in the following morning to get us up for the morning lighting. I slowly slithered out of my bed, grunting. When I reached the floor, it was freezing, causing me to rise like a sloth and slug myself over to my vanity next to my bed. "Coco, you have to get up." I began to shake her. "Now! Coco." She stuck her little tongue at me, which caused me to continue shaking her until she fell out of bed. I began laughing hysterically as she jumped to her feet and gave me a grim stare. With sagging eyes, I announced, "This is the longest week ever!" It felt like it would never end, but we couldn't complain, considering we got ourselves into this mess.

As the next few days passed, we jumped out of bed and prepared ourselves for the day. It was chilly outside, so we put on our coats and left. After we finished, it was finally time for the rest of the students to wake up and get breakfast. At breakfast, I told Lulu to "Stay here and watch from a distance. I am very close with Mr. Henry, and maybe I can speak to him about this."

I slowly approached Mr. Henry and asked if I could speak to him privately. Mr. Henry told me I had to wait until his free time later that day because he was busy in the morning. I felt hurt, considering he had never done that before. After he walked away, Lulu walked up to me after watching him send me away. I faced Lulu and muttered, "What could be happening with that? I need to talk to him about this. This is an urgent matter!"

Lulu whispered, "I'm sorry, Ruby, but I agree. I have never seen him do that to you before. Maybe we should follow him." I concurred.

After about ten minutes of chasing him around the school, he finally stopped behind the trash bins in the back and went to talk to someone. It was an unrecognizable man. He wore glass to cover his eyes, a long brown scarf to cover his neck, a black outfit, and a tall hat.

"I can't hear anything they are talking about," Lulu faintly spoke to ensure Mr. Henry didn't hear us.

"Neither can I, but that is why I have this," I expressed as I pulled out a tiny wire with a small bulb made of carbon on the end of it.

"Ruby, what is that thing?" Lulu exclaimed.

"This device makes things louder that are too far for us to hear. I call it the hearing piece."

"That's an interesting name for it. So, how does it work?" Lulu responded.

"It works by putting it in your ear and then facing the bulb piece out in the direction towards what you want to hear. Here, I'll show you." I showed her, and we finally heard what he was saying.

"Lincoln will be at the Sheldon Hampton theater at the...." Mr. Henry murmured, then stopped because he saw us.

We ran to our first class, hoping maybe he didn't. We sat and prayed that he wouldn't say anything when we arrived. Then he walked in.

"Hello, class. Is everyone alright today? Before we begin, Ruby and Lulu, may I see the two of you for a few minutes in the hallway." Mr. Henry voiced.

We had slowly risen from our seats and made our way outside, ignoring all the other students making "ooh" noises. "Now, what were two clever girls like yourselves doing following me around?" Mr. Henry enquired.

We both had blank faces, and I said, "Nothing, we were not doing anything. We just got a little lost, that's all." Wow, that was the first time I had ever lied to him.

"You got lost? How? The both of you have been here for a few months?"

"I don't know, we just did. I'm sorry for bothering you." Lulu wailed with tears in her eyes."

"Lulu, you don't need to cry. I'm not mad. I want to know why you were following me. Ruby, do you have anything you'd like to say for yourself?"

I shook my head, and then Mr. Henry questioned, "What did you want to speak about earlier?"

I debated if I wanted to tell him. I mean, what if he is in on this? But I couldn't imagine him ever killing anybody.

I have known him my entire life, so I should probably tell him, but maybe not everything.

"When we went to the white house, I learned that someone was going to try to assassinate Abraham Lincoln. I want to try and stop it from happening." I briskly voiced.

"Ruby, I can assure you everything will be alright. It would be best not to worry about Abraham Lincoln because nothing would happen to him. Now I would like the both of you to rejoin class so that we can begin," Mr. Henry sharply mentioned.

I stood there with a blank expression. He walked into the class, and I wondered what was happening. Is he a part of this plan? Why won't he let me learn about his assassination? Why is he dismissing it? Now that I have tried to tell him I must do this on my own. Well, with Lulu and Willie, of course.

It was finally Friday, the last day of lighting the candles. During our free time in the afternoon, we discussed how we were getting to the train station. At this time, I knew I had to lie to Mr. Henry again. I felt horrible about it, but he didn't know. So, I went up to him and told him, "Mr. Henry, this weekend, Mom and Dad invited Lulu, Willie, and me to our house in Boston, and I was wondering if you could take us to the train station later today?"

He smiled and stopped what he was doing, "Well, of course, I can. I'm glad you are trying to repair your relationship with them."

I smiled back and nodded.

It was finally time to leave. Once we arrived at the train station, he took us inside the nondescript brick building and up to the person over the counter to help us get on the train. I insisted that he leave and we could do it ourselves since I already knew everyone at the station, considering my parents owned this railroad business. Additionally, we get free tickets. He agreed, waved goodbye, and left.

I uttered to the ticketer with a lovely emerald outfit and an interesting little hat, "Good evening, Ms. Miller. My two friends and I were invited to visit Vermont, and my parents are there this weekend. We would like three tickets, please."

She was charming and handed them right over. We walked on the train, trying not to act suspicious. Once we found our seats in an open cabin, we slept for the night, knowing we would arrive in the morning.

When the sun shined through the cabin glass, we had awoken. It was eight in the morning, and a new train attendant I had never met came in to give us breakfast. She handed each a chocolate chip muffin, a banana, and a glass of water. Then she sat down next to us as if she was about to start a conversation, holding her cart with her left hand. I looked at her as if I low-pitched and grumpy, "Hello, children, my name is Ethel Wood. Now, where are the three of you young ones going?"

Willie, Lulu, and I turned toward each other and shook heads, indicating that I would speak. "Um... We will visit my parents' house in Middlebury, and these are my friends."

"Are the three of you traveling alone?" asked Ethel solemnly without taking her eyes off of us.

"Yes, but my parents will pick us up when we arrive. Also, I don't mean to be rude, but we just woke up and wanted to eat our breakfast peacefully. So, if you don't mind, please let us be?" I softly and sarcastically answered.

"Why, yes, of course. Carry on with your breakfast." Ethel communicated with a suspicious tone in her voice. She didn't stop staring at us as we exited the train car. It was quite unsettling. I think she went to tell someone that we were alone.

I rose from my seat, scooted over to the door, and slid it shut so she had a lower chance of hearing us. Then I locked it, and Lulu released the silence by stating, "That was a close one. What if she figured out that we were all alone? Also, Ruby, what if she watches us leave the station?"

I quieted her quickly to ensure no one else would hear and continued, "It's okay. Keep your guard low, and we will be fine. We are all pretty small, so when we arrive, I will go to some random person and hug them. Then, I will call them Mommy or Daddy, depending on the gender. Ethel will probably watch us exit, so after she turns away from us with our so-called "parents," we will make a run for it."

"But Ruby, you don't know anyone," Willie bit his fingers, and his posture laid low.

"I know, but look at me. My sister is right! I look like I'm six, and it'll be adorable!" I mumbled as a slight smile edged out from my mouth.

Lulu, Willie, and I laughed. Finally, after another hour, the train chugged slowly to the station, and finally, we arrived in Middlebury, Vermont. As suspected, Ethel watched us when we first got off the train. So, I went up to the first woman I could see, who had long brunette hair and a straight posture, and shouted, "Mommy, mommy! It's quite good to see you again! Oh, how I have missed you so much. I love you, Mommy!" Then I hugged her tightly. Ethel nodded and turned away.

After that, the woman got down to my level and expressed, "Little one, are you lost? I am not your mother, but I am happy to help you find her."

I turned towards her with the biggest grateful smile and squealed, "No, I'm not, but thank you, you just looked like her for a second. Sorry for bothering you. I will be going on my merry way now. But thank you again!"

She shrugged her shoulders, and we left. We walked past the train, through the store, and onto the dirt road. On the street, I approached a tall, hairy, green-eyed man and asked, "Pardon, sir, I don't mean to bother you, but could we trouble you to give us directions to the Sheldon Hampton Theatre?"

He said, "I would be happy to take you there myself."

Thinking that was a little suspicious, I muttered, "Umm... No, thank you. Can you please tell us the way?"

"You know this is a scary world for young children like yourselves. I believe it would be best if you didn't get lost or kidnapped. I am happy to take you there or help find your parents."

I watched Coco sign, "Ruby, don't go. It's a trap. He will hurt us."

I agreed and murmured to him, "Um... No, thank you, sir. You know what? I see our parents now. We should get going." He grabbed my arm, gave directions to Lulu, and let me go. That was quite a bit terrifying, but it turned out fine.

We began walking, and after about an hour and a half, we were panting and stopped. We appeared to be in an unusually unsafe feeling town. To the left of me, in the distance, I saw bandits destroying a post with Mr. Lincoln's face on it. They were protesting against him. Willie's breaths scattered, "Ruby, they are destroying my father's posters. They are breaking down the town. We have to stop them! It isn't right!"

I nodded and thought for a second. This could be dangerous, but Willie is correct; it isn't right! I began heading to their location, but Coco grabbed my hand and held me back, "I don't know if that is such a good idea. They don't look very friendly. They could hurt us. There are a lot of psychos here, Ruby."

I pointed towards them, "They aren't doing the right thing, though."

Coco shook her head and sighed, "They may not be, but some things are best left alone."

Coco was right, but I didn't want to let Willie down. One of the bandits, who had filthy clothing and what appeared to be one eye with a few teeth missing, saw us and then approached.

We gulped and slowly backed away, then ran. His bandit friends, unfortunately, were faster and caught the three of us. "Now, what would children like yourselves be doing here? We saw you talking about us. Didn't your parents ever teach you it is rude to talk behind people's backs?"

We all stayed quiet as the main one-eyed one grabbed my arms and put me in front. "Well, answer!"

I gulped, "We didn't mean to be rude. We just thought it wasn't the right thing to see you destroying Mr. Lincoln's poster and making a mess."

He sneered and blew out steam into my face. Then, spit a Coco-sized loogie to the ground left of me. "You believe in this fool's plans." Sneered again, "He should be shot," then yanked me out of his hands and threw me to the ground. "The three of you shouldn't be playing around here. Go tell your mamas I said this man is a vazey scoundrel who deserves to drop dead."

I knew this probably wasn't the best choice, but "And what if we don't? It isn't right. He is trying to help and give people more freedom. Don't you want freedom?"

He got down on his knees and hopped over me, "Freedom? This little twit says freedom. How is he gonna give us more freedom?"

"To all the enslaved people. Don't you want to help them? Or would you prefer to be a Southerner?"

He spat again, "I will never be a Southerner. Those filthy creatures can go die in hell."

I glanced at Lulu to see her nails biting her arm and Willie's hands clenched with Lulu's. I looked back over to this man. I don't think they should die. I just think they need to learn a new perspective, "So we..." I shook my head back and forth, "more or less agree on something."

He dragged me from the ground by my dress. "I guess you're right, child. Get the hell out of here, and then maybe we will reconsider the value of Mr. Lincoln's life."

I puffed, "Please don't think like that. How would your mama like it if she heard you thinking about murder, huh?"

He held his head low as I continued, "Go on, Mr. Whatever your name is. She wouldn't like it at all, now would she?"

He slightly shook his head, and his single eye filled with a tear. Or at least, I thought I saw a tear. His henchmen dropped Lulu and Willie, and they allowed us to leave.

Right before we began to run in the other direction, the big one-eyed one yelled, "You are a brave child. I respect it. We shall reconsider our choices."

A small smile beamed across my face, "Thank you."

We turned away and headed for the other direction. I took a fast glimpse backward to see them cleaning up their mess. "Ruby, you did it! They don't seem to hate my father anymore!" Willie hollered with a gleam in his voice.

We continued for another twenty minutes before I asked, "Lulu, are you sure this was how he sent us? This shouldn't be taking this long."

It felt like it had been hours in the scorching heat, and we were exhausted. We were in the middle of this small town and sat in front of an ice cream shop. On the window, there was a sign that stated no pets allowed, but we wanted to take a break and eat ice cream. Because of this, I told Coco, "You need to pretend to be a new toy; therefore, we can go inside there. It is too hot out here, and I will get whatever flavor you want." She agreed, and we went in.

We sat down at the end of a large rectangular flat table. The owner and his wife came up to us. They were this young family with two kids helping behind the counter. We knew we were in a poor neighborhood, but I had never seen any children ever have to work before. It made me rethink how fortunate, lucky, and appreciative I was to be born into an affluent home. The wife faced me and asked, "Good day, children. Are you traveling alone?"

I hesitated, "Yes, we might have gotten a bit lost, though. We are trying to find our way to the Sheldon Dock Theatre but have been walking for hours. Our parents are waiting for us there. We got lost at the train station back in Middlebury, but I feel we are going the wrong way."

She had a worried look on her face. She responded, "Well, children, what are your names? The theater isn't too far north of here. It is about a five-minute horse ride. I am happy to take you there."

Lulu, Willie, and I smiled. Then I said, "Thank you, but that won't be necessary if only you could give us the directions. Also, I am Ruby, this is Lulu, and this is Willie."

She verbalized, "Great! It is nice to meet the three of you. I'm Alice. Your monkey looks extremely realistic. I have never seen any toy like that before. What is its name, and where did you get it from?"

I tried to be all cute and uttered, "Oh," I stuttered, "this is Coconut. I got her when I was very young, and I take her everywhere. Also, I don't know where I got her from because my mother bought her for me. I'm sorry."

She smiled, "That is alright. I was looking for a unique toy for my daughter's birthday. So, what may I get the three of you today?"

Lulu answered first, "Peach, please," then Willie, "I'll have the citron, please," and finally me, "Plain vanilla is fine, thank you."

She swiped the cloth attached to the door as she entered the kitchen. About five minutes later, she came out with delicious cold confections. As she looked the other way, I handed some to Coco. Then their daughter watched Coco move. "Look, Mama. The monkey is real!" I anxiously muttered.

Alice came to us and said, "I am very sorry for my daughter. She has a vivid imagination. I can take your dishes for you now since you're done. Thank you for coming today, and because all of you are adorable and respectful, it is on the house. When you leave this shop, turn right and keep going straight until you see the wooden horse. Once you do, turn left, and it is on the right of the green-colored tower."

"Thank you for your help," Willie said.

I didn't want to leave her empty-handed from the kindness she had shown us. I decided to leave her with a large tip because of the kindness in her heart and because they needed it much more than I did. So, I grabbed two octagonal 50-dollar gold slugs from my pocket and placed them on the table when she wasn't looking for a note of gratitude. We headed out, and after twenty minutes, we arrived at the theater.

When we did, there was a large crowd of people. We snuck through them and behind the stage. "Look, there is my father. Let's go talk to him!" Willie exclaimed.

We ambushed him from behind, and I welcomed, "Good day, Mr. Lincoln."

As he turned around, he replied with "Good da…" and stopped and faced Willie, then me with an intrigued look. Why did he stop? "Hello, Willie."

Willie stared and exclaimed, "Hello, Father."

Mr. Lincoln continued with, "Hello, Ruby."

My eyes widened as if I had seen a ghost. "I don't mean to be disrespectful, but how do you know my name?"

"Well, Ruby. I have heard much about you and Coco from my good friend Henry Jones."

"Oh, well, I guess that makes sense. Did you know I was going to come?"

"No, I didn't, young Ruby. Willie, you never told me you were going to be here either. Why aren't you in school? What can I help you with?"

"We need to talk to you about something significant now!" I hollered.

Lincoln looked at me and whispered something to the guy next to him. It must have been his protector. Then the man started sending people out of our view, and Lincoln faced us, especially me, and stated, "Follow me."

I was baffled that there must have been hundreds, if not thousands, of people there, and he sent them away to talk to us. We followed him to this small room, and he locked the door. "Now, Ruby, Willie, and other child, what may I have the pleasure of speaking to you about?"

"I don't mean to scare you or put you in shock, but someone is going to try to assassinate you during the presidential convention at the Wigwam!" I whispered, practically cutting him off so no one else would hear.

Lincoln stared at Willie and me confusedly and vocalized, "Ruby, how and why do you think this?"

I felt very nervous about what I was about to tell him, but proceeded to anyway, "I know this because I was in the room with the assassin. On the day of your big rally at the Wigwam, a man named Marshall has been hired to assist President James Buchanan in assassinating you. They will be dressed as an usher. The letter mentioned they would climb the stairs and shoot when everyone cheered at approximately 9:08 in the morning. So, Mr. Lincoln, I must advise you to proceed cautiously or not attend this major convention. The current president doesn't want you to become the new president. Your life is in danger!"

Lincoln scoffed and shook his head, continuously watching the door to ensure no one else would enter, "Oh, little one, do not worry. Nothing is going to happen to me. I must attend this convention to be elected as the Republican candidate. I will take the three of you back to Miss Holmes' Academy. Also, Ruby, it is not okay to make up lies. I understand you are brilliant, but not everything you hear or see is true. Let's go."

"Wha... Bu... I... No! Mr. Lincoln, I'm not lying, someone is trying to kill you, and I need you to be prepared.

Please, you have to believe me!" I yelled in a deep tone with squinted eyes, pursed lips, and frowned eyebrows.

He glanced at me and pushed the three of us toward the door. I couldn't believe that he didn't believe me. I get it; I'm tiny, but I am mighty! I am just trying to protect him from danger. I'm not going to let this happen!

As we were leaving the building, a woman stopped Lincoln. She was small and slender, with brown eyes, brunette hair, and a platinum dress covering herself. Her name was Abigail Taylor. She faced Lincoln and asked, "Where are you going? Sir, you need to be on stage in ten minutes. Who are these three children?"

He hesitated, "You are correct, Allie. I forgot this is the current situation. Children, I will take you back to the Academy after this. Allie, can you watch these three young ones, for now, to ensure they do not get into any more trouble than they are already in?"

She smiled, "Of course! I love kids and am happy to watch over the three of them until you return."

I had a straight face. You have got to be kidding me! I didn't need some cherry watching over me. I am perfectly capable of handling myself. We came from D.C. by ourselves, didn't we? Oh, the disadvantages of being a kid. What can I do? I'm only nine!

She smiled at us and asked, "Are the three of you hungry? I know where to get the best sausage and fried potatoes."

I gave her a disgusted look because I didn't want to go with her. I didn't know her, but my stomach was growling. "You know, little one, I can hear your stomach grumbling. You do not have to be nervous. I won't hurt you. I know it can be scary meeting new people."

I wasn't scared of meeting new people; I was irritated, that's all. There wasn't much I could do right now, so I sighed and nodded. We went down the block and walked into a large shop that smelled of fried dough balls. I used to have them a lot when I was younger, but the last time I ate one, there was a bug in it, and I almost threw up. It's not a pleasant memory.

Abby sat us down, and then a woman with a darker figure, beautiful looks, and puffy hair who works in the shop approached us with four plates of sausages, potatoes, and dough balls stacked in her arms. "Hello, child and madam. I, Lucille Roberts, will be serving you today."

She didn't seem to have that much of an education since she couldn't speak very well, but she was lovely. She pounced behind the counter, filled cups of water, and returned to the table. "If you need anything else, just ask."

How did she know what we wanted to order? Maybe there was nothing else that they served. Oh well, who cares? We started to eat. It tasted like heaven! I have never had such good sausages before. Maybe they are not made of natural beef and something else. You know what? It's probably for the best, I don't know.

We ate for about thirty minutes. As we were finishing up, we handed Ms. Roberts the exact change with no extra money for the poor woman to keep. As they left, I headed to Ms. Roberts, and she stopped me. "Little one, where are you going?"

I knew she wouldn't want me to pay her for her service since she hadn't paid her before, even though she deserved it, so I lied, "I am going to get a napkin from her."

I approached Ms. Roberts, who towered over me with a precious smile, "Hello, Ms. Roberts. How do you do?"

She had fear in her eyes as she flinched and hesitated, "Good, I get everything right? I'm sorry if I didn't. Here, I give your money back."

I was questionable but stated, "No, everything was absolutely perfect! I am here to get a napkin."

Once she handed one to me, I wiped my mouth and hid the money inside. I smiled, "Here. This is a little extra for you and your family, but shh," I covered my mouth with my right pointer finger, "don't tell anyone."

She gave me a funny look and then looked down and smiled. She deserved it. I'm pretty sure she was enslaved. I didn't care; she was lovely, and I wished she wasn't enslaved. She didn't deserve to be. No enslaved people deserve to be. They are people, too, and should be treated with respect!

She put the napkin in her pocket, and I ran to catch up with Allie. We headed back to the Sheldon Hampton

Theatre. When we saw Mr. Lincoln, he looked like he was verbally beaten up and ready to leave. He was finished with his speech. So, we left and hopped on a horse carriage to return to the train station.

When we arrived at the train station, we took the first train back to D.C. We arrived late Sunday night and headed to the Academy. Mr. Lincoln led us straight to Miss Holmes' office, which is when I knew we were in trouble.

CHAPTER EIGHT

In School Suspension

We slowly walked into Miss Holmes' office. For whatever reason, I noticed a small charm that looked like a golden blue balloon, but I didn't give it a second thought and continued focusing on Miss Holmes, "Good evening, Miss Holmes! How are you?" I queried nervously, sighing, knowing that Mr. Lincoln would tell her about where we had been.

Honestly, being in trouble didn't bother me too much because I was more focused on the fact that he didn't believe me. I'm trying to help him, not the other way around. If I didn't care about the safety of the possible future president, what kind of a patriotic American would I be? Miss Holmes invited Mr. Lincoln into a different room.

"Now, children, please wait here for a few moments while I talk to Mr. Lincoln." Miss Holmes answered in a very stern voice.

She has used strong voices before, but never like this one. Unless we were in trouble, and believe me, I've had my fair share of getting in trouble plenty of times. After about forty-five minutes of painfully waiting in her office, playing jacks on the floor with Coco, Lulu, and Willie, they exited. They hugged each other, and Miss Holmes then said her goodbyes. "Thank you, Abe, for bringing them to me. I assure you I will make sure they are never unattended again."

"I appreciate it!" Mr. Lincoln verbalized softly as he wore his big, black stovepipe hat. He turned towards Willie and opened his mouth as if he was about to say something but didn't mutter anything. We watched as he took off his black stovepipe hat to show respect for Miss Holmes and exited.

Before Miss Holmes reached her chair to sit down, her gaze faced me, then Willie and Lulu, "William and Lulu, you may leave. I want to talk to Rebecca alone." Miss Holmes whispered in one of the scariest tones.

Oh no! Considering she used my full name, I knew I was in trouble. My head crouched down into my shoulders, but that didn't stop me from saying, "What?! That's not fair. Why are you only going to scold me? I didn't do anything wrong? Well, I did, but it's not fair!"

"Miss Ledger, I know you were the leader of what had happened because I know you, and in the past, I had a brilliant child in my custody like you. I'm not foolish. Additionally, you are always the one who comes up with these preposterous plans. So, Lulu and Willie, you may leave." Miss Holmes uttered.

I knew she thought I had messed up at that point, but I knew I didn't. I wasn't sorry for trying to warn him about being assassinated. Miss Holmes continued, "Rebecca, you can't go on these missions alone. I understand they are fun for you, but this is a life-or-death situation; you could have gotten seriously injured or killed! For starters, you lied about going home to see your family. When you left two days ago, I called your parents with the telegraph you made for them. They were frightened when I told them you were missing and not on campus, so I panicked and searched your room. I found a map of your plans about Mr. Lincoln inside your room and knew you had gone to find him. So, I telegraphed him and told him you were coming and to watch out for you, but Rebecca, you can never do this again, do you understand?"

"No, I don't understand, Miss Holmes. All I did was try to help. I know someone, well, not just someone, but, ugh .." I took a deep breath and continued, "I know something bad is going to happen to him, and I went to tell him to warn him, but he didn't believe me. Miss Holmes, I can't just sit here and do nothing! I have to do something! I'm sorry I lied, but I knew you would say no if I asked to go. So, I went anyway. Besides, whatever will happen to him will happen in a while, and I need him to be prepared, but he is not going to be because he doesn't believe me."

"Ruby, stay out of this. I understand this detective stuff interests you, but I need you to stay alive, not just for me but for your friends, family, and Coco. Stay out of it! I promise nothing will happen to him as long as the HIA has something to do with it. I promise he will be okay."

I had a strange look as she mentioned the HIA. "HIA? Miss Holmes, what is the HIA, and what do they have to do with this?"

"It is nothing important. Just forget that I said that, but I am serious, Ruby; you must stay out of his life and everyone else's. The only life you should worry about is your own, and maybe Coco's too, but STAY out of this. Do you understand me?"

"But–" I voiced, trying to get her approval.

"Rebecca!"

I crossed my fingers behind my back and stated, "Fine. I'll stay out of it."

She gave me an intense look, shook her head, stood up from her desk, and wrapped herself around the corner of her desk, "Thank you. You must remember that with every action comes a consequence, and because of these serious ones, there are serious consequences."

I sighed and let her continue, "You will have detention for one month and suspension for a week. This also means no Mr. Henry lessons. Once you are done with your core classes, you will sit in the den outside my office for an hour. You may do your homework or work on one of your crazy inventions. I do not care, but you must stay silent. I don't want you talking to anybody during this time. Am I clear?"

My eyes started to fill with tears. I can do detention, but no, Mr. Henry's lessons. This wasn't fair! I couldn't let Mr. Lincoln die, and yet I got punished for trying to save him. I guess I did break the rules, but still. It's not right!

"Now, young lady, I'm sorry for these, and I know they are harsh, but I need you to be safe. I need you to learn. You may leave now."

I slowly draped my arms next to my sides as I reached for the door, but before I left, she removed herself from her desk, and hugged me, then escorted me out of the room. When I walked out the door, not one or two, but all three serpent sisters stood outside laughing at me.

'Aww, does the poor wittle Wuby want hew mommy... Look at you in your tears. You're such a crybaby, Ruby!" Emma, the egotistical maniac, screeched like a banshee.

I wanted to pounce at them but decided it was for the best that I didn't. So, I released my clenched fists and took a deep breath, "Don't you have something better to do than make fun of people you are jealous of? Why don't you go and pick on someone your own size and caliber? Like a gorilla."

She snarled at me and left.

I went to my room and started thinking about my next plan for saving Mr. Lincoln. I wouldn't let him be assassinated if I had anything to do with it. Lulu was on her bed when I entered the room and asked, "What happened? Are you okay?"

She hugged me, as she could see I was visibly upset.

"Yes, I'm fine. But, unfortunately, I got suspended for a week, detention for a month, and no Mr. Henry's lessons until the end of the suspension." I answered in a salty tone.

"Well, at least you've learned your lesson. So, it won't be that bad."

For the first time since we met, I disagreed with her and gave her the dirtiest look I could make with my face. I could not believe she had just mentioned that. So, I thundered, "You were also a part of it; it's not fair that you didn't get into trouble as well. Also, no! I haven't learned my lesson, so I just wait. Mr. Lincoln will be saved. I just have to figure out how. After that, I will be the best detective in history books!" I smirked heinously.

Lulu questioned suspiciously, "What are you going to do now? I mean, what can you do? I bet Miss Holmes will probably keep a close eye on you..."

I cut her off. "Exactly. She will keep an eye on me, but not you or Willie." The evil smirk appeared on my face again.

We both got ready for bed and went to sleep. The following morning, we went to the room filled with sausages, bread, fruits of all colors and shapes, and croissants. It was marvelous. I wondered why we were having such a bodacious breakfast. Then it hit me. Today was the first day of the parents' weekend. I had completely forgotten about it. Today, we had to showcase what we had learned, and I knew that if my parents found out I got an in-school suspension, I was done for. I didn't have a choice, though. I was stuck in my room all day except for meals. I just hoped that they would think the trip was too far to visit.

On my way back to my room upstairs, I decided to take a little detour. I passed the great silver ball on the west side of campus. It was in a beautiful meditation greenhouse with thousands of flowers ranging from daisies, magnolias, peach blossoms, eastern redbuds, swamp milkweed, eastern red columbine, etc... Hoping I would see Willie there, as I knew he loved to go there to relax and meditate. Instead, I saw Lulu with the one and only President, James Buchanan. What is he doing here? He wasn't supposed to be here. Also, what is he doing with Lulu? As I got closer to listening, the only thing I could make out from Lulu was, "Don't worry, Uncle, I will make you proud."

Then they turned and might have seen me. At that moment, I ran as fast as I had ever run. I made it to my room in a record time of three minutes.

When I arrived, I faced Coco and whispered, "President Buchanan is her uncle? But wait, doesn't that mean she might be working for him? For all we know, she could be behind his assassination. Do you think it's possible she was always this way? Coco, I don't know if we can trust Lulu anymore."

"See, Ruby, I told you from the beginning when we first met her. I don't trust her. There is a reason why she couldn't learn to speak Capuchin, and it's because I have been slowly switching up the way I speak to you as I speak with her. Therefore, she could never understand. I believe she is dangerous, but we can't confront her now."

I agreed. Then Lulu walked into the room. Buchanan was gone. I pretended to be doing a puzzle on the floor with Coco. "Hello, Lulu, how are you? Are any of your parents going to be here this weekend?"

"Hi Ruby, umm… No, they won't be, but I saw my uncle. Unfortunately, he left, but I should get going. They still have activities for students whose parents aren't here. I'm sorry you're stuck here all day."

"That's all right. I will do my thing all day, alone, as you know."

"Okay, bye. See you later, Ruby."

I waved back to her with a fake smile on my face. I had more important things to do. After a few minutes of debating whether or not I should escape, I decided I needed to. I snuck into Mr. Henry's office and hoped he would be there; luckily, he was. I came through his back window and sat in his chair. When he turned around, I scared him. "Oh, good heavens, Ruby, I didn't see you there. What are you doing here? Aren't you supposed to be stuck in your room all day?"

I didn't know how to respond, so I froze and stared at him momentarily; after a few minutes, somehow, I found the words to say, "I had to see you. I'm sorry I lied about the other day, but I couldn't wait to change Abraham Lincoln's fate. I had to do something myself. I might be tiny, but I am mighty!"

He smiled at me, "I know you are. You are a feisty little beast who doesn't stop. Additionally, I don't blame you. When I had a mission that was calling my name, there was nothing that would stop me from going. You know you remind me very much of..."

Then he stopped. "Of? Mr. Henry, of who?"

"Never mind, child, it's not important. So, tell me about your adventure. Do you know what you want to do next?"

I told him what had happened, "Why do you think he didn't believe me? I don't understand. Do you think it is because I am a child?"

"No, Ruby, it wasn't because you're a child. As you mentioned, Ruby, he knows who you are primarily because of me. Ruby, Lincoln cares about you; it wasn't because you're a child. I promise. He didn't believe you because he has a history with James Buchanan. They go back about thirty years, and he knows Buchanan like I don't. But Ruby, I need you to understand that I believe you, but what you're budding into is an exceedingly dangerous matter. You should stay out of it and let the adults handle it."

What? How could he think that?

"Now, Ruby, please return to your room before I report you to Miss Holmes."

I got up and left. I wanted to punch my pillow or cry when I arrived at my dorm. I didn't understand why the one person who let me go on missions and help me didn't want me to be a part of this. "Coco, do you think he has something to do with this?"

"I don't know, but someone is coming," Coco replied.

It was Willie. "Willie, it is great to see you." I jumped into his arms, "I got an in-school suspension and detention, and no Mr. Henry studies for the next week. But I will not stop until I save your father. I can't let him die. It is too vital that he stays alive."

"Ruby, I agree. We can't let him die; he's my father, and we must do everything to protect him. Please, Ruby, you are a genius. Please help me save him." Willie uttered in a soft voice.

"Don't worry, Willie, I will protect him," I muttered.

He was the only one I could trust until I figured out what was happening with Lulu.

Before Willie left, "Ruby, wait! I have something for you." He reached into his little bag and pulled out a musty-looking journal, "I stole this from my father's bin. I think it may be his journal. He hasn't written anything past February 19."

I didn't want to take it because I felt bad, "His journal? Willie, isn't this private?"

"Technically, yes, but it may help you learn more about him. Please, Ruby, take it."

I held my eyes to the floor for a few moments and debated whether or not I should take it, but ultimately, I agreed, and he handed me the journal.

That night, as I laid on my bed, I couldn't help but wonder what Mr. Lincoln had to say. I knew it was wrong, but I decided to read it.

CHAPTER NINE

Abraham Lincoln's Journal

May 19, 1838

I don't know exactly where to begin. I have never written a diary before, but only one of my dear lady friends says that writing my thoughts down may help me clear my head more, so here I am, writing this journal. She says I should write my feelings out and go back as far as I can remember. Maybe I should begin with my childhood...

I was born on February 12, 1809, in Larue County, near Hodgenville, Kentucky. My name is Abraham Lincoln. I don't have a middle name. I think people who have middle names are unique. I am a six-foot-four-inch tall male with hazel-gray eyes and am slender. As a child, I was in poverty, living and working on a farm with my family. For enter-tainment, I would read next to the fireplace. As a child, I became the first in my immediate family to read and write by borrowing books. Some of my favorite books include Pride and Prejudice, Frankestine, and many others written by Jane Austen. My mother and father wanted to help me, but unfortunately, they were illiterate. My mother died when I was nine, and my father remarried. As I grew older, I became a flatboat navigator, storekeeper, soldier, surveyor, and postmaster.

When I turned eighteen, I became a part of the Hartford Agency.

"The Hartford agency?" I sat up from lying on my stomach, "What on earth is that?" I hollered to Coco as she shook her head and moved her shoulders.

"Keep reading, Ruby!" Coco sat beside me and leaned against my body, with her little arms shaped like an "L" since she leaned on her elbows.

I stumbled into a mystery mission when I tried to stop a shooting that nearly killed three people. The agents noticed this when they approached me and asked if I wanted a job. I agreed and decided to go into law enforcement to cover up this significant commitment.

When I turned twenty-five, I was elected into the local government of Springfield, Illinois. I considered this place to be my home because I grew up here. This was the first time I learned I wanted to be in the court of law, so I decided to teach it, and then opened a practice and earned the nickname "Honest Abe."

"Honest Abe?" My eyebrows lifted. I knew that nickname from the papers, "That's so interesting! I never knew that is how he became Honest Abe."

June 15, 1838

Yesterday, a tall British man in a blue suit from London, Great Britain, walked into the Supreme Court to watch. I knew he was part of the organization because he had a small red and blue pin with a silver border on his suit pocket–the middle of the shield is an "H," the "I" strikes through the middle, and the webbing on the top and bottom are "A's." Lastly, a white, blue, and red tri-triangle symbol is in the middle.

I was trying to fight for two indicated murderers in a medical malpractice case, and I won. At the end of the case, the tall British man approached me and asked, "Why would you fight for those murderers?"

I could only reply with, "Sir, this is because I don't believe the murderers were in the wrong when they killed those people. The public is shown how these murderers were only killed because of their race, but I looked deeper into this case, which is why I fought. I believe in this country and want to fight for everyone in it... What is your name, and what are you doing in my court?"

"I respect that very much of you, Sir. My name is Henry Jones–"

I readjusted my position to make myself more comfortable as I stuck my nose further into the book. "Mr. Henry knows Mr. Lincoln? Coco, Mr. Henry isn't saying as much as he is letting on? He knows something that we don't..."

"Keep reading, Ruby."

"I am from London, Great Britain, and I found your case fascinating. I would love to speak with you."

"Of course, Henry. Follow me."

Henry followed me for a few blocks to a small, unique building only for a particular organization based in London and Washington, D.C., but with branches worldwide. This is where I have done all my work. The inside of the building is exquisite, with multiple fountains and statues at the entrance. As you head to the right, there is a library full of thousands of books. To fully enter the secret organization, you must find the book copied as "Lockie Topography of London." Then, you pull on the tiny opening on the side of the book and place the minor circular key inside. After that, you move back, and it opens the bookshelf to a very different room.

When we entered, many people dressed in suits spoke into a telegraph machine that sends signals worldwide within minutes. Others were doing paperwork, and some were working out in the physical training area. As we passed them, we headed to my office. When we arrived, I offered Henry a glass of water. He politely agreed, and we began to discuss.

"Sir, what has made you come to America at this time?"

"Well, Abe, the HIA has sent me here to work with you to stop the Vanderbilts."

"What do you have in mind?"

Henry continued, "Well, as you know, the Vanderbilts are among the richest families in America, but their wealth is believed to have been collected through blacklists and not only railroads. I want you to help me stop them from continuing these illegal acts."

As I picked up today's newspaper, I stated, "Alright, well, in the newspaper, it claims that Vanderbilt's net worth increased by a few billion through supposed cow catchers, but those aren't big in the market yet. Because of this, I believe they got their money elsewhere."

Henry smiled.

"What is our plan?" I asked in a soft voice.

Henry continued, "First, we must be certain that they truly got their money from somewhere else before we can accuse them of anything. Once we do, we are legally obligated to arrest or fine them enough to ensure they don't repeat it. We have to keep our eyes on them. If we let them go, they will get richer, continue these illegal acts, and buy more enslaved people they neither need nor have."

After the meeting, we set up a control system in his office with a camera to watch them. The HIA was the first to create the camera, but it wasn't considered officially invented until one of our agents stole it and showed it to the public in 1816. His name was Frenchman Joseph Nicéphore Nicépce. We set it up in his office after we went to his house as "friends."

Cornelius Vanderbilt and I used to be old friends. I was one of the people who helped him build his fortune. So, I contacted him, and we decided to have dinner to reconnect.

June 19, 1838

When we entered the house, it was a three-bedroom, three-bathroom home. Although it wasn't enormous like his house is in the present day, it felt cozy. Each room was beautifully decorated with ornaments, tapestries, and gorgeous paintings. There was a little fireplace that had branches and flowers of lavender burning. It smelt lovely. When we sat down, we chatted about his business. Vanderbilt responded, "My business is going very well. We just hit it big with our cattle catchers."

"How did you get these cattle catchers?" I replied with wonder.

He shrugged and moved on to the next question. He invited us to his office to see what his everyday life looks like on a day-to-day basis. It was nice to see how he was doing. Later that week, we went to his office and set up the camera without him noticing. I don't believe he ever found the camera. As we watched him do his malicious acts, we learned that he had bought parts from the United Kingdom and was importing them for his business. This was considered illegal at the time because it was done during the time of the Aroostook War. This was a war between the British and Americans about the boundaries between the state of Maine and the British Canadian Province of New Brunswick.

Henry and I decided that we needed to confront him now that we had proof. Our only problem was that he could sue us and the HIA, causing a loss in our jobs and the HIA's faculty's jobs, but we felt that we didn't have a choice.

June 20, 1838

Today, we confronted him, "We have evidence to believe that you are smuggling illegal iron into federal America. Fortunately for you, we don't want to report it because we are old pals, but we need you to stop."

He was shocked but didn't fight. Instead, he responded, "Yes, I have been doing such acts, but I don't see why they are illegal. I am not stealing them or buying them on the black market. I am buying them from a friend I have known for many years, and even though the Aroostook War is ongoing, it will never break that friendship."

"Would you care to reveal their name and contact information to telegraph them to confirm this?" Henry said with a severe tone in his voice.

"Yes, of course. Her name is Cordelia Wellington. Her husband owns one of the largest iron and steel industries in Britain. The telegraph wire line that connects to their office is line 555-231. They should answer in the morning if you send it out now." Vanderbilt communicated.

I sent out the telegraph, and indeed, he was right. First thing in the morning, I received a message with the correct information. He wasn't doing it illegally, and there was nothing we could do about it, even though something still didn't seem right.

June 27, 1838

A few days passed, and Henry Jones was going home. I asked to go with him, and he was congruent. So, we left that evening and arrived on a boat named the S.S. Rebellion about a month later. The ship was a massive steamboat with many rooms for guests. On deck, I had worked on many proposals for how to run for president in the present day. I wanted my term to last and my name to go down in history as one of the greatest presidents that will ever be recorded.

July 29, 1838

When we arrived in England, it was very bare. Many workers were on the loading docks, and many poor pedestrians were living in the streets, with rodents and measles everywhere. I knew I had to keep my mouth shut because they would try to kill me if they found out I was an American.

We jumped on a horse and headed towards Henry's house in London. It was a small cottage with a brown roof and white walls when we arrived. It had two stories and, fortunately, had a lavatory in the house. This meant that Henry had some wealth to his name. As we entered, there was a lovely young lady named Violet Sherrinford. She had brunette hair, blue eyes, a thin figure, and was quite beautiful if you ask me.

"Welcome to our humble home. I am Violet, Henry's fiancé. I understand you have had a long journey, so why don't you put your gear down and join me in the kitchen for some tea?" Violet enquired, watching me.

I quickly responded, "Thank you, madame! I appreciate you letting me rest here. As you know, I am a HIA agent along with your husband."

As the day went on, she explained what she does in the organization. I learned that she is also a spy. "Are you the first female spy in the company?"

"Why, no, I am not. Henry's and my good friend Millie Hartford's family was the first."

"Well, that is lovely. I am delighted they are including women in this industry. Since no one would suspect a woman to have power, you are perfect." I said vigorously.

August 15, 1838

I stayed with Henry and Violet for quite a while before I returned to the States. When I returned, I had a new perspective on life. My goal while there was to see how Queen Victoria was leading her people, and I was utterly shocked by how poor the economy was. When I returned to America, I knew its people deserved better, so I put more work and effort into everything I did.

I skipped through multiple pages until I found something interesting and useful because he went on and on about his experience in England. Quite frankly, it was irrelevant and boring.

June 18, 1849

Over the past eleven years, I have visited London multiple times to see the Jones family. For now, I believe this will be my last trip before their child is born. Based on old wives' tales and how Millie is doing, they think it is going to be a girl. She is due sometime around May.

"A girl, Coco? Why hasn't Mr. Henry ever said he had a daughter?"

"Maybe something happened to her?"

"Maybe..."

It has been over a year and a half since Theodore Jones, Henry's first child, was born. He is a little boy with brunette hair and bright blue/green eyes. He is a sweet, tiny tot. He looks just like his mother.

"That's Theo, isn't it?" Coco whispered.

"I believe so."

However, on this trip, I learned that Violet had impure intentions. She was having an affair with another man. His name was Morland Holmes, and he was not a good man to anybody else but her. I tried to intervene because I cared for Violet and Henry. This outraged me, especially the way I discovered this. It was on a mission with Violet, as someone was trying to assassinate Queen Victoria from the side of Buckingham Palace. The mission was successful, but in the end, Violet went somewhere, so I followed her. She was kissing Morland like a fool. I confronted her, and she made me swear not to tell Henry, but how could I not? He was my closest friend.

"Miss Holmes had an affair with Mr. Henry, but why would they still like each other?"

June 21, 1849

Today, before I return home, I have to leave a note about what happened.

June 25, 1849

Two days ago, Henry found it and was furious with Violet's actions as he loved her very much. He told me he would get together with Millie to compensate for this anger.

September 22, 1849

As the past few months flew by, Henry and Millie fell in love.

Coco and I kept skipping through pages because we felt they weren't that important, which is why I haven't written every detail of his journal.

May 29, 1850

As I predicted, their sweet little girl was born earlier this month. From the moment I first saw her, I knew she was the brilliant child of Henry and Millie Jones. She looks just like her mother. She was the prettiest little girl I had ever seen.

"Coco, look at the time stamp of when he wrote this. It's around my birthday. I know this may sound vazey, but what if I am his daughter? I mean, it would make a lot of sense. I do look more or less similar to him, and I am just as brilliant as he is. Also, the fact that he knew who I was when we went to warn him makes a lot of sense if he already knew what I looked like."

"But Ruby, that can't be! Besides, Mr. Lincoln said that Mr. Henry told him about you–"

"Yes, exactly! He also said that he has been great friends with him for many years. I just can't help but wonder." I muffled under the covers, trying not to alert Lulu.

Coco puffed, "Ruby, you are forgetting that your parents raised you. They have always referred to you as their daughter. Why would they lie to you?" Coco replied.

"I don't know… Let's just keep reading."

July 15, 1850

Shortly after her birth, she exhibited the signs of a child genius. She was the most gifted little girl I had ever met. I saw her earlier today, and she was babbling, starting to roll over, crawl around, and examine lights and gadgets.

December 28, 1850

Henry told me recently he has decided to forgive Violet and is trying to return to her. I strongly discouraged this, but unfortunately for Millie, he had an affair with Violet.

March 12, 1851

Millie found out a few days ago that Henry had had an affair with her. She told me she decided it was best that he did not raise the poor little girl. She wants to leave him and the HIA. She feels done with her work for the time being and only wants what is best for her daughter. Still, she doesn't want the girl to be a part of the HIA, so she is thinking of sending her away to hopefully protect her from all the chaos the HIA brings.

April 15, 1851

Millie telegraphed her sister two weeks ago to look after and raise the little girl. They recently replied with a yes and are going to fulfill this request.

June 16, 1851

"Coco, do you see what is happening? Now I really can't help but wonder if I am that little girl."

Coco gulped, "I don't know, but Ruby, your mother doesn't have a sister. Only a brother, remember?"

I scrunched my eyebrows, "While that may be the case, maybe she does have one, who she never talks about. I mean, she hates her brother; I could only imagine she would hate her sister as well. That is if she has one."

"You should ask your parents."

I shook my head and whispered, "Coco, if she hasn't said anything so far. I couldn't imagine she would say anything if I confronted her. She would probably lie."

Coco agreed, and we stuck our faces back into the journal to continue.

The little girl recently left the family about four weeks ago. I met her recently here to take her to her new family. As for Henry, he still loves his daughter more than anything, but now he can't be with her. He doesn't want to overlook this; therefore, he wants to follow the girl to her new home to ensure she gets the life she deserves.

August 29, 1851

Trying to put aside the thoughts of the Jones family, I have decided to start my campaign and continue my life.

I wanted to read more about her, but that was all he wrote. I flipped about seventy pages to reach where it said 1857 when the little girl came up again.

February 14, 1857

Over the past few years, Millie and Violet have once again become incredibly close friends. Recently, Violet moved to America with her three children, Theodore, Mycroft, and Sherlock, because Millie asked her to be near the girl to protect her. She knew that the little girl was growing more intelligent with each passing day. Violet bought the previous academy from her relatives and turned it into Miss Holmes' Academy.

Although I never watched the little girl grow up, I view her as a niece because I am very close with her mother and father. I knew she would be just like them from the day she was born. Especially how similar she looked to her mother. She has the same elegance.

"Coco, the little girl, lives here in America. Do you think we should ask Miss Holmes about her?"

"We can go to her later today."

We skipped another thirty pages until we reached the present.

February 19, 1860

Earlier today, my son, Willie, and his friends visited me at the Vermont Convention. The little girl Ruby said that someone was going to try and assassinate me. I honestly don't believe her. The reason for this is that I know James Buchanan, and even though he has a streak of jealousy, I don't believe he has it in him to kill me.

We go back many years. I first met him when I was eighteen years old. He was thirty-six. Initially, He was part of the HIA until he was banished in 1827 due to illegally smuggling money into his bank. I was the one who turned him in, but we both agreed that it was for the best. He never faced jail time because he promised to become a better person. I helped him in that way. We spent multiple months working on what he could do better. This was when he decided he wanted to become president, but he never intended to kill anyone. Although he did commit some illegal acts in the past, it doesn't make him a murderer.

Once we arrived at Miss Holmes' academy, I approached Violet. Of course, I wanted the best for these children, but I didn't want her and her friends to kill themselves over something exceedingly foolish that would not happen. Fortunately, I knew they were coming because Violet sent me a telegraph about their appearance so that they would be safe. Violet mentioned that the little one Ruby is the mastermind; honestly, this doesn't come as a surprise because she is a prodigy. Even though the child is only nine years old, she doesn't have nearly as much knowledge as she thinks she does; I don't want her getting herself in trouble or, worse, killed. I debated whether or not to tell Violet about Ruby's naughtiness, but ultimately, I decided it was the best solution.

I shut his journal because that was the most recent page he wrote. He clearly wrote his last journal entry on the train ride back to school. "Coco, we must learn more about this girl."

Coco agreed, and we both went off.

CHAPTER TEN

I'm On to You Lulu

I hid the journal in my pillow case so no one would find it. Then, Coco and I strolled along until we reached Miss Holmes' office. We figured we should go to her first because I feel like Mr. Henry would have said something to me before, but he didn't. Once we arrived at her office, we knocked three times before she said, "Come in."

She glanced up at us with a cup of tea in her left hand and a newspaper in her right hand. "Hello, Ruby. Do you have a reason for this visit, or did you just want to talk to someone?"

"I have an actual cause."

She nodded her head and asked me to sit down. I was a bit nervous, but I needed to learn more. "So, Miss Holmes, I just discovered something shocking from Willie. Well, actually, Mr. Lincoln. I found this... speech, you could say.

In the speech, it said that you and Mr. Henry used to be together. But I already knew that, so that is not why I am here. I am here because it says that Mr. Henry remarried another woman named Millie. It also stated that Millie and Mr. Henry had a daughter together, and she was born in the same month I was." I could see her eyes widening with fear, "So, Miss Holmes, I was wondering. If there is any relation between her and me, It also stated that she moved to America and that you bought this school to be near her."

Miss Holmes choked on her tea, "Ruby, where did you find this speech? You know not everything you read is factual."

"I know; it's just the girl seemed to have some similarities to me, and I couldn't help but think that she was me."

"Ruby, I promise there is nothing you need to know about this girl. Who she is is confidential. Alright? She is nothing you need to worry about. I promise. Besides, don't you think that if you were the girl, Mr. Henry would have told you, or your parents would have told you that you were adopted?"

"I guess so, but–"

She cut me off, "No 'buts' Ruby. Do you honestly think if Mr. Henry had you as his daughter, wouldn't he make that very clear?"

"I guess so, but I am his favorite student, and I was back at home as well."

"While that may be the case, your siblings are very rude to you. He has good reason for you to be his favorite."

"I guess so." That wasn't the answer I was hoping for. I held my head down, trying to process the information. "Thank you, Miss Holmes. I don't know what I was thinking before; I was just being vazey, that's all." I think she could tell I was disappointed by the low-pitched softness in my voice.

"Have a nice evening, Ruby."

"Bye, Miss Holmes..."

I couldn't stop thinking about the journal, but I had to return it to Willie to give back to his father. I couldn't think about this right now; I had to focus on his assassination. I promised I would.

As the rest of the week of detention went on, I built a detector to see if someone had metal on them. I broke a piece of metal from the bottom of one of the chairs in the cafeteria and hid it in my dress. Then I went to the kitchen, disassembled the oven, and rebuilt it without one of the smaller heating coils. I wrapped the metal disk in the copper coils and attached a small stick to the side of it to hold it. I think I will call it the silver shaky detector. Now, I have to test it. I handed Willie a metal button and held my silver shaky detector to his chest. It started to shake. "Yes, it works!" I announced, jumping to my feet and dancing in a little circle with Coco. I was intensely happy it worked. I wasn't surprised I could do it, but it was relieving.

By the end of my punishment, I had invented many objects similar to the silver shaky detector. It is perfect because when I go to Chicago, I can hold it up to people to see if anyone has metal on them. I will tell people that it is a project for school that shakes when it likes you. People are vazey; they'll believe anything. I know it. Now, all I had to do was figure out the exact plan on how we would stop the assassination from occurring.

That night, Lulu gave me a picture of the supposed culprit before bedtime. It had the name Elijah Devon written on it. Coco and I hid under our covers with a small closed candle to see, "Coco, maybe there was something wrong about Lulu. I think she is trying to lead me astray. This picture you see is fake, not real, and since Lulu is gifted in drawing, I believe she created this to lead me in the wrong direction. If you hold it up to the candle, You can tell by the direction of drawing marks."

"Why would she tell us that unless she works for Buchanan?"

Coco nodded and signed, "I don't trust her!"

"Coco, I think you're really onto something."

"I'm glad you finally believe me," Coco stated with a look of curiosity. I shook my head because I believed her before, but not as much as I do right now. I guess Coco is trying to look out for me.

As the weeks passed, we started formulating our plan. Finally, we decided to make our new meeting place at the

"Secret Garden." We call it that because it is in a more or less hidden location behind the school and down the trail toward the beginning of the forest. It is a meditation garden filled with many beautiful plants. It was peaceful, and nobody could hear us when we were there at night. It was the perfect place, better than our previous hideout. "Okay, Ruby, what is your major plan?" Willie gleefully cheered.

"This is what we will do. The assassination will occur on Wednesday, May 16, 1860, at 9:08 a.m. That is three days after school ends for the summer. We will tell Miss Holmes that your dad, Willie, wants us to watch his congressional speech as he finds it important and that we should also come along. Due to this major event, we will only be gone for the long weekend before we have to return to our houses. We cannot miss our opportunity to find the murderers. I guess that they will be wearing some usher worker uniform. It looks like a black and white suit with a white tag saying usher. You will go up to each person with these silver shaky detectors and hover it over them."

"Wait, Ruby, what if they don't let us? Also, what if they won't be wearing the worker uniform?" Willie questioned.

"Just wait for me to finish, but to answer those questions. Number one: look at us; we are all adorable; they won't say 'no' as long as we say it's for a school project. Number two:–"

Lulu chimed in. "Wait, we are girls. Won't they think we are odd?"

"Just say it checks the fabrics of clothing. It's not that difficult to understand. Now, to continue what I was saying before I was so rudely interrupted," I snapped a disgraceful look at Lulu, "I know they will wear an usher uniform because they have to. This is because nobody will suspect an usher worker to be doing this. Also, it will make James Buchanan look like he had nothing to do with it if they can't find the man who shoots Mr. Lincoln. Besides, President Buchanan can say he has no idea what happened, and it will be easier to play it off. So, both of you must trust that I know what I am talking about.

Now, continuing with what I was saying." Another sharp look at Lulu, "We also have to look for a person who looks like they are armed. It is not going to look like a gun. It will look like a pen, so we have to be careful. Once we find the perpetrator, I will take him down with my pocket spy. I will make sure he is stunned. This is when one of you gets the police to come in. I will have Coconut tell you the coordinates of the exact location. Then, Willie, you must watch the president and see what he does. Make sure he doesn't leave so that he can be arrested. Also, most importantly, make sure nobody ever discovers we stopped him.

"What, why? That doesn't make any sense. Wouldn't you want the credit for it?" Lulu enquired.

"No! We don't. I thought about it, and if we got the attention, someone might come after us. It isn't safe." I faced away from Lulu, inching to the butterfly statue in the center of the secret garden. After that, we had to take the first train back to our homes and get back before dinner. Do all of you understand?" I questioned in a snarky voice.

They both answered, "Yes."

When we concluded our meeting, we snuck back into the dorms and went to sleep. Since the following day was Saturday and we, of course, had no classes, I asked Lulu if she wanted to come to the park with Willie and me to test the new kite my mother had sent us. She responded, "Maybe in a little while, Ruby. But why don't you go ahead? I will meet up with you soon."

I agreed and went off on my merry way. After I left, she took my telegraph out and put in the number of President James Buchanan. She started by writing to him that I was onto her. Then she wrote the exact plan we were doing but told him he couldn't change it because I would know it was her if he did. Then, she erased the data on the telegraph and went out to meet with us.

Before dinner, she returned to check if he had received her message and was pleased that he did. Then she erased what he wrote; therefore, I would never find out what was happening. Luckily for me, I suspected that she might have used it, so I put beads in the back of the device, and every time someone used it, it would drop a new color bead to the person who used it. I created this facial recognition device by drawing pictures of the people who knew about the machine –I was brilliant at drawing– and put this fantastic gear into it that would take a picture of the face of the person and compare it to the drawing. Then, it would drop a bead corresponding to the person. Willie's were blue, mine were purple, Lulu's were yellow, Miss Holmes' were green, Mr. Henry's were red, Coconut's were orange, and everyone else's was white. I knew she had been through my stuff, but I still didn't know why. I didn't want to confront her about being a betrayer because she might change the assassination plan, so I asked her, "It is okay if you did, but did you use my telegraph machine?"

She lied, "No, I didn't. Why?" I stared into her soul and headed for my bed. I think she could tell I didn't believe her, so she decided to come clean, "Wait, Ruby, I did. I'm sorry I lied. I was just nervous that you wouldn't let me use it. I used it to write to my parents to see how they were doing."

"Okay, you can use it, but please ask first next time," I hollered.

Why would she lie to me? Every day I'm with her, I feel she keeps becoming increasingly suspicious, but what can I do?

The next few weeks started to fly by like a bird heading to the south during the winter seasons. Spring break was in three days, and I wasn't ready to go home yet. I didn't want to see Clara, Charles, or anybody else. I wasn't in the mood to be made fun of again for my inventions or my uniqueness. I was happy at school. It definitely didn't help that Mr. Henry wasn't going home to teach me.

Instead, he said he was going to meet with a close friend in Maine for the next week, and he was sorry for not being able to be there for me. I wasn't having it. It was not a good thought that I had to go home alone without someone who cared about me. But what could I do? How bad could it be? Maybe my siblings will finally stop making fun of me, or perhaps, like always, they will be the rude, vazey scoundrels I have known them to be.

I didn't try in class the following two days. I hoped Miss Holmes would notice and invite me to go home with her, but I was mistaken. So, I decided to take matters into my own hands and ask her: "Hello, Miss Holmes. What are you doing for the break?"

"Hello Ruby, I'm meeting with Mr. Henry and one of my old friends. What are you doing?"

"Oh." She could tell I looked down. "I will be going to see my amazing family," I screeched sarcastically.

She definitely could tell I wasn't excited, but that was okay. "I'm sorry, Ruby. I know how difficult it is for you at home, but you should try to make the most of it. I would have loved to have you over, but I have a crucial meeting. I hope you understand. I will, however, take you to the train station with me tomorrow morning and make sure you hop on the right train. If that's alright with you."

"Okay. I understand. Thank you for thinking about me, though. I appreciate it." I responded solemnly and then went to pack.

The following morning couldn't have arrived sooner. When we arrived at the train station, a small group of people held up signs for Mr. Lincoln. As I headed to the ticketer, a person with a knife came out and tried to stab some of these pedestrians. Miss Holmes noticed the chaos shortly after I did and tried to get me to the train as fast as possible so I wouldn't have been a product in the stabbing, but I needed to do something about it, so I took out my pocket spy and handed it to SPIDER to go and inject the culprit with.

Miss Holmes held me back, but I needed to stay there. I directed SPIDER to the culprit and had it climb up the slight pole near next to this bloody mess. Then it slowly reeled down a vial of this sleeping medicine, and at the right moment, when the culprit opened its mouth, it spilled it into it. The culprit coughed and gagged before passing out. Don't worry, I didn't kill him; I just made him fall asleep for a few hours, which is the perfect amount of time for the police to take him to jail.

I led the SPIDER back to me and hid it in my pocket. Then, I freed myself from Miss Holmes' grip and raced over to the pedestrians. I ripped off a piece of my jacket and used it as a tourniquet so the stabbed child wouldn't bleed out. The mother of this poor child who was stabbed held her daughter tightly. "Thank you," she whispered.

Miss Holmes raced over as fast as she could to get to me as I faced the poor mother. "I'm sorry for your daughter. She will definitely need immediate medical attention." I paused briefly, "Can I please ask you a question?"

The mother hugged me with bloody hand prints. "Anything," she said as her eyes filled with tears.

"Why did he try to hurt you? You didn't do anything?"

She had a sad giggle, "You are courageous, little girl. We were rooting for Mr. Lincoln, but this man was against him and didn't like our response. So, he tried to go into a rampage."

By the time Miss Holmes made it to me and saw the bleeding. She instructed me to go to my train and watched as I walked away and boarded it.

The conductor took one look, "Oh, the Ledger child. Your parents have told me to keep a straight eye on you, young one."

I faced him in disgust but proceeded onto the train. I headed straight for a window seat and saw that Miss Holmes helped care for this poor child to make sure she didn't die. I wasn't able to see much more because the train chugged too far out of the station for me to see anything.

Before the train ride was over, I found another little girl who was sitting with her mother. She was probably about three years younger but the same size as me. I asked if I could switch dresses with her so that Mother would not panic, but the girl's mother said no. I knew I needed to bribe them, so I grabbed a pocket full of gold and asked again. The mother instantly agreed and hugged me, then kissed me on the cheek.

I thought it was a little odd until she said, "Thank you. This money will help my family immensely." She then turned towards her daughter and instructed her to change out of it. Within a few minutes, I was in this new yellow dress. I had never really worn yellow before since normally my clothes are purple, sometimes they can be pink or blue, but never yellow. I thought it was quite pretty.

After five hours of traveling, I finally arrived home. The conductor took me to the new nanny for my siblings. My parents had replaced Gibface Gerty because she tried to steal a precious ornament from the Christmas box a few weeks after I left for school. This nanny had dark skin, hair, dark eyes, and a slender figure. She was beautiful, but I didn't care too much as I cared more about who she was on the inside, so let's see. "I will assume that Mother and Father are too busy to pick me up today."

"Yes, little girl. They are busy with your siblings' competitions today. Your sister is in a beauty contest, and your brother has a game today. My name is Liri, but you can call me Louie since nobody can pronounce it. I am from–"

"Let me guess, Albania or some Hebrew-speaking place?"

"Why yes, good guess. How did you figure that out, little Rebecca–" she responded.

"My name is Ruby, not Rebecca, Liri. And I figured it out with your strong accent. Am I right?"

She said in a dark tone, "For starters, little one, I do not care what your name is. Your parents say your name is Rebecca. Therefore, that is what I will call you. Also, my name is Louie, not Liri, but you surprisingly pronounced it correctly."

"Well, of course, I did. I speak Hebrew fluently. I speak eight languages and won't respond if you call me Rebecca."

"Well, too bad, Rebecca, I will make your life a living hell. Now I see why your parents say you are a special little one. You're the one who thinks you are too smart for everyone else. Why can't you be more like your sister? This is going to be a horrible week for you."

She was already comparing me to that koala. But, for being exceedingly beautiful, she was such an unlicked cub. So, I just stared and nodded. Then we headed off to my house.

CHAPTER ELEVEN
Spring Break

When I arrived home, the house looked a little different. New doors, chandeliers, tapestry, and paintings of my family lined the walls. It was like I walked into a non-religious shrine. It was wild. The first thing ludicrous Liri said after we walked into the house was, "Go to your room, Rebecca, and keep your filthy, creepy, ugly monkey away from me. If you leave your room before your parents come home, we will have a problem. Do you understand?"

I put on a fake smile and voice and answered, "Yes, of course, I understand. Why wouldn't I? I mean, as you stated, I am 'too smart for everyone else,' so I will prove that."

She watched me as I ran off to my room. Luckily, when I got inside, my parents didn't touch or move anything this time. Well, that was except for my toolbox. They didn't know that the last time I was here, I replaced all the tools in the toolbox with fake ones that didn't work and put the real ones in the cellar under a floorboard under my bed in my room. I crawled under the bed to retrieve all my excellent tools but opted not to build any device just in case my mother came in. Instead, I was going to make a dress. I know a dress, how unlike me, right? Well, it won't be just any dress. This dress is going to be perfect for assassination day. It will have every pocket and weapon holder; nobody will realize I have them. I will also conceal my silver shaky detector in the pockets underneath; therefore, nobody will see it.

After about two hours of measuring and drawing the blueprints of this dress, I decided to sneak out of my room to my mother's room to get silks for the dress. Then I heard a chime from the front door bells and the sound of my loud, sinister siblings. Mother was home.

"Good evening, Louie. I see you have returned from the station. Did everything go well? Is my beautiful little girl here?" Mother softly spoke in a calming voice.

Did she just call me beautiful? I am so lost. Maybe she missed me. But I decided to wait in my room for my mother to see lackadaisical Liri get in trouble.

"Yes, I believe she is upstairs. You know how children are—especially this one. You were correct. She is a brilliant little girl." Lakey Liri had retorted.

Mother nodded and headed up the stairs to my room, where I was "playing" with my dolls and dresses. Then she walked in.

"Oh, hello, mother. How are you on this fine day?"

She ignored me, ran over, picked me up, and gave me the world's largest hug. I was shocked. I never knew she had loved or missed me this much. "Mother, I can't breathe. You are squeezing the life out of me."

"Oh, I'm very sorry, Ruby. I have extremely missed you! It has been a long few months, and I am glad you are back home for the week." Mother verbalized as she looked around the room and saw what I was doing.

This was like an entirely new woman, but it had only been a few minutes since I had been back. I know she will return to how she was before sometime this week.

As Mother examined the room, she turned her face towards me and asked, "Ruby, sweetie, what are you doing?"

"I am making a dress. I was taught how to do this in sewing class. Why?"

Her face lit up. This was the biggest smile that she had ever shown me. It was pretty terrifying, actually. She even started to tear up a little. I grimaced and enquired, "Mother, can you please purchase some materials for me to make this dress? Because I only have old ones that are falling apart."

Her face lit up as she exclaimed, "Of course! I will take you right now. I am exceedingly happy that your school is teaching you to be the proper young lady I know you are and that you are dropping all of your maths and science nonsense."

And there it was. My mother said girls are only good for their looks and nothing else. She was such a fussock, but what could I do? I just smiled and nodded. I've learned that with the not-so-brilliant people, all you have to do is smile and nod, and you will get your way. She picked me onto my feet, and we headed to the automobile. She called Father to drive as she didn't know how. What a surprise, a woman doesn't know how to drive. One day, I will learn, but I need to play it off and try to get them to teach me.

"Father, may I drive with you by sitting only on your lap? I want to do this so I can get closer to you. If you let me do this, I won't ask again and be a pain in your butt. Also, this way, I can still be your precious little girl since you will be the one driving, of course?"

Mother and father looked at each other and commented, "Why yes, Ruby, I think that is a marvelous idea. I want to spend as much time with you as possible since you're home."

He picked me up, placed me on his lap to help steer, and we went to the market. When we arrived, Mother took me to the most expensive silk store. I wasn't surprised, though. She always wanted the best materials. She approached the store clerk and told him, "This is my daughter, and I want to get the best materials for her. She is learning to make a dress for her class. What can I purchase from you?"

He eyed me repeatedly and said, "Hello, little girl. I didn't know they let children of your age make dresses. Typically, children are about nine or ten years old before they learn to sew their first dress, but I guess it is good to start them young. So, how old are you? Five, maybe six?"

My mouth hit the flour; He thought I was five! Are you kidding me? I am not that small. This isn't fair, but life isn't fair.

"Sir, my daughter isn't five or six years old. She is almost ten. Why don't you help her choose her fabrics? She is very capable of doing that on her own." Mother howled with strength.

My mother just stood up for me. Who is this woman, and what has she done with my actual mother?

"Why yes, of course. I am thrilled to help her. What kind of colors do you normally like, little one?"

"Um... I like Egyptian blue with hints of white lace. I want my dress to be primarily blue with lace on the sides of the chest and the dress's skirt. I also want to make the middle a striped blue and white bow. I have already planned out this dress, and I want it to look perfect to impress my mommy." I only said that last piece to make me sound even cuter. Therefore, my parents would buy exactly what I wanted.

"Oh, of course. She is adorable." Then he went and got the materials.

"How does this color look for you?"

My eyes lit up as I responded, "I love it! May I please get it, Mommy and Daddy?" as I swayed back and forth with a big smile.

They agreed, bought the materials, and we went back home. Before I could race upstairs, my mother invited me to the kitchen to show her my cooking skills, but I respectfully declined and told her I would help her tomorrow. She replied, "Okay, Ruby, go and make me proud with your dress. Dinner will be ready in an hour."

By the time the hour was over, I had finished the bones of my dress with the help of Coconut. Then Mother called me down to eat. The only thing I had left to do was put in all of the secret compartments that would sit under the dress. I've always said, 'brains over brawn,' which works well for me in this circumstance. Especially in this case, since I enhanced my sewing machine. All I had to do was put the pieces in front of the device, and it would look at the blueprints of what I had made and automatically sew it for me. I loved my intelligence! Honestly, I couldn't imagine what life would be like for a vazey person. I mean, how difficult must it be for them? I guess it gives me hope for the future for how far I'll go. Oh well, who cares? I'm bloody brilliant!

I headed downstairs to the dinner table. There were five main courses to pick from and an assortment of sides. There was a giant duck covered in some "special" sauce, or at least that is what my mother says. As well as beef Wellington, masked angelfish, golden alligator, and fried chicken. The fried chicken was personally my favorite. On each side of the table were green beans, potatoes, carrots, and roasted Brussels sprouts. I loved Brussels sprouts! I know I am the weird kid who enjoys my vegetables, but they are suitable for me as long as they are adequately cooked and in the right season. Unlike when I came here last time, they taste amazing!

After I sat down, my mother started speaking. This was odd because we typically began eating before anyone spoke, but I was interested in what she had to say. "Today, we are celebrating the return of our young little Ruby for the break."

My sister started giggling like a hyena with a rash on its bottom that wanted to be removed. I gave her the death stare and asked, "What's so funny, Clara? Miss me?"

She snarled, "No, I didn't miss you. I'm glad you live somewhere else. At least now the true girls live in this house."

What did that even mean? My sister was such a cherry. "True girls? I am a girl, just a girl genius."

She struggled to come up with an insult. "I mean the people who look like a princess and not like the little...."

Then she paused. I don't understand how I got all the brains, and she got none. "A little what? What? Did a cat get your tongue? Aww, oh no." I rolled my eyes.

"Rebecca, that wasn't very nice." Mother barked.

"What? She insulted me first, but you know what, it's fine. I won't insult her again. This shows that I have something known as class. Ever heard of it, Clara?" I expressed with a smile that reached from ear to ear.

Mother shook her head at me, and then Father chimed in, "Ruby, please just eat your dinner."

Oh, come on. Of course, I'm the one who gets blamed.

Then Charles said, "Ruby, you know I've noticed."

"What?" I snarled at him.

"I've noticed that in all the months you were gone, you are still as short as a penguin. Incredibly tiny and petite. So, what happened?"

I bit my thumb at him. From Shakespeare, this meant the same thing as sticking your tongue out. "Nothing happened. I am just a slow developer, that's all. Also, what is your problem? Can't you ever be nice for once? I mean, all you are is a flummox."

"I am not a flummox." He turned towards Mother and Father, "Wait, what is a flummox? Also, is biting your finger supposed to mean something? Man, you are stupid!"

I started chuckling at him. God, how was I born into this family? I was curious if I should tell him the actual meaning, so I didn't. "A flummox is another way to say..." I hesitated, "brilliant." Then, I whispered under my breath, "Yeah, I'll go with that..."

He returned a dirty look and shrieked, "Mom, Dad, that isn't what it means. She is fooling me." But my parents didn't know the true definition either. Therefore, they couldn't scold me. Flummox means that he is a failure. He didn't have a bright future, but that's not my problem. So, for the rest of dinner, we all sat quietly. Well, that was until the last five minutes when my sister yelled at the top of her lungs, "Ruby, you literally ruin everything. Nobody wants you to be here because we used to have very intellectual conversations over the table when you weren't here, but now it's all silence."

"Intellectual? Okay, Koala, oops, I mean Clara, what does the word intellectual mean?"

She stood there momentarily and retorted, "It means, um... it means..., oh, whatever you know what it means."

As she answered, I rudely nodded, sipped my drink, and laughed when she couldn't finish. "Ruby, don't laugh at your sister. Please go to your room and stay there because you are grounded." Mother announced hesitantly.

What! This wasn't fair! She started it. Well, I guess that answers the question of who this new mother of mine is and replaces it with the mother I know and love. Whatever, I pushed my seat away from the table and marched upstairs. Even though I didn't care that I was grounded, this meant I could spend the next few days without being bothered, so I guess it was a win-win situation.

When I got back to my room, I began the final steps to finishing the dress:

1. I sewed in the final compartments and put small pieces of lead that I got from under the table during dinner time.

    a. I got Coco to unscrew it. I also got it from the tiny compartments in my drawers, but most of all, I got it from my brother's complete toolbox since I only had aluminum in mine.

2. I aligned the entirety of the dress with it, so if anyone tried to shoot me in this assassination attempt, I would survive. As I've learned, lead is bulletproof.

I learned this because when I was at the Academy, I built a gun, which was taken away... But that's not the point. When I had this gun, I went outside and shot a post that was made of lead. Instead of the bullet penetrating the shaft, it bounced off right back at me. Luckily, I jumped out of the way fast enough. Therefore, nothing happened, but it was a fun story. Well, at least to me. That was the reason I got it taken away. Mr. Henry saw this event occur, and he walked up to me and said, "No more guns for you. Not until you learn to use them the proper way."

It was a fair thing to say. Finally, after two hours, I finished the dress and tried it on. The good news was it fit perfectly! Even though it was done, something felt like it was missing. I'm just glad that I measured myself correctly, and it fits! Also, for being full of lead, it didn't rattle when I walked, and it wasn't too heavy either, which meant I did it accurately.

Additionally, it was very comfortable to move around in. Which was surprising, but at the same time, I have always worn dresses my entire life; therefore, I was used to them. Now, the ultimate test: how did it look? I walked to the other side of my room with a large glass, bejeweled mirror. Then I heard a voice behind me saying, "You look beautiful."

I jumped out of instant fear. It was Mother. When did she walk in? How did she stay so quiet with the oversized cabooses she calls heels? "I am very sorry, Ruby. I didn't mean to scare you."

"It's fine. May I help you with something?" I asked in a subtle voice.

"No, I just came to check on you and wish you a good night. How do you feel being back?"

"It's alright, I guess. I mean, I am grounded, and it's only the first day. So..." I sarcastically chirped.

"Ruby, you deserved it. You scolded your sister."

"She started it! Besides, I'm the younger one; shouldn't she be a role model to me?" I shouted with all my might.

"Ruby..." Mother took a deep breath and patted me on the bed, calling me over, "Okay, little bug, come here. I want to tell you something, but first, let me help you get ready for bed."

She scooped me into her arms, helped me take off my dress, and put on my sleepwear. She then put me on my bed and tucked me in, ready to tell me a story. I wondered what kind of story it was. Maybe it was some fairytale! I love fairy tales, but I don't think she has it in her to do a fairy tale. Let's see, though...

"Ruby, I want to tell you why I treat you quite differently than your siblings. So, hush up, little one, you must stay real quiet."

I nodded. Wow, I can't believe she was admitting that she treats me differently—what a shocker.

"Ruby, I treat you differently because I don't always understand you. You are my little girl, my baby girl, but you are different. You love these stupid things in history, maths, and science. You remind me of someone I know and was incredibly close to."

"Wait, who?" I chirped.

"Hush, little one, let me finish. I will tell you the story of someone who used to be very near and dear to me. This is the story of a young voyager named Molly."

"Molly? Is that her real name?"

"Little one, I won't continue unless you hush up."

"My voice is now silent, as is Coco's. Isn't that right, Coco?" I swiped my fingers across my mouth and threw an invisible key across the room. Then, I faced her, and we both agreed.

"Now, as I was saying, this is the story of a young voyager named Molly. Molly, like me, was from a place far away from here."

"Mother, do you mean London, Great Britain," I asked. She had a slight look of anger.

I continued, "Sorry, Mother, I promise to be quiet. Please continue."

"Molly and I were raised together. Growing up, I was pretty close with her, but I never understood anything she said, just like what you say sometimes. She was just as brilliant as you, always curious about the world and its people. Her goal in life was to become a detective like yours. She was always highly brilliant at seeing the most minor details in things you wouldn't even imagine were there. I remember she invented this machine with wheels on the bottom of it, and you could sit on it. She put gears into it like an automobile and could ride it down the street. I don't remember what she called it, but even though it was pretty fascinating, I grew enraged with jealousy of her and her intelligence because I couldn't understand how she could do that and spend hours creating these odd new things every day.

As the years passed, we grew closer and closer until one day, she fell off the face of the map for months. She got herself in a mess she couldn't clean up. Then, one day, she returned with a baby girl. As time passed, her daughter grew to be one of the most brilliant kids in the world, if not the most brilliant. Like you."

"Mother, why are you telling me this story?"

"Because Ruby, I love and care about you, but I don't want you to go on these missions. I don't want you to disappear as Molly did."

"But she came back! She was fine, wasn't she?" I yelled back.

"She was extremely different. It was as if she was an entirely new person. Ruby, I don't want to lose you. So, I am kindly asking you to stop this detective nonsense."

"But mom, what happened to the girl? I mean, is she still here today? Can I meet her? Can I meet Molly?"

"No!" I jumped back a little; she could tell she scared me, but she didn't mean to, "Ruby, I'm sorry, but I can't let you meet them. Please, I ask you not to do whatever foolish thing you will probably do. I am very nervous that you will get yourself killed, and I would never forgive myself if you died. I treat you harshly because I don't want you to end up like Molly. Please, Ruby, listen to what I say for once in your life, and don't do anything foolish."

I thought for a moment, but I couldn't promise. I needed to help Abraham Lincoln. He was in danger, and I couldn't let him die, no matter the cost, even if it meant my disappearance. How bad could it have been? She came back, even though she was a different person. But still, she came back.

"Now, little one, do you remember the song I used to sing to you to fall asleep before you left for the academy?"

Oh my gosh, I forgot. I loved that song! I used to hum it all the time until my mind went straight to saving Mr. Lincoln.

"Here, Ruby, why don't I start?

Sapphires may glow, but Rubies sparkle.

Listen to the screech of the owl mumble.

Pick the one with the glowing chest, but be careful for the poisonous rest.

Once all is found, it'll lead the way.

But be wise because if not, the reapers will get you.

Good night, my little gem."

"Goodnight, Mother!" I hollered.

Then she left. I couldn't stop humming the song. It was beautiful, and even though it didn't make sense, do any lullabies ever really make sense? After a few repetitions of the song, I thought about Lulu and why she would give me a picture of a guy named Elijah Devon. Then I had it!

I began to poke Coco to wake her up; after about three pokes, she roared, "Ruby, stop. I'm trying to sleep!"

"I know, but I have found some fathomable evidence about Mr. Lincoln's case. Think about it like this: Lulu is working for Buchanan, right? Well, what if he told her to lead me astray from the truth? However, as time passed, she began to like me and wanted me to succeed because she knew that killing Mr. Lincoln was wrong. Still, if Buchanan found out she was trying to help me, he would probably do something terrible to her. I mean, if he is capable of assassinating Mr. Lincoln, I can assure you that he is capable of hurting her as well. What if she knew that I was onto her? Therefore, she decided she would try to give me a clue without being too obvious, knowing that I'd figure it out!

As it was discovered, the picture she handed me was one of her drawings, which wasn't real. Right? She also told me that 'Elijah Devon' was his name and that he was a Russian with white hair and green eyes. I don't know how I didn't think of this before, but in Russian, the name 'Elijah Devon' isn't pronounced Elijah Devon. It's pronounced 'Eliyah Dyevon,' so what if Elijah's name isn't Elijah Devon, but it is Eliyah Dyevonn?"

Coco smiled as she caught on very quickly; then she shouted, "It's an anagram!"

"Exactly! It's an anagram. If you rearrange the letters of Elijah Devonn, you get Elya Nidyevon, like my professor. Also, there is another thing: the first day Buchanan came and visited me, I had a class with her when she mentioned, 'Always live with your guard up,' which is exactly word for word what Buchanan said to Marshall before he left. And the saying 'always live with your guard up' is uncommon. I had never heard that before that day.

Additionally, if I remember correctly, Buchanan had a string of white hair on his shirt, and now that I think about it, he had a dab of red lipstick on the side of his neck, which is the same kind that Professor Nidyevon wears. You can tell based on the brick shade, and nobody else wears brick-colored lipstick except for Professor Nidyevon. So, it would make the most sense, and nobody would suspect a woman to do it.

"Ruby, that's genius, but if we tell Lulu that we figured it out, couldn't something bad happen to her?" Coco screeched ecstatically.

"Yes, we just have to play along as if we don't know anything." I squealed right before falling asleep.

The following morning, I woke to the sound of my brother ripping apart my room.

"Umm, excuse me, chump, what are you doing?!" I shouted at the top of my lungs to him.

"I know you have it in here, tiny. You always take my things." He responded in a low, deep voice.

"I have no idea what you're talking about at all. Maybe if you could give me a clue and didn't rip my room apart, I could help you."

"I'm talking about my toy car. I wanted to show it to my friends, but you probably took it!"

Okay, I did take his toy car, but to be fair, it would be a surprise for him. I was going to replace it and put a little wired steam engine in it so it could actually move around, but you know what, why should I do that anymore? So, I got up, went to my locked drawer, and returned it to him.

"See, I knew you took it, you little twirp. Stay out of my way before I make sure you disappear," he yelped, then pushed me as hard as he could onto the ground.

I debated whether or not I wanted to get him in trouble but chose not to. It was easier to stay in my room or sneak out and walk around. A few moments later, Liri walked into my room. "Good morning, Rebecca. Although you are grounded, your mother instructed me to get your smart-alec rump ready for the day because today we are going to the docks and feeding the birds some bread."

"Are you kidding me? The docks, I don't want to do that; you can't feed birds bread. There are natural preservatives in it that can make the birds severely ill. I refuse to do that! I'd prefer to be locked in this room or walk around and do my own thing rather than be with you. Thanks!" I muttered in a harsh tone.

I didn't want to go. Besides, I had better things to do than feed the birds, like build my telescope or weapons or invent anything else under the sun.

"How dare you back yack at me, child. You will do what your mother tells me you must do, and that is final!"

Then she went to my dresser and pulled out the dress I had made last night. I yelled to her, "Fine, I will go to the docks and watch the birds but not feed them, and I won't wear that dress. Pick a different one, lady! Besides, if my parents are paying you to watch me, doesn't that technically mean you have to be nicer to me so I don't get you fired?"

She hung up the dress and picked a different one. It was very pink with little purple flowers on the collar and sleeves. I sighed and then went to her to help me put it on. Then she sat me down and did my hair. Finally, after thirty minutes, we were ready to go.

When we arrived at the docks, it was beautiful! It was sunny, the water was glistening, and the ducks were floating in a circle. There were even ducklings. It was adorable! I ran up to one of them and sat down. The mother duck trusted me enough to sit on me, and the babies followed. It felt like I was in duck paradise. First, I started laughing hysterically and then crying. I couldn't keep it together because I couldn't remember a time as happy as this one. Liri began to smile, but she didn't want my outfit to get all dirty, so she came up and tried to pick me up, but I refused. After a few minutes, she stopped trying.

"See, Rebecca, this isn't that bad. Besides, you can look through the binoculars over here," Liri told me.

I walked over to her but was too short to see through it, "Louie, I'm too small; I can't reach it!"

She picked me up, and finally, I could look through it! Ah ha, that's it! There was a little piece of brass inside. I could get the brass and use it if I took it apart. It could melt just enough to turn it into a piece I could rub against the assassin. This will mark him and make him sick for a few days, but he will not die. So, after he goes to prison, he won't fight. Of course, I will measure how much I am putting on it, and I can't cut myself with it; otherwise, I will be in trouble. This should work! As she held me, I took off my bracelet, which had a secret little pick that could be used as a screwdriver. I started unscrewing it, but I couldn't open it with Liri standing there; I decided I needed to make her go away. I had to be nice because it would only take a few minutes to get it out before she returned.

"Louie, I'm hungry. Do you see that shop over there? Can you please, please, please, bring me something to eat?"

She replied, "Yes, but you have to come with me. I don't want to leave you here alone; it's not safe."

I had to think of something, "Oh, Louie, please! It's so pretty out here; besides, you can practically see me from the shop itself. Pleeeeeeease!" Then, I used the puppy dog face. It always works because I'm adorable!

"Fine, I will get you some food, but you can't move! Do you understand? If your parents find out I lost you, they will kill me, and then I will give them an actual reason to kill me by killing you."

My eyes widened as she said that. She is very dramatic! I hollered, "Yes, of course, I won't leave, I promise!"

"Okay, you are too smart to be kidnapped anyway, but you are tiny. I will be keeping my eye on you the entire time!"

"Thank you, thank you, thank you!" I yelped as I hugged her.

She scratched me off her and responded, "Okay! That's it, revolting little grasshopper, stay here," she was off.

In the next five minutes, I entirely removed the binoculars with Coco's help and put them back together. I managed to get the brass piece I needed and stuffed it in my pocket. She returned with a large scoop of Neapolitan ice cream. It wasn't my favorite, but that's alright. It was still good.

After I finished it, we returned to the house, and I went to piece it with my unique dress. As the end of the week was approaching, every day seemed to be very similar to the previous one, where Liri would take me out, and that was the end. By the end of the week, I became bored with my family, but at least, for the most part, they played nicely.

Finally, it was Sunday morning, and I was returning to school. Mother and father took me to the train station themselves. Before I boarded, my mother and father picked me up and held me in their arms. Mother whispered in my ear, "Remember, don't do anything foolish, and be the good little girl I know you are! I will see you in a few months for summer break." Then they put me down, and I went on my merry way. I had my dress, brass, and everything I needed to accomplish my first major mission. It was perfect!

When I arrived at the station in Washington D.C., Miss Holmes, Mr. Henry, and their friend. She was gorgeous, with brunette hair, a slender figure, and violet eyes, like me. Then I whispered to Coco, "Coco, look. Maybe she is Millie Hartford from Mr. Lincoln's journal."

Coco veered her little head towards the violet-eyed lady.

I had never met anyone else with violet eyes before. Unfortunately, they didn't let me say anything to her and wished her a farewell back to England. I had many questions and tried to ask them on the way back to the Academy, but they didn't answer. I wondered who she was. Maybe she was the woman from Mr. Lincoln's journal who had a daughter. Which now gives me more reason to believe that I am Mr. Henry's daughter, which would make her my mom, but if that is the case, I would have to prove it first.

Right now, I need to focus on Mr. Lincoln's assassination, but I will return to this issue and find out who she is. Once we finally arrived at the Academy, I ran to my room, put my stuff down, headed to dinner, and went off to sleep.

CHAPTER TWELVE

President Buchanan Visits the Academy

The following morning, I woke up to Coco jumping up and down on me like she was some type of a kangaroo. "Coco, stop! What are you doing?" She didn't respond and crawled under the covers. Then she hugged me for dear life as if she had seen a ghost.

What was going on? I went under the blanket, and she began signing to me, "Ruby, I'm sorry for jumping on you, but I just saw him. Buchanan is outside of the window. But something seems different about him. I think he knows you figured out his plan. He even got close enough to the door where I heard him speaking about how he was looking for you, Ruby. Someone must have told him. Do you think it was Lulu?"

Now I understood why she was petrified, "Coco, if I run, then he will know that I know, but if I stay, it might not be safe. Right now, I can't go anywhere or do anything because if I do, I will get in immense trouble; I have to play it as if I don't know anything."

She agreed, and we both got out of bed. I dressed and put Coco in her cute little uniform; then we went to breakfast. I sat down to eat, looked to my right, and the President walked in. The entire school stopped what they were doing and dropped their silverware. While looking at me, He whispered something into Miss Holmes' ear, but she shook her head. I wondered what he was saying to her.

After breakfast, I was heading to my first class when Buchanan approached me with no other accomplices. I tried to ignore him by continuing to walk, but then he uttered, "Ruby, isn't it?"

I stopped in my tracks and turned around towards him. He had a little red mark on his collar and white hair on his shirt. It must have been from Professor Nidyevon, but I couldn't let him know I knew, so I responded, "Yes, may I help you with something?"

He continued with, "I remember you from the White House. You know, little girl, you made a significant impression on me with your brilliance. I haven't seen a child or anybody as intelligent as you in many years. Well, at least since I was much younger. I am fascinated by you and would love it if I could come and spend some time with you this week on campus."

I thought for a second. Then Coco vocalized, "Don't do it; it must be a trap!" I agreed, but what could I do? He would know I might have known something if I told him no.

So, I had to say, "Yes, you may. I am heading off to hair and makeup, which is my first class. You are welcome to join me, but I think you will find it boring. I know I do."

He smiled, "No, I think it will be entertaining. Don't worry, child. I would love to watch it."

I'm not going to lie; that kind of creeped me out, considering he was a grown man, but he was also President, so if he tried to hurt me, well, it wouldn't end well for his career. On the way there, he seemed slightly nervous; I wondered if I had scared him. I mean, even though I am tiny, I am mighty! Maybe he saw that. As we entered the class, he stopped me and asked, "So, is this monkey your pet?"

"Yes," I answered silently.

"Aww, isn't that adorable? Earlier, I saw you communicating with her as if you could understand her. What was happening there?"

Oh no! Do I tell him I can speak, monkey, or do I lie? Okay! I got it, "No, I can't; it was just in my imagination. I mean, I am a kid. Sometimes, I like to pretend I can speak, monkey, you know?" I was trying to play stupid.

Unfortunately, as I was saying this, the abominable Ackers were passing and voiced, "Wait a minute. Aren't you the president guy of our country?"

I gave them a stupid look and smacked my forehead. They were such chumps.

Then he responded, "Why yes, girls, I am."

"Umm, what are you doing with the little six-year-old? Haha. I mean, she is very annoying. Wouldn't you rather spend some time with us, the people who actually matter in life?" Caroline smirked.

He looked in disbelief and stated, "You know it's not nice to insult the people who are smarter than you because one day, you're probably going to end up working for them. Don't ever insult this child again, or I will make sure your parents have a difficult time with their payments in the next year. Also, to answer your final remark, no, I would not rather spend time with you, as I am very interested in what this little one has to say, so if you don't mind, please carry on with your business and head to class."

They gulped in fear and then walked in. Did he seriously stand up for me? How interesting, I think he did. "Why would you do that? You don't know me or anything about me. So, why would you stand up for me?"

Buchanan thought briefly and continued, "Because I don't like bullies. I find them to be repulsive and very aggressive. Additionally, the smallest ones are always the toughest. I was a small child like you once, and we must stick together. You're just like me, Ruby."

But, I wasn't like him, even though I was small, he was a killer, but he didn't know I knew. I wonder why he was being exceedingly lovely to me. I mean, maybe he was different than I thought. Maybe there was something else about Mr. Lincoln that I didn't know why he was assassinating him. Assassination is not the way to go, but what if I am missing something?

During class, we learned how to make the proper ball gown makeup; about halfway through, Mr. Buchanan left. I didn't know why, but maybe he got the information he needed. I also didn't understand why I needed to learn this, considering we didn't have a ball. When I was finished, I looked in the mirror, and I looked like a clown. Another girl in my class laughed at me, but only because the Ackers told her to. I didn't blame her. Professor Nidyevon asked me. "Ruby, what are you doing with your makeup?"

I sighed, "I don't understand how to do that. It's not my thing."

"Well, Ruby, if you don't complete this, you will get an F for the class. You have ten minutes to learn." She declared before walking away.

Are you kidding me? I wanted to cheat, but that wasn't right. Although she never said I couldn't have Coco do my makeup. I mean, monkeys have very steady hands. So, I called Coco, "Can you please help me?"

She nodded, stripped my face, and redid it. To me, it was perfect. Then the bell rang. Professor Nidyevon approached me and stated, "Well, it's not perfect, but it is good enough to pass. I give you a C."

What! A C, are you kidding me? I sighed. At least I passed. As I entered Mr. Henry's culinary arts, he spoke to Buchanan. Once again, they were whispering, and I knew they were talking about me because they mentioned my name at least three times. But what could I do? I couldn't just tell them they were talking about me. Ughhh, it was frustrating. Then Buchanan left, and Mr. Henry walked over to me. "Ruby, I understand that you know Mr. Buchanan, but I need you to stay away from him and out of his life. Do you understand?"

"What! I didn't do anything that's not right!"

"Ruby?"

"Fine, but to be clear, he came to me, not the other way around!"

Mr. Henry smiled and continued with the class. Over the next few weeks, Mr. Buchanan came to the Academy multiple times, and he watched me like a hawk each time. It was creepy. But I carried on with my life and was prepping for the assassination day. As it got closer and closer, I began to be a little nervous because what if my plan didn't work out the way I wanted it to? What if my plan doesn't work and my parents are right? What if I needed to stop with this detective business? NO, STOP, RUBY! I mustn't think that way. I can do this!

About two weeks before summer break, I noticed some of my gadgets were not working. I decided to take them apart and realized they were fake. Why would anyone take them, and how did anyone besides Lulu and Willie know they even existed? I wonder if Lulu had anything to do with it. So, that night when she was gone, I searched her stuff, but they weren't there. I wondered where it all went, but I had to keep it on the down low. If I said anything, I would probably get in trouble for having them, so I rebuilt them again and didn't tell anyone. Fortunately, they weren't stolen this time.

The following morning was the last time I saw Buchanan on campus before the end of the school year. I first saw him walking the campus before class, but as I was exiting, I saw him with Lulu again! As I got closer, Lulu claimed, "She is onto me; you have to be careful; you can't come here again."

This time, instead of standing in silence, I decided to confront them. "Hello, Mr. Buchanan and Lulu. I didn't know you knew each other. How are the both of you?"

I think she knew what I was doing; Lulu became anxious as she expressed, "Um… we met each other a few weeks ago on campus. I love politics, as you know, and I wanted to get to know him more."

I couldn't tell if she was joking or not. "Why did you call him uncle then? I heard you a while ago, and I'm just confused."

She hesitated for a second, then replied, "Oh, that's because you know, like Uncle Sam, well, of course you do, Ruby. You're the smartest person I've ever met; this is just like that."

Was she serious? Uncle Sam was created in 1813 because of Samuel Wilson, who supplied meat to the American troops during the War of 1812, and he was nothing like that. So, I brought that up, and Buchanan responded with, "Well, I found out that Lulu's family needed extra food because her family isn't as fortunate as yours is, so I supplied it to her, and they encouraged me to be called Uncle Buchanan."

"Well, I guess that makes sense. But, Lulu, why didn't you tell me you needed help? My family would have been delighted to assist you. Although my family is a bunch of wankers, they care about my friends."

She looked down and then at me. "It was because I felt ashamed; you're right, Ruby. I should have told you."

I was still a little skeptical, but if she was telling the truth, then she really needed my help. That night, I telegraphed my parents to send her family some money. A few days later, they said they sent her family a couple of thousand dollars. It was a nice gesture.

Or at least I thought so until Lulu came up to me yelling, "Why would you do that? Ruby, I don't need your parents' money. My family can get by on our own."

"What? I was trying to help you. Why don't you want my help? It's not like I shot someone or hurt your family. I was only trying to help!" I thundered in a loud, firm voice.

She sighed, "Ruby, I appreciate what you do, but I need you to stop with this nonsense, okay? I get that your family is rich, but I don't need your help. So, from now on, don't do anything like that again, do you understand, shorty?"

I couldn't believe what I was hearing! All I was doing was trying to help, and she replied shorty! "I am not a 'shorty!' Okay, I am, but I can't believe you just said that to me. You know I might be tiny, but I am mighty! All I was doing was trying to help you, and I don't need your criticism. I wouldn't have done it if I didn't care about you!"

I could tell Lulu felt terrible. She ran out of our room and slammed the door. I was very furious at her rudeness! I couldn't believe what I was hearing or seeing.

To blow off some steam, I opened my toolbox and began to build whatever I could piece together. As I was rummaging through the metal scraps, barbed wire, and other chemicals in bottles I had, it hit me. "Coco, everything that the perpetrator was using was from that box that was in the White House, but that box was supposed to be mine, and when we went there that time, Miss Holmes didn't seem shocked that I snuck into the room, which could mean that she probably knew what was in the room and knew I would be safe, which means that she knew that the box was mine.

What if Miss Holmes knew much more than she was willing to give off? I mean, she must have known! She knew about my necklace; I wondered what else Miss Holmes was hiding. So, what if she knew what was going to happen to Lincoln? If she didn't, she wouldn't have also mentioned, 'You must stay out of this; it is too dangerous for you.' Or at least she said something like that. How did I not piece this together before? But if all of this is true, I can't go and confront her; I mean, she would tell me again to stay out of it. I need to do this with Willie and Lulu."

Coco concurred, and then we went to the secret garden. Lulu was sitting there planting. That's where she always went when she was frustrated. I slowly walked in. "Lulu, I'm sorry for trying to help; I didn't mean to make you feel poor or left out. I know your family can fend for themselves."

She smiled at me, "No, I'm sorry, Ruby. I shouldn't have gotten mad. Your family was trying to help, and I appreciate it! I should have said thank you. So, here it is, thank you!"

We both hugged, and she looked around as if she was worried someone was watching her. Then she continued, "Ruby, the day is coming closer and closer. We only have a few days before we leave for the assassination." She leaned in as if she thought someone was spying and whispered in my ear, "I figured something else out. The second guy that you heard, the Marshall guy, he's not going to be the killer; he's just going to be the driver. There is a third person, and it's a man, or at least I think it is; he has long white hair. It is in the picture that I have given you. I believe he is a Russian that Buchanan is using. This is because nobody will suspect an older man to kill. It's perfect!"

Even though I already knew who the culprit was, I put the world's largest smile on my face because this meant that Lulu felt bad for hiding this information from me. She knew what she was doing was wrong, so I played dumb and continued with, "How did you figure that out?"

"Well, you know how Buchanan has been coming here every so often. I would talk to him about his plans for the future."

I had never been more proud of Lulu in my entire life than at this moment! She was right. This was brilliant!

After our little confession session, I had to go to Mr. Henry for his class. Today, Lulu and Willie decided to join me. We were learning about the Acadian Expulsion that occurred between 1755 and 1778. About 10,000 Acadians were deported to many places around the Atlantic because they refused to sign an oath of allegiance to Great Britain.

"Mr. Henry, why didn't they just sign it? I mean, wouldn't that have been easier?" Lulu questioned.

"Well, Lulu, the Acadians believed that they were protecting themselves from the insanity of the empires; they also wanted to preserve their religion. Ruby, I know you understand this, but Lulu and Willie, you must never let anyone control you. Even if it's difficult, you must fight for what you believe in. The reason why I am teaching you about this event is because the Acadians didn't stand down and never ended up signing it. They stood up for themselves, so must all of you, even if someone says it's too dangerous!"

Then he winked at us; I believe he secretly knew our plan and only told me to stay away from it to be a "good" mentor.

After class was over, we headed to dinner. Willie said, "Does he know? I mean, does he know about our plan?"

"I didn't tell him that, but I think he might. To be completely honest, I don't know, but he is always mysterious with me like that." We all laughed.

As the end of the school year approached, there was a small ceremony to celebrate. We were required to wear lovely attire and go to the great hall. When we arrived, the boy's academy was even there, and each person had to sit in an assigned space depending on their year. I was in my youngest year. Therefore, we were on the far right, while the oldest students were on the far left. It seemed like a graduation.

As we all took our seats, Miss Holmes walked on the stage. She had a giant cone-shaped thing; I like to call it the sounding cone because it amplifies your voice. "Good morning, students! As you know, the year has come to an end, and I am so proud of each and every one of you. Today, we celebrate all of you moving forward into the next year of education with a great feast and a scroll of your accomplishments and grades from the entire year. Some of you are graduating this year and moving on to your university careers, while others are just beginning their journey here at Miss Holmes' Academy. I have watched each and every one of you grow throughout the year/years, and it is amazing! I am exhilarated to see what each of you graduates accomplish in your lives, and I hope that the skills we have given you have prepared you for those. So, we will start by handing out the graduates their scrolls first and then make our way down towards the first years."

After a grueling hour of waiting for our scroll, it was our turn. Miss Holmes handed everyone else's before she got to mine. Before she gave it to me, she pulled me to the side and whispered, "Ruby, I am so proud of how far you've come this year. When I first met you, you had a lot of hatred for this school, and I knew you didn't want to be here. However, as time passed, you learned to accept it and see its goodness and everything else. I am especially proud of how much you've grown as a person. I know it is difficult for you to follow instructions sometimes because you are an incredibly accomplished little girl, and I just wanted you to know that I truly care for you, and I know you'll succeed! But, you must remember, Ruby, in a world full of darkness and despair, you must be a flame, or the horrors of society will consume you in an instant.

Here is your scroll. I'm proud of you, kid."

I smiled at her, taking in everything she said, and responded, "Thank you!"

Mine didn't look like everyone else's white parchment scroll with her signature on the bottom. Well, on one side, it did, but on the other, it didn't. It was in the format of a riddle. Or, at least, I believe it was a riddle. The message stated:

"Beyond the walls of time, my bear will shine.

Killers don't smile without intent, so be careful of what you mean.

Don't be shy, and learn to speak before all your brains will leak.

Be careful on your journey before it's too late; inside my office, a special roll with bake."

I showed it to Lulu, Coco, and Willie. "Maybe there is something in Miss Holmes' office," Lulu told me.

"Or maybe it was in Professor Nidyevon's office." I screeched as we all ran towards her office.

When we arrived, we ransacked the place but found nothing. Don't worry, we put it back as if we had never been there. Then we decided to go behind Miss Holmes' office because there was a room full of clocks. That I always referred to as the time room. We found one of Miss Holmes' carved bear statues with a closed candle on top of it. "This must be what she meant by '*Beyond the walls of time, my bear will shine.*' It must be, right?" Willie curiously questioned.

"It's the only thing that makes sense. Let's open its head!" I enthusiastically yelled.

"Ruby, why is its head?" Lulu chimed in.

"Because the next line of the riddle was '*Don't be shy and learn to speak before all your brains will leak,*' it must be where its brain would be, which is in its head."

Unfortunately, it was locked; we tried to pick it up, but it didn't work. It was okay, though, because I had the idea to use my key necklace. It opened astonishingly quickly. I wonder what other places my key fits. I guess the "*Don't be shy and learn to speak before all your brains will leak*" part of that speech was when the animal died before it had the opportunity to screech. On the inside of the brain were three train tickets to Chicago.

"Miss Holmes knew all along what my plan was, didn't she," I questioned curiously.

"Of course she did, your Ruby Ledger, the Detective! She must want to help you."

I smiled, and we took the tickets and went on our merry way.

The following day was leaving the day to go home; it was Monday, May 14, 1860. When we arrived at the train station, Miss Holmes was there to say farewell. "Ruby, I'm glad you found my surprise. Please promise me you'll be careful where you're going. Now, Ruby, I told your parents you would stay with me for a few days after school ends, and I will then take you to the train on Saturday night. Remember, don't miss your train, but accomplish what you have to! A man named Allan Pinkerton will meet you in Chicago and guide you. Best of luck, little Ruby!"

I smiled, gave her the world's largest hug, then thanked her for everything and calmly yelped, "Don't worry, Miss Holmes! Everything will be alright, I promise. I can't wait for next year!"

She smiled back, and Lulu, Willie, Coco, and I were off to Chicago. This was going to be a long week, but it was going to be great!

CHAPTER THIRTEEN

The Assassination of Abraham Lincoln

After about seven and a half hours of traveling, we finally arrived in Chicago. The train station looked immensely different in the Midwest than in the North. In the north, as you would exit, there would be many tickets but not carts of food and snacks because people, on average, were poorer, so my family is one of the richest. Here in the Midwest, they were much more organized. Many people have carts of snacks, treats, and food. It was amazing! I had never seen anything like it before in the United States. When we got off the train, a conductor walked up to us. His name was Allan Pinkerton. He looked like an average-aged man with very little hair on each side of his head, dark brown eyes, and nice clothing. He also had a weird pin on his chest that looked like the three triangles.

It was odd because I'd seen this before on the bottom of my key and at Miss Holmes' and Mr. Henry's offices.

I thought he would ask us something stupid like, "Hello, children, may I ask where your parents are?" Instead, he said, "You must be the three children I am taking around Chicago and showing the convention's location to. Miss Holmes sent me to help the three of you."

Then he pointed to Willie, Lulu, and me and continued, "You must be Willie, Lulu, and you, the little one, must be Ruby. I can tell by your cute little rosy cheeks."

Subsequently, he showed us unusual forms of identification to prove he was the right man. I had never seen any identification cards before. I think I will call it an I.D. for short. It must be something new or maybe something related to the HIA organization.

We all smiled. I don't think I had been more grateful then at this moment because I realized Miss Holmes truly understood me. When we arrived at the hotel, it was highly secretive. On the top of the building read, "Hexing International Auberge" in black lettering with a gold rim.

There were a bunch of people in suits, even women. It was terrific, but Allan told us to ignore them. As we were walking upstairs, I saw the same woman with Violet eyes who was with Mr. Henry and Miss Holmes after a break. She was talking to another woman. As we passed her, the only thing I could make out of what she was saying was, "Are you sure this is a good idea not to let anyone else handle this? If it weren't for Ruby, we wouldn't have discovered this dangerous mission, but I don't feel comfortable letting her do it on her own. Maybe we should step in and let one of the other agents do this. I can't let anything happen to Ruby. I don't want to lose her. I can't lose her."

Why would she say she can't lose me if she doesn't know me? Now, I am even more inclined to believe that I am probably her daughter, but I couldn't confront her now, no matter how much I wanted to. However, I could spy on her.

I listened for a few minutes before she saw me. I tried to run, but she called me down before I could get far enough. So, I slowly walked up to her. This was the first time I was talking to a woman who could possibly be an important figure in my life. My only question is, if I really was her daughter, why would I not be with her, and why would Mother and Father have raised me? Why wouldn't they ever tell me that I was adopted? There are just too many things going on and not enough time to figure it out!

As I headed down the stairs to her, I thought she would yell at me for eavesdropping, but instead, she came down to my level, picked me up, and hugged me as hard as possible. Then she kissed me on the head and lowered me down. I didn't fight her because something about her made me feel safe, probably because I was related to her.

She had tears in her eyes, "You know, little Ruby, for the future, when you sneak up on someone, don't let them know you're there. If they see you, you can't run. Otherwise, a person will be suspicious of you. You must stay put and act like nothing is happening, alright?"

I smiled, "Thank you! But what's your name?"

I waited a few minutes, but unfortunately, she didn't respond. I have a feeling she is Millie but I can't be for certain. Not until she tells me. I could tell it was very difficult for her to keep her identity a secret from me. You could see it in the way she looked at me and hugged me.

As I walked upstairs to where I was supposed to be, I heard her mumbling under her breath, "She has grown much to be exceedingly beautiful and precious. I can't believe she will be ten on Friday. Even her little cheeks are still as bright as ever. I love her more than anything."

That night, I couldn't stop thinking about her. I liked her. She was kind, loyal, and caring.

The following morning, I went downstairs to see if she was still there. The lady at the front desk approached me, noting that I was becoming visibly upset when I couldn't find her.

"Child, I know you're looking for her, but she is not here. She left last night but will return on Friday before leaving for her home in London. I'm sorry."

I held my head down for a few seconds. But I guess it was for the best. She couldn't be on my mind now. I needed to focus on my mission, so I returned upstairs, and a lovely lady named Florence helped me prepare for the day. She was in her mid-twenties and was deaf. But she managed to speak very well because she went deaf when she was three due to an ear infection. She could also speak sign language fluently and could communicate with Coco. She was like a hero! Additionally, she is the head of the HIA in Chicago.

It was the day before the assassination, Tuesday, May 15, 1860. We went to the Convention Center to scope it out so we would know our surroundings for the assassination tomorrow. The outside reminded me of a prison with the American flag on every point. Inside was a long hallway with stairs on each side leading up to the balcony and doors for people to enter the convention room. There were thousands of seats, a terrace on top of the entrance with central pillars connected to the ceiling, and posts on either side of the stage, holding the conventional area from falling to pieces.

As we searched around, I tried to find the best angle where a shooter would hide and the best exit for the perpetrator to leave. Finally, we decided that the best place was probably on the suitable top balcony because it was not only closest to the exit of the stairs but also the exit of the building, as there was a door on the side that led out to the road. So, it was the perfect place for an assassinator to make their shot. After we left the convention center, Allan took us to the Pinkerton National Detective Agency, also known as the PNDA. When we entered, there were many interesting people in gear with weapons.

"Mr. Pinkerton, did you invent this agency since it's named after you? Also, why did you take us here?" I mentioned as I looked around.

"Why yes, little Ruby, I did. I am America's first official certified detective, just like you want to be, and I can tell you will be one hell of a good one. You need patience, little one. I took the three of you here to ensure you will not get hurt tomorrow."

"Mr. Pinkerton, how do you know what is happening tomorrow?" Lulu responded.

"I just do, Lulu. I can't tell you too much about how or why, but I need you to trust that, alright?"

We nodded and walked down the hall into his office. He went behind it and opened his cupboard with a key. He pulled out a little toolbox and handed it to me. Then we left. We went back to the hotel and our rooms. He told me to work on what I needed and that everything was in the little box. After that, he walked away, and we were alone. I opened the box, and it shined bright like a star in my head. It was full of everything I could ask for.

"Ruby, what are you going to make?" Willie smirked wondrously.

"I am going to replicate the pen gun I saw." Replying with a stern voice.

Lulu asked, "Why?"

"Well, because I am going to replace the real one so that the perpetrator uses the one that won't work, but it will be very realistic. Therefore, she will believe it does."

Willie and Lulu faced each other and smiled. "That's genius!"

"I know," I replied candidly.

After about an hour of working, I finished! It was perfect! I can't believe this is happening. We walked downstairs and had dinner. Everyone was extremely welcoming. After dinner, we headed back upstairs to prepare for tomorrow's big day. I started feeling butterflies in my stomach, and my hands began to sweat. I had never felt this way before. "Ruby, are you nervous about tomorrow? I mean, what if we fail? What if we won't be successful?" Lulu stated with a low, anxious, and scared voice.

"I am, but don't worry, it will work. I promise!" I gulped and lay down.

I began to breathe heavily, but quietly so no one else would hear. Why was I highly nervous? I had never really been scared before. Why now? This wasn't a good time to be worried. Coco could tell I was anxious, so she jumped on the bed and snuggled beside me. At that moment, she was like a doll children slept with, but I liked it. I loved moments like this. She was warm and cuddly and gave me a sense of purpose and place. I knew I could do it. Or at least I hope I can...

That night, it was challenging to sleep. I must have woken up about five times. The first few times, I went to the window and watched the stars shimmer for a few minutes, then went back to sleep. The last time I woke was 6:03 am, and I was ready to be vigilant. I couldn't go back to sleep again. This was it. The possible future president would be assassinated in three hours and five minutes. We weren't leaving for another two hours, so I went to the window again and sat under the shimmering sky. Coco came up and muttered, "Don't worry, Ruby, today you will be an American hero. You can do it! I believe in you. You just have to believe in yourself." I smiled at her.

Finally, another hour passed by, and everyone woke up. It was time to get ready. I went to my suitcase and took out my unique dress. Then Florence came into the room to do my hair. After she left, I grabbed my special replicate pen, and we were ready to stop the assassin. We grabbed muffins on the way to the convention.

Once we arrived, the stands were packed with people. I noticed Mr. Buchanan walking into a back room with Mr. Marshall. He grabbed him by his arm. I wonder what discussions they were having with each other. I bet it was to reiterate their plan.

Now that you are all caught up with how I got myself into this situation, it is time to find out if I really was able to stop him.

By the time we navigated around him, it was already 8:37 am. We took a deep breath and started looking for the perpetrator with our silver shaky detectors to find the real assassin. A few people asked us what they were, but we just mentioned they were an art project from school, and nobody bothered us. When I got past the backstage entrance, I saw Mr. Lincoln again.

"Hello, Mr. Lincoln. How are you?"

"Oh, hello, Ruby. You came here to watch my speech; is that correct?"

I thought briefly and responded, "Yes, sir, but I also came to warn you again. Are you sure you want to do this today?"

He answered quickly, "Don't worry, Ruby, nothing will happen to me, alright? I am safe."

I nodded, and he sent me off. It was now 8:58 am, and we only had ten minutes to find the perpetrator. We headed upstairs toward the balcony. When the first announcer came in, "Ladies and gentlemen, please rise for the early morning announcements."

"Our republic of people is..."

Time was running out! I watched Mr. Buchanan like a hawk after he exited his room, and it seemed like he was giving a signal by touching the bridge of his nose and swiping down repeatedly in the direction of the right end of the balcony. That is probably where the assassin is standing. I was getting roaringly nervous because it was already 9:00

am, only eight minutes to his death. Even though I have pinpointed the assassin's general direction, I still have to find her; at least I know what she looks like, so it shouldn't be too difficult. However, there was an ocean of people between me and her.

Mr. Lincoln began to give his speech. I started to breathe heavily, and Coco started singing Mother's lullaby. It calmed me down. As I looked up again, I saw her. Professor Nidyevon. I looked to my left and right and told Willie and Lulu, "Go get the police and meet me in the front where they will escape, and I'll get her."

I walked right behind her and watched as she grabbed the pen from her coat pocket and twisted it in some odd way. I guess that is just how the pen gun works... I used my shaky detector on her. YES! I found it. I grabbed my pen from my pocket, instructed Coco to watch Buchanan, and then hugged her while saying, "Доброе утро, профессор Смит. Какдела? Я так взволнован, наблюдая за этим важным событием, кто будет избран!" Which meant, "Good morning, Professor Nidyevon. How are you? I am excited to watch this momentous event of who will be elected!" Then I hugged her and replaced her pen with my pen.

She had disgust in her eyes and exclaimed, "почему да. Почему бы тебе не бежать сейчас" Which meant, "Why yes. Why don't you run along?"

So, I did, but before I did, I "accidentally" scratched her with my brass to mark her. It left a brown residue on her hands. It was 9:06 am, and only two minutes remained until she tried to make her move. Coco grabbed the collar of my dress as she pointed out that Mr. Buchanan was leaving the site. He seemed to act like there was an emergency in his family and he needed to exit, but I knew his real motive. He made a sprint for the exit without alerting others of his true plans.

Finally, as predicted, it was 9:08; she grabbed the pen gun from her pocket and tried to shoot. The only thing that came out was water; I walked right up to her, shook the real pen gun in my hand, and then said, "Are you looking for this?"

You could see her enragement in her eyes, "You little twit, you switched it, didn't you!"

I smiled while waving the pen gun in the air, "Indeed," as loudly as possible. She then alerted Buchanan of the failed assassination, and Coco said that his face looked absolutely flushed as if he had seen a ghost, then completely turned to fire.

He rushed towards the stairs exit, as I ran! She chased after me down the stairs. Fortunately, I was small and could fit through the crowd of people. Otherwise, she might have caught up because my legs were much smaller than hers.

When I got outside, Marshall was in wrap-around hand chains, and she tried to turn around and escape. Luckily, a police officer was behind her and knocked her out. Then, the rally stopped to get Buchanan from the audience, who aborted the mission and began to run in the opposite direction. I watched as a police officer tackled him to the ground. Lulu, Willie, Coco, and I raced over to him, and as we reached him on the ground, trying to struggle his way out of the officer's grip, he shouted at Lulu, "Luella Grace Hughes, I have never been more disappointed in you in my entire life."

By the end of his sentence, the police got him to his feet and escorted the three of them on horses to the prison. I did not know her full name was Luella. It was quite a unique name, though. After a few minutes of pause in the discussion, they decided to finish the convention. After the convention, I went back to the hotel only to see a news-paper that stated, "Earlier today at the Republican Con-vention of 1860, President James Buchanan planned to as-sassinate Abraham Lincoln this morning. Nobody knows who stopped the perpetrators, but President Buchanan will no longer be allowed to run again, as committing murder is a major felony. Thank you to the person who stopped them. You are a true hero!"

When I read that, my heart melted into my chest! We were heroes. I stopped them with the help of my best friend, Willie, and technically, Lulu; even though she did the right thing in the end, I am still a little hesitant about her! This was the new best day of my life. That night, Allan and Florence asked me to come downstairs without Lulu and Willie. Of course, I followed their instructions. Mr. Henry and Mr. Lincoln were there. I wondered what he was doing there. When I descended the steps, they stood with a cake that read "Welcome to the HIA" written on it.

As I read it, I asked, "HIA? What is that? I've heard of it before from Miss Holmes, but nobody has ever explained it to me. Also, how did my metal box end up in the White House?"

"The HIA stands for Hartford Intelligence Agency. It is a secret organization that recruits detectives like yourself to go on missions and stop crime. Henry and Abe have been a part of this organization for many years, and it takes a special person to join—especially one as intelligent, wise, and discerning as yourself. We would have never found out about the planned assassination if it hadn't been for you. We took it into account.

At first, because you are only a child, we wanted to handle it, but Violet and Henry convinced us to let you do it with supervision. They believed in you! This was your test to see if you belong here, which you do. They were entirely right about you. And before you ask if we helped you, we did not. Abe had no idea what was going on. It would have been unfortunate if you weren't able to stop the assassination from occurring because we weren't going to do anything to save his life. It was entirely in your hands, Ruby.

Now that you have proven you are as courageous as a dragon, we would be honored to have you as part of the HIA. We will have your big inauguration on Friday if that's okay with you.

To answer your last question, your box was stolen from a ship called the S.S. Rebellion. You traveled this ship when you were a baby to get to the United States. It was unknown that it was in the White House until you mentioned it. After Buchanan was arrested, the HIA authorities took it to Mr. Henry's home for you to have there." Florence humbly exclaimed.

As I heard this, I smiled and cried a little. This was the best moment of my life. I know I have stated that a lot, but this indeed was, and the fact that I will be inaugurated on my tenth birthday meant the world to me. Additionally, now I can look through my box.

"Also, one more thing, Ruby, I think you would like to know that you are officially the youngest member in history to join this organization. I can't wait to see what you do next!" Florence voiced with a giant smile that spread across her face.

"Wait, I have one question. Why aren't Lulu or Willie here? They helped me, too. Even though Lulu tried to betray me, she made it up in the end." I exclaimed before mumbling, "Even though I still have mixed feelings about her."

"Well, Ruby, you were the true mastermind behind the plan. We elect people who are not only brave enough to go on the missions themselves but also the ones who create their missions, the tools they need to be successful on the missions, and the plans to stop the rebellions. You are the only one who did all three. That doesn't mean they can't join in the future. It just means, as of right now, you are the only one who has proved yourself."

I guess that made sense. "I feel bad for them, though. If they attend the inauguration ceremony on Friday, will that upset them?"

Mr. Henry said, "Well, if it does, and they are not proud of you but instead jealous, then they may not be your true friends."

I nodded. I still felt guilty, but I was ecstatic.

Allan faced me and commented, "If it makes you feel better, we can make them honorary HIA agents, but not actual ones this way. So, all of you get the credit you deserve."

I concurred, smiled, and went upstairs to invite them to have cake with me. For the rest of the night, I explained to them what the HIA was and that they were honorary members. All of us were living the life we wanted. Or at least I was.

Later on, Mr. Lincoln walked up to me. I asked him, "Did you truly know about the assassination and were just playing it off, or did you not know?"

He responded, "I truly didn't know. I never thought that he would attempt to assassinate me. See, I have been friends with him since I was about eighteen years old. After multiple years of friendship, I caught him illegally smuggling money into his bank account. I assume he never forgave me for that. I never thought that it would result in murder. I am here today to thank you for everything you have done for me, Ruby. You truly are your parents' daughter. I will make sure that when I become president, I will make this country the best that it can be, and I am all grateful to you. I am sorry I didn't believe you before, so I hope you can forgive me."

I smiled, "It's no problem; it's just an everyday adventure of my life! Additionally, I do forgive you. But I have one question. Why does everyone say I am 'truly' or 'definitely my parents' daughter.' I mean, how could I be? My parents only want me to be a 'normal' girl. How could I be anything like them? I am nothing like them! I don't even look like them, well maybe a little bit like my mom, but, actually, no, I don't! Why do you and so many others keep saying that?" I responded, hoping that he would confirm anything about Mr. Henry and Millie.

"Well, Ruby, even though you don't see them now as your parents, they are! And you are very much like them, whether or not you like it. One day, you will view the same, but until that day comes, you must trust that you are their daughter. Ruby, I wouldn't tell you this if I didn't care. I need you to trust what I say."

"Okay… I trust you." I mumbled.

Maybe he's right. It isn't easy to know that my whole life could be a lie and that no one is telling me. Also, if it isn't, it is hard to hear that I am similar to my parents when I don't see myself in them because I don't understand them. I never have. Maybe I should let it go and let life take its path. I know everything will turn out how it's supposed to, and I have to trust that, as I trust him.

Unfortunately, it is now bedtime. Before falling asleep, I asked Lulu, "Can you please tell me the real truth behind how Buchanan knew you? Also, why did you switch out my replica pen for a real one and then switch it back at the last second?" Don't worry. I figured it was real before anything happened. Therefore, I switched it, but as she switched it to the original, I switched it again to be the fake replica.

She looked terrified and surprised, "Maybe tomorrow, but for right now, let's go to sleep. You are a real hero, Ruby, and I am fortunate to have you as my friend. I hope you know that, and I am very sorry for everything!" She started to cry.

Even though I knew she was a bit of a traitor, I comforted her, but she was still my friend and had been there for me through everything. I couldn't betray her now.

As I was about to go to sleep, Lulu whispered, "Ruby, do you want to know the whole story?"

"The whole story? You mean, why did you lie?" I crossed my arms as Coco crawled onto my chest and curled into a little ball.

"Yes."

Coco smiled at me as she cuddled up in my arms, "Yes, I would."

"Okay, here it is."

CHAPTER FOURTEEN

Is Lulu Hughes Really My Best Friend?

*S*o, Ruby, as you know, my name is Luella Chloe Hughes, but I go by Lulu because I think it is a much more beautiful name. I was born on December 28, 1849, and am from a small rural town outside of Pittsburg, Pennsylvania. I have one sister named, who is three years younger than me, and a brother named Lewis, who is three years older. Lewis attends the boys' school. Then there are my two parents: my mom is named Amanda, and my father is Adam Hughes.

My family is Reform Jewish. My mother grew up orthodox but switched to reform because it became difficult to afford. She wanted us to fit in better, considering there is a lot of antisemitism worldwide.

Ruby, if you didn't know, there are three main types of Judaism. The reform people pray on certain holidays, but we don't keep kosher. Then there are the conservatives who light candles and go on with their day just like everyone else but are kosher and will pray on the Sabbath, also known as Shabbat. And lastly, there are the orthodox. These people don't burn any candles or do any work on Shabbat, which is from Friday night to Saturday night.

When you see three stars in the night sky, that means Shabbat is over, and that is when we have havdalah. Havdalah is basically when you light a candle, sing, and smell specific spices such as cinnamon. Being orthodox, you are one hundred percent kosher, meaning that a rabbi must approve that everything you eat was killed with respect. Kosher meats are slaughtered by slitting an animal's throat rather than hitting it over the head with a hammer. Honestly, I don't know how slitting the poor creature's throat is more humane, but I didn't make that decision.

Everyone in my family is skinny, with red hair and blue eyes. Because of this, my parents call us their little golden lion tamarins. They like to say we are their little monkeys because we love to climb around and have fun. It's adorable! For entertainment, I used to love to play outside with my siblings with balls and sticks. The three of us love to pretend that we are going on missions to many foreign countries and solve the world's mysteries. I also read many stories to keep me entertained.

My family has always been proud of our endeavors and encouraged our brilliance. All three of us are intelligent, just like them. They are great parents who genuinely love me dearly. They find that education is more important than anything else–other than mental health–but they always say that to fit in, I must learn about beauty and care for myself. So, my parents sent me to Miss Holmes' Academy. That wasn't the only reason they sent me there, but until I explained that later, my brother also went there, and apparently, my mother knew Miss Holmes from a while back, but they weren't that close. Miss Holmes promised that she would give me a proper education in addition to the education of beauty. Each of us can speak four different languages. We speak English, Spanish, Yiddish, and Hebrew.

Not like you, Ruby, who can speak eight, but I have to say I was a contributor, considering I taught you Yiddish, and you quickly picked it up and speak fluently now. I don't understand how you are so brilliant; I wonder if being that smart hurts your head.

I giggled, "My head doesn't hurt, but thank you for the concern. I think all of my brains just fit perfectly in there."

My family wasn't poor growing up, but we weren't rich either. We were somewhere in the middle class. My family could afford to keep us healthy, get proper vaccinations, and go on vacations, but not too often. We lived on a farm and grew our food, such as corn, wheat, oats, barley, soybeans, sweet potatoes, potatoes, tobacco, peaches, apples, and pump-

kins, depending on the season. We also have multiple animals. We have two cattle for milk, three horses to get places, a bunch of chickens for eggs, many ducks for eating, and three sheep for their wool.

Because of our farm, my family owns a local grocery stand to hide our family's secret. It is our town's number one grocery stand; therefore, my family has some money. You may be wondering what our family's secret is. Well, all of us were spies from an agency known as the Dupin Agency. Le Chevalier C. Auguste Dupin was a French detective who came to America to solve some of the most prominent cases. Because of this, he began the agency. My parents are considered the best agents of the organization. However, our organization is against the other major one.

About thirty years ago, my second uncle, President James Buchanan, joined my family's detective agency after being kicked out of another organization. I am not allowed to know what the name of the other one was, but supposedly, they have some of the strongest spies.

After Uncle Buchanan joined the agency, my parents followed and became the top agents there. In my family, we must enter when we turn eight years old. So, I am new to the whole spy thing. My first few missions were minuscule compared to what my current assignment is. In the beginning, I had to stop a few burglaries in my local town, which were a piece of cake, but it wasn't until this mission that I took being a detective seriously. I knew my uncle would try to assassinate Abraham Lincoln because he told me, and my agency instructed me to help him. There was some brawl that went on between the two of them about thirty years ago, and Mr. Lincoln was the person who got him kicked out of his old agency; ergo, he decided to get even.

My uncle knew about you, Ruby, from before you joined Miss Holmes' Academy. My mission was to find you and become friends with you so I could find out all the information about your family and your organization to ensure the assassination attempt didn't fail. I didn't know that I would become best friends with you. We have many similarities, and I have never met a girl like you before. You don't care about foolish girl things; rather, you do what is best for you, and I completely respect that! You are kind and loyal, and to top it all off, you are absolutely brilliant! You have invented many of the most prevalent inventions in my organization.

Not only that, but you literally taught yourself how to communicate with a monkey when you were three years old by using vocal manipulation and studying how Coco speaks. Then you associate sign language with words, or whatever Coco's noises are. I mean, who can do that? You are a much better detective than anyone in my family has ever been or ever could be.

When I first got to the academy, I had to look for you, but little did I know that you would be my roommate. The first words from your mouth gave me that feeling that you were the one. After about a day, I determined you were the girl because you were the most intellectual pupil. You were the only one who didn't care about beauty but instead about history, math, science, and English. You discussed pacing and running away from school with me. You also loved learning new languages and dialects and building gadgets that people could only imagine. You are gifted, and it was so obvious!

We got along very well, and I genuinely enjoyed being around you. I never wanted to hurt you. You became more than a friend but a sister. Unfortunately, as time passed, my uncle constantly contacted me to inform him about you. I even got myself to be invited to your house for Christmas break. Your home was lovely and large. I had never been in a mansion of that size before. However, what amazed me was how rude your family was to you. Your parents didn't believe in you, which made me feel horrible because you are brilliant, but they were blinded. Shortly after Christmas break, I knew you were onto me because you became more concealed about everything that you did, while at the same time, you still gave me enough information that I needed to share.

As time went on, I got closer and closer to you, but I didn't want to help my uncle anymore because you genuinely cared for me, and he didn't, or at least maybe somewhere deep down on the inside, he did, but he never really showed it. To him, all I was was his puppet. I didn't want to be that anymore; therefore, I decided to become a double spy. During this whole experience, I learned that there is nothing more important than my friends and family; for this reason, I knew I had to help you.

A while back, I decided to give you a photograph of a guy named Elijah Devonn. I drew the picture and told you it was some Russian guy with white hair and green eyes. I knew you were smart enough to figure it out; as predicted, you did. If Uncle Buchanan found out I had done that, I don't know what he would have done to me, but I don't think he is smart enough to figure that out. So, I hope you can forgive me for my sins.

A few days ago, when we went to the Wigwam to look for where the killer could be, my uncle showed up, so I left for a few minutes. He handed me another one of the pen guns. He stated, 'Just in case Ruby tries to switch it.'

He also said that if this plan didn't work and you stopped him, he would murder my family, and I didn't want that to happen; I had to decide between you, my best friend, and my family. Of course, I had to pick my family, so I switched the replica pen gun you built to a real one my uncle gave me, hoping you wouldn't notice, but you did. However, I knew it was wrong. I knew that I wouldn't be able to live with myself if I knew I was a part of the reason that caused Willie's father's death. I knew my family's lives were on the line, but as long as your plan worked, there was nothing that I had to worry about because now everyone is against my uncle, and he is in prison.

Additionally, Abraham Lincoln doesn't deserve to die! I don't know why my uncle got kicked out of his organization, but it was probably for a good reason. Besides, Mr. Lincoln would be a much better president than my Uncle Buchanan. I also know that Mr. Lincoln was only doing his job. It amazes me how someone could be horrible to him just because he did his job correctly. Mr. Lincoln was an excellent, innocent person who was against slavery and loved Jewish people. While my uncle, even though he is morally against slavery, he is contemptuous towards Jews, which makes no sense considering my family is Jewish. Still, he is my second uncle, so we are not directly related. Also, with the slavery thing, all he did was try to maintain the peace between the states of anti-slavery and those for slavery. He definitely could have done a better job as president, but who am I to say that?

So, Ruby, I am very sorry for lying about everything! I didn't want to hurt you, but I had no choice. I hope you can forgive me.

Tears pranced down her face. I hugged her and responded, "You did what was right to protect your family, which is important. Lulu, remember what I am about to tell you. Mr. Henry once mentioned, 'You can't let your emotions take over your case. That is your first mistake.' But you tried to help your family. How could I be mad at that? I wish I had a family as caring as yours. I hope you don't do anything like this in the future because I can help you, and

I want to help you. However, I will say that it may take some time for me to fully forgive you because you could have completely been part of the reason that our future president was assassinated."

She looked down and smiled at me, "I understand, and I will work hard to try to help you trust me again."

We hugged each other for a few minutes as the rest of the people in the room watched and yelled, "Aww, see, that's a true friendship right there."

Lulu and I shrugged our shoulders and laughed. We were back to being best friends again. Whoopee! Then, we returned to our room to prepare for the day.

The Inauguration

Today is May 17, 1860, and tomorrow is my tenth birthday. I am incredibly excited! Well, except for one thing: I was still terribly small. As I gazed around the room, sulking about my size, Florence walked in.

She could tell I had a bothered look on my face. "Hello, Ruby! Oh, sweetie, what's wrong? What's saddening you?"

I initially didn't want to say anything because I felt that it might have been stupid to her, but it wasn't to me. "It's not that important," I put my head low and held on to Coco tightly, "but tomorrow I will be ten years old, yet I am still practically only four feet tall. It's just that nobody ever takes me seriously. It's not fair! I want to be big like you."

She smiled at me, "You know, Ruby, when you're older, you're going to miss being small, but if it makes you feel better, being our youngest and smallest agent makes you our best one."

"How so?" I questioned.

Florence smirked and encouraged me out of bed without any hesitation, "Well, nobody suspects you as an agent. So you can blend in very well. Also, even though you're small, it doesn't make a difference because you have the biggest brain and are the most brilliant child I have ever met. Maybe even the most brilliant person, so don't let the fact that you're tiny ruin your day. I mean, you always say that you may be tiny, but you are mighty! Don't let anybody take that away from you. Besides today, we have much to do to prepare for your inauguration tomorrow."

I took everything she was saying in, "I guess you're right; it's just it has always bothered me, but that's alright. You are right; I may be tiny, but I am mighty! Thanks for this conversation. I can't believe I will still look like a six-year-old at the ripe age of ten. Also, intelligence isn't defined by the size of your brain, but rather the amount of crinkles it has."

She helped me finish getting ready for the day. After we were done, she took Lulu, Willie, Coco, and me to the horses outside. When we got there, she told Lulu and Willie, "Unfortunately, the both of you can't come with Ruby and me today because whatever we are doing is secretive, but Allan will take you both to the docks for you to relax there."

They willingly agreed and went off. Then I turned towards Florence, "Florence, what are we doing that they can't come with us."

Florence peeked her head around the corner to watch their horse carriage leave. "Well, Ruby, today we aren't leaving the hotel. We must make them think we are because they can't see what is happening here. So, we will sit in the horse carriage and wait a few minutes for them to leave fully."

After their horse carriage went far enough out of the visible eye, Florence picked me out of the other horse carriage, put me on the ground, and followed her back inside. "Florence, if Lulu and Willie know what this place is, why can't they know where we are going?"

She replied, "Well, only agents can enter."

We walked behind the receptionist's desk. She had placed a unique key in a keyhole on one side of the desk. Then she continued, "Ruby, please tell me you still have the key necklace your parents gave you because this is the only one you will receive for safety reasons."

I reached it from under my shirt, "Yes, I always have it with me. I never take it off. But, wait, what does this key have to do with the HIA?"

She said, "Well, this key was specially created for you. When you were born, your parents knew you would be an agent, even if they didn't necessarily want you to be. It was just a matter of when. You were the most intelligent baby that we had ever seen. You were babbling and building with blocks from the moment you could sit up. We knew we would recruit you one day, so we made this key that could get you into and out of any lock, but this key will only work for you."

Wait, that didn't make sense, "Florence, how could it only work for me? It's just a key."

She smiled and continued. "On the back, you may have noticed your fingerprint. Well, there is a lock inside the key, and when you place your finger into the wedges of the fingerprint, it unlocks the key, making the key only usable to you. It is a very advanced technology, ahead of its time."

My mouth dropped to the floor. That was the most fantastic thing I had ever heard.

She said, "Ruby, you see that little hole at the end of my desk? I want you to fit your key in to help me unlock the opening to the HIA. So, we can get to where we are going." Florence excitedly.

I took out my key and wanted to test this fingerprint thing. I put my finger on the key, and lo and behold, it worked. The middle rhombus-shaped piece of the key's bow pulled itself inside, only leaving the two dragon sides. My eyes widened. It was supremely unique! Then Florence mumbled, "Ruby, I understand you are excited, but you must never unlock it publicly because people will try to take it from you. You must be extremely careful, do you understand?"

I nodded and exclaimed, "Yes, I'm sorry, Florence."

She looked kind of guilty for just telling me off, but it was okay. "Ruby, now please insert your key into the small hole, and on 'three,' we will turn them. One, two, three."

It worked! "Miss Florence, if there aren't two people here to turn the keys, what do you do?"

She responded immediately. She always has the quickest responses. "Well, Ruby, you typically only need one person to do it. I was showing you how to do it. This is how we always teach our recruits."

That made sense to me. Florence removed the yellow carpet under the desk as we talked, revealing a trap door. It opened independently, and we headed down the tiny, narrow staircase. When we descended the stairs, there was an entire space with agents of all kinds, weapons, and tools, which was amazing! Whoopee! I didn't know what I was expecting before, but it definitely wasn't this. This was incredible! There were even moovos and closed candles surrounding the place. "Wait for a second, Florence. There are closed candles everywhere. I always thought I was the inventor, but who was it if it wasn't me?"

She looked around and smiled. "You were, actually. Mr. Henry told us about your inventions, and many of them are implemented here. You were the first to figure out the closed candle mechanics without them blowing out due to the lack of oxygen and how to relight them. This place used to be lit up by many normal candles. So, thanks to your inventions, you are already changing the world."

Wow! I am astonished I did that. I couldn't believe a significant organization like the HIA would use my inventions. I don't have the words to express how incredible this is!

As we got to the first floor, the very first thing I had to do was to be measured for the bulletproof clothing that I was going to receive. I walked to the measuring station, and a lovely lady showed me many designs of dresses that she had in mind, but the best part was all of them had pockets. I picked the stunning blue, pink, and purple dress designs. She measured me from head to toe and then went to her coworkers to make them. She told me, "Your dresses will be ready by the end of the day for all of your future missions."

I couldn't stop smiling. This place felt colossally magical. It felt blisteringly surreal. It was great!

Then, we went to the weapon sizing station. There were weapons of all kinds that you could only imagine. Some of which I would have never thought to turn into a gun. There was this dishwasher that was known as a dishwasher rocket. It was phenomenal. When we got to this station, a person approached me and asked me to lift as much as possible. He handed me multiple different weights. The heaviest one I could lift was the one-hundred-pound one, even though I only weighed about fifty-five pounds. Then he told me, "Ruby, I just needed to see how much you could lift at once without breaking yourself. For being so small, you are quite strong, which is excellent because once you start training and learning to fight, it will come in handy."

Am I going to be taught to fight? Like truly fighting the proper way? My eyes widened so vastly you could see the back of my pupils. "Wait, but aren't most people that I fight going to be bigger than me? Because if you look at the physics of it, I would always lose, wouldn't it?"

He laughed at me, "No, little one, it doesn't matter the size of your opponent. If you have the proper technique, you will always win. Additionally, since you are so tiny, you will probably be faster than your opponent, giving you an advantage."

I gave him a funny look, "But physics says otherwise."

Florence started laughing. She got down on one knee to be even with my eye level and responded, "I promise you, if you know what you are doing, you will always win. Besides, it's much harder to hit you because you are a petite little girl, so don't worry."

I believe them, even though that's not exactly how the world's physics works, but it's alright.

After we were done with the weapons station, Florence directed me to the fingerprint and blood station. "Ruby, even though we have your fingerprint and blood type on file, we must get it again for safety reasons. This will help us find you if you ever get kidnapped or lost." She assisted me into the massive chair as the finger printer walked over.

"Why do you have my blood on file? What does blood have to do with anything?"

"Ruby, an official figure in this organization, discovered multiple years ago that people have different-looking blood if you look at it under a microscope. It helps us identify people, but you must keep that more of a secret, okay?"

I glanced around the room, "Okay..."

Wait a second. When she explained this, the first thing that came to mind was my mother's story of Molly, who was probably Millie Jones. I really want to get more information about her. Especially since Mother mentioned that she was a detective, Florence could help me. "Florence, I have a question. My mother said that she knew someone once named Molly. Molly was supposedly a detective, but then, one day, she disappeared. Was she part of this organization?"

Florence was intrigued, "Ruby, your mother is Margaret Ledger, correct?"

I could tell she was thinking about the question, so I nodded for her to continue. I just assumed they knew everything about everyone here.

Florence thought for a minute and vocalized, "Well, Ruby, yes, I did know Molly. She is our strongest agent here. She very much reminds me of you."

I smiled and quickly expressed, "Well, one day I will be the best, don't worry!"

She smiled and laughed at me. Then I got finger-printed, and 20 ml of blood was removed from my arm. This may seem small, but it is the maximum they can take with my weight class. I felt slightly lightheaded afterward, but Florence gave me a cookie and apple cider, and I instantly felt better.

Unfortunately, after that, we were done down there. I wanted to stay longer, but Florence took me back up-stairs and said, "Don't worry, there are other locations I am sure you will spend hours at."

She was right, but for right now, I don't know how I will be at another one. Moving on... I can't count my eggs before they hatch. It was about three in the afternoon, and Lulu and Willie were returning to the hotel. When we got back together, we all asked each other, "How was your day?"

Lulu and Willie were the first to respond by saying they had a fabulous day. Behind them, Florence signed, "Don't tell them what you did. You must make some-thing up."

I agreed and told Lulu and Willie, "I visited the Chica-go History Museum. It was a new museum opened only four years ago, in 1856. They had some pretty interesting exhibits there."

Willie responded, "That's amazing, but why couldn't we go with you there?"

I was quick on my feet and exclaimed, "Oh, that's because they didn't like children in some of the exhibits, but they knew Florence and said she could only take one person at a time. If I knew that would happen, I wouldn't have gone. I'm sorry."

They both faced each other, "It's okay, Ruby. I'm glad you had fun, though!"

Later that night, while we were having dinner, Lulu and Willie were distracted because they brought in a baby goat to play with, while Florence pulled me to the side and took me upstairs. When we arrived, she took me to my room, and two cases were on my bed. They were the typical brown suitcases with black metal sides. They were in excellent condition. I must open the cases with my key to get to the HIA equipment section. See, there were two sides to it, and if I opened the case without my key, it would open a part of the case that looked like a standard suitcase to throw people off, so they wouldn't be suspicious. There were just some regular clothes, scarves, gloves, socks, and ribbons for hair. It was a setup to conceal the critical part.

Florence then told me to open the correct area. When I did, one of the cases was filled with dresses. There must have been at least eight in there. I don't understand how they fit in there, but they were all lovely, each different from the last. I tried one of them on, and it fit perfectly, so I didn't have to try the others.

Florence picked one of them up; "Ruby, tomorrow you must wear this one, alright? All inaugurates have to wear these colors." It was black, blue, and gold. It was pretty.

I then closed that case and opened the other one. It was full of concealed weapons but didn't weigh much. Many looked like toys because I was a child, but there were other odd ones. There was the pen gun, the pipe dart, the flower-shaped pocket knife, two prominent and tiny ball gown masks (one for me and one for Coco), dice grenades, the game of jacks needle grenades, rubber duck sirens, brass yoyo for knocking people out, button spikes, lipstick gun, and many other secret weapons. Then, there were some weird cans of food like canned peas, cherry tomatoes, black beans, sardines, and other odd ones. "Florence, what do these food ones do, or are they all just normal food?"

She smiled and screeched, "You can't eat those! See, the canned peas are little bombs. You sprinkle them on the ground, and they will explode, but you must be careful not to blow yourself up. They only work when you activate them. Each one has a little button; once you press it with your key, you must throw it at least fifteen feet away. You will have ten seconds before they explode. However, they have an explosion radius of ten feet, so you must be precise with them. The black beans are built similarly, but instead of exploding, they release toxic fumes into the air, which is what the masks are for. The cherry tomatoes have acid inside of them, and the sardines are also toxic, but they won't make you sick; they will blind you; therefore, please be very careful. All of these items look like they are for children because when you are on a mission, no one will suspect you are an agent, so your parents don't take them away from you. Just make sure you don't let anyone take this, and don't EVER open this part of the case with someone inside the room with you."

This was by far the most unique gift I have ever received. "I understand, Florence, I won't, don't worry."

She told me to open the case with the dresses in them, but the case had already been opened, so I was confused. She pointed to the top of the case, separating the hidden stuff from the usual wear. There was another little keyhole, so I opened it, only to find many tools and gears for inventing and building objects. This was the best birthday present I had ever received! I hugged her with all my might.

I closed the cases before Lulu entered our room and ensured they were locked. I mean she could still be a reason that important information could get leaked in the future. Then, Florence left to give us space before the big day tomorrow. I can't believe this is happening! As I got ready for bed, I panicked again, just like right before the assassination. So, many thoughts came into my head: what if I wasn't good enough for this agency? What if I make a mistake and war begins because of me, or what if I don't have what it takes to be the best agent? By this point, I started to panic silently in bed. Lulu was fast asleep, and Coco was cuddled up next to me. Tears began rolling down my face, and I accidentally fell on Coco. She arose from her cute slumber and wiped away my tears.

She knew this was going to happen. "Don't worry, Ruby. Everything will be alright! You are going to be an amazing agent. Just wait and see. I mean, you were the only one who could stop Lincoln's assassination. You will be fine. I promise."

I took a deep breath and thought about what she had said; I was probably overthinking this. After about an hour of laying in bed, my eyes finally shut for the rest of the night.

I woke up the following day at the crack of dawn. I lay in bed for a few minutes, thinking about the day in just a few hours. Of course, I was very excited about my inauguration and my birthday! Fortunately, unlike the night before Mr. Lincoln's planned assassination, I could sleep throughout the night.

I had to be very quiet when I rose out of bed because I didn't want to wake Lulu. Until I realized she wasn't in the room. What? Where could she have gone? I wanted to see where she was, but when I got to the door of my room, it was locked from the outside in. I also noticed that my hair had already been done and that there was a small note on the door. It read,

"*Good morning, Ruby! Today is not only your special day because you are being inaugurated into this agency but also because you are turning ten years old! We understand that you always love a good challenge. We have locked you in here with Coco to figure out how to escape. Most importantly, these are the rules:*

1. *You must wear your inauguration outfit, as you can see your hair has already been done.*

2. *All of the objects that you need to escape are in the room.*

3. *You will have until 8:15 in the morning to escape. Otherwise, there will be consequences.*

4. *Don't judge a book by its cover.*

5. *Most importantly, Have fun!*

I will not give you your first clue, but I will give you a hint. So, think about what your body needs and I will see you shortly, Ruby!

(By the way, all agents apart of the HIA are tasked to escape)."

I looked at the watch on my wrist. It was currently 7:15, which meant I only had one hour. This was going to be extremely fun. My first thought was to go to my unique suitcases, but someone took them out of the room. So, I sat down and took a deep breath. What does my body need? Coco's little stomach started to rumble. "Ruby, we need food. There must be a clue where the food is."

We both ran to the food cart, but before Coco could put small tomatoes in her mouth, I slapped them out of her hands. "Hey Ruby, I was going to eat that!"

"Coco, stop. Remember the fourth rule, 'don't judge a book by its cover,' a metaphor recently used in George Eliot's book *The Mill on the Floss*. It means don't judge everything by the way it looks. Looks can be deceiving. We have to test it to see if it's real food first. I mean, it could be a bomb." So, I grabbed the tomatoes out of her hands to check if there was anything in it, and lo and behold, it wasn't food; it was a candle.

Coco's eyes widened as she came to this discovery. She couldn't believe she almost ate a candle. "Maybe we have to burn it."

"Okay, but we must find a fast way to burn it; otherwise, it will take a millennium. But wait, hold that thought. She said we could use anything in the room, so Coco turned around. We can remove the closed candle and encapsulate the oxygen to make this candle burn much faster."

We ran to the other side of the room. It was currently 7:25, and the time was ticking down. I used the little clip in my hair to hold Coco's long fur back and unlocked the candle. It worked much faster than anticipated, which was a good thing. Then, I set fire to my tomatoes in a controlled environment and put the glass shield on top. I removed about 95% of oxygen by adjusting the oxygen intake in the tight space. After about three minutes, the candle was completely burnt. There was nothing inside; nothing happened. Then I went back to the food cart, and this was the only thing that was not food.

So I tried it again, but this time, I realized it had a particular smell. It smelled like herbs. Why would it smell like herbs? Then I pieced it together. Of course, herbs can cover the scent of blood. Maybe it's supposed to be like a vampire. So, we went to the next part of the room, the cupboard with a little bat drawing on the wall. I used my key to open it, and a little map fell out.

The little map was in Latin, saying, invenire specialis pectus ut effugere, which meant *finding the unique chest to escape*. "It couldn't be just any chest, could it, Ruby?"

I went to one of the large chests, but nothing was there. It was about 7:45 a.m., and we only had thirty minutes left. "Ruby, another way to describe a chest is a seat of feeling. What if it is in the window because that is where we sat both nights, gazing at the stars."

I smiled, and we went to the window. At this time, I realized the window seat could open again. It needed my key, but it still opened. Inside, there was a telescope. I pulled it out and put it on the window sill. When I looked through it, I saw a note that stated, "Happy birthday, Ruby. Your last clue will lead to your escape. How many stars are there in the observable sky?"

As of what we know today, there are 100 billion. That could be the passcode to escape. I ran to the door and put the numbers and letters' 1,0,0, M' in the lock. M is billion in Latin. Unfortunately, there were two slots for safety. These were some of the newer locks that were created recently with letters. Maybe they were referring to how many we could see, about 2,000; in Roman numerals, 2,000 is MM.

I put in MM, and the lock fell to the floor. Finally, after about thirty-two minutes and fifty-four seconds, we escaped. It was very dark in the hallway. I wondered what was happening. Then, I was blindfolded from behind by Mr. Henry. He said his name so I wouldn't get nervous, thinking I was being kidnapped, and we went on our merry way. After about an hour of being blindfolded, we arrived in the middle of nowhere, Illinois. It was a gorgeous and antique building. On a giant sign, in large letters, it stated, "Congratulations, Ruby!"

Then Florence walked up to me. "Wow, Ruby, you got out of that room quite quickly. For most agents, it takes them about twice as long as you; brilliant job!"

I smiled, and then we walked inside. There were many people there, probably about fifty. Supposedly, all of the agents on the East Coast were here. I walked onto the stage when I got to the front of the hall. Lulu and Willie were sitting in the front row. Then, on stage, there was Mr. Henry, Miss Holmes, and the violet-eyed lady. For the first time, I had a bit of stage fright. I was pretty nervous, but it was alright. I knew I was meant to be here and in this organization.

I sat next to the violet-eyed lady when I settled on the stage. She whispered to me, "Happy Tenth Birthday, Ruby!"

I looked up into her eyes. She knew it was my birthday, which only led me to believe that everything I thought about before was true, but I couldn't think about that now. It wasn't important at the moment. I had to keep my focus on what was happening at the moment. Florence approached the front of the room and shouted, "Ladies and gentlemen, thank you very much for being here to inaugurate our youngest agent into the agency. Today, on her tenth birthday, this brilliant little girl stopped James Buchanan's plan to assassinate Mr. Lincoln. From the day this child was born, we knew she would be a perfect agent, and now she has saved the life of our future President, Abraham Lincoln. Ruby, please stand up, raise your right hand, and repeat after me."

I walked over to her, and she continued, "As part of the HIA, I will be trustworthy, loyal, respectful, diligent, and honest. I will never betray the HIA and put my whole heart and energy into helping the world's people, and no one can stop me or tell me I am not good enough. So, by touching this HIA shield, I am officially a part of the HIA."

After repeating each sentence, I touched the shield. It was surreal! Finally, I was appreciated for everything I had done. To finish the ceremony, the violet-eyed lady approached me and put the little pin on my dress. She said, "When I first saw you, I never wanted you to be a part of my hectic life, but seeing you now at ten, I have never been more proud of you! You're an incredible little girl who is a force of nature, and never let anyone stop you." I smiled, and she gave me a bear hug. She began to cry and then left.

I felt horrible for her. I could feel a solid connection to her, and I wished she would have stayed longer, but she didn't. I'm glad she came to watch this.

After the ceremony, there was a large party for my tenth birthday. Lulu and Willie attended before we had to leave tomorrow. It was exhilarating; then, Miss Holmes walked up to me out of nowhere.

"Hello, Ruby. I want to congratulate you and tell you how proud I am of you. I am delighted you made it here and am excited to see what light you will spread on the world. You are an amazing kid, and I am honored to have you in my school. Now that you know about this agency, next year will be a little different, and I hope you won't lie to me again about where you are going."

I cackled, "No, I won't. I'm sorry, Miss Holmes. I just wanted to tell you that the academy is my home, and I want to attend every year until I graduate!"

She smiled, hugged me, and walked away. As the day went on, it was finally ready for bedtime.

Before I entered sleep, Mr. Henry entered the room and sat on the edge of my bed. "Hello Ruby, how are you? I am immensely proud of you; I told you that you can do anything if you put your mind to it."

I chuckled, "I never doubted it for a second, Mr. Henry! This was the best birthday ever!"

He grinned and left for the night. The following morning, I packed up my new gear before returning home. I was upset that I couldn't stay longer, but I needed to return to my parents' home. It will never be my home again because Miss Holmes' Academy is mine. Mr. Henry walked Lulu, Willie, and me to the train station and sent us on our way.

As the hours passed, we finally arrived in Massachusetts. When we arrived, we took the first carriage out to the house. Finally, after twelve and a half hours of traveling, I only wanted to eat and go to sleep, so I did.

CHAPTER SIXTEEN

My Whole Life is a Lie

The following day came quickly. I think it was partly because, as time passed, I started to think about Mr. Lincoln's journal and the little girl. When I woke up, my mother was in my room watching me. I'm not going to lie. It was pretty creepy. "Good morning, Mother. I don't mean to be rude, but why are you watching me sleep?"

She hesitated but then replied, "Good morning, Ruby. You came home so fast last night you barely got to say hello."

I didn't feel like talking to her now, but what could I do? "Oh, I'm sorry, I was just exhausted from returning from school. It must have slipped my mind."

She laughed a little, "Ruby, how was your inauguration?"

I froze briefly, "How did you know about that?"

"Even though you may believe I am clueless, I know much more information than you think I do." She paused, grabbed a brush, and headed over to my bead to help me with my hair, "Ruby, I am delighted you are home, but is there anything you learned at the academy that you didn't know before?"

I had no idea what she meant; of course, there were some things, but she didn't need to know about them. "No, Mother, there isn't anything I can think of right now."

She gulped and then did my hair. I wanted to go downstairs to get some breakfast. However, before I reached the stairs, SPIDER fell out of my pocket and crawled into Mother and Father's room. As I entered to get SPIDER back, I saw Mother's vanity open, so I decided to go look in it. I saw a small, suspicious-looking box and was intrigued.

I decided to grab it and headed straight to my room.

After I arrived, I crashed onto my bed and opened it carefully. There was a lot of dust, causing me to cough. After opening it, I saw an older-looking piece of paper. I wiped the dust away, turned it over, and saw the top of the letter labeled, *'Certified Copy of an Entry of Birth'* at the top. I had never seen one of these before, so I kept reading.

'Birthed within the district of British London in England.

London, England? Is this Mother's birth certificate? I knew I had to keep reading.

Columns 1 2 3 4 5 6 7 8 9 10

No. 1 When and Where born: London, The Kingdom of Great Britain

No. 2 Name, if any: Rebecca Annarose Jones

No 3. Sex: Female

No. 4 Name and Surname of Father: Henry Giles Jones

No. 5 Name and Maiden Surname of Mother: Millie Juliana Jones

No. 6 Occupation of Father: Professor of students

No. 7 Signature, Description, and Residence of Informant: Millie Jones. Lovewell, New Road, London, Greater London, W8.

No. 8 When birthed and registered: May 18, 1850, July 14, 1850

No. 9 Signature of written: Henry Giles Jones, Millie Juliana Jones

No. 10 Name entered after registering: Rebecca Annarose Ledger'

After reading my name, I crumpled the piece of paper as it crashed to the floor. My eyes were pools, and I turned to silence as a friend.

I felt like I couldn't breathe, but at the same time, I had a feeling this was the case. All my suspicions were right. That woman with the violet eyes was probably Millie Jones, meaning she was my mother, and Mr. Henry was my father. You know, I had a feeling that I was the little girl from Mr. Lincoln's journal, but there was a slight piece of me that I never actually thought would be me.

Maybe because I didn't necessarily want it to be. Why would Mr. Henry not want to raise me by myself? I just don't understand. What did I do wrong? I don't understand. And I've wondered why I am incredibly different from my family. It's because I'm not a Ledger; I am a Jones, which means Mr. Henry was my father. How could I not realize that these people who raised me weren't my true parents? I am typically a pretty perceptive person, but I guess for the first time ever, I actually felt my age. Now I know what it means when they say kids are kids and they miss many things in life. I never wanted to put myself in that category, but I guess I am ten, after all.

Then Mother walked in with a little cake to celebrate my birthday. But she wasn't my mother. She was an imposter. "Hello Ruby, what are you—"

"W-w-what is this? Y-you aren't my mother. You lied to me! How could you?" I paused, trying to gather my thoughts, "Mr. Henry is my father. What is wrong with you?"

Mother dropped the cake and rushed over to me to grab me while calling Father into the room.

"I'm adopted? Why would you lie to me? Why didn't I get to live with my real parents? Why did you try to raise me? It makes sense now why you treat me differently than your 'precious' children. It's because I'm not one of them!" I cried.

She cried as well while grabbing my arms. "Ruby, I am very sorry we didn't tell you sooner, but I am ready to tell you the story now. Don't blame Mr. Henry for anything. He didn't do anything wrong. Your parents were trying to protect you, but they couldn't anymore."

"Protect me from what?" I screeched back, but no response came my way, so I got up to run out of the room. Mother grabbed me and sat me down.

I tried to fight her by slapping her, but she didn't stop holding onto me until I stopped fighting and promised I wouldn't run so she could explain everything. "Ruby, I know you are upset right now, but I am giving this to you because you must decide. When you were first born, you were born to the two greatest HIA agents in the world, Henry Jones and Millie Hartford."

"Wait, wasn't Hartford your surname before you married Father?"

"Patience, let me tell my story! Henry and Millie were a part of the HIA, just like you. Henry had a wife. Her name was Violet Sherrinford, or as you may know, Miss Holmes. She and Henry had a little boy named Theodore, who they adored. Unfortunately, Violet had an affair after he was around a year old, so he wanted to leave her. By this point, Henry had eyes for my sister Millie, and after a short period, they fell in love, got married, and had you. They

knew that you would be just as peculiar and brilliant as they were because even when you were the size of a pea, you were babbling, walking, and doing things babies your age couldn't.

When you were a few months old, Henry returned to Violet, and Millie was furious. So, she telegraphed me because she didn't want to have anything to do with him. Millie is my sister, and I was always jealous of her because she was brilliant. You remind me so much of her. Just like you, she is gorgeous with her bodacious violet eyes.

She gave you to us, and we adopted you. Millie wanted us to promise that you would never have anything to do with the HIA because it wasn't safe. However, when Henry found out you were coming to America, he couldn't leave you. He loves you too much and knows we wouldn't know how to raise a child like yourself, so he offered to become your teacher.

We agreed but told him not to encourage the missions or ever tell you that you were his. Unfortunately, he couldn't help it. You were your parents' daughter. The reason why I treat you differently is that I never understood you. I wanted to, but I couldn't. Even though I still don't, Ruby, I have always loved you like my own. At first, I thought I wasn't going to, but as time passed, you became my daughter, which is why I am hard on you. If I didn't care, I wouldn't push you so much.

Also, your father and I intentionally sent you to Miss Holmes' Academy. We didn't think it was fair to hold your *unique talents back. So, when you fell that day trying to help us, we acted like we were mad to send you away to a place we knew you'd love. If you want to go to England and visit your biological mother, I am willing to let you go with Mr. Henry. You can leave soon if you'd like, and you have the option to stay there, but I will say I will miss you. So, I am very sorry we lied!"* Mother exclaimed in a melancholy tone.

I couldn't stop crying. She kissed me on the head, cleaned up the mess from the dropped cake, and left the room. What should I do? I have the opportunity to visit Millie and truly learn what she is like. However, as exciting as this might sound, I had to think about it. I wonder if Clara and Charles knew.

I sat in bed for a few more minutes before getting up and going downstairs. I had to talk to Mr. Henry because he lied to me, too. I also needed to speak to my cock-eyed siblings.

I ran downstairs to the kitchen, where my two siblings stuffed their faces with cake. I sat down next to them, where a new nanny was working. She had brunette hair and brown eyes and looked like a baby doe. I faced my siblings and asked, "Where did Louie go?"

Clara had a revolting look, "Of course, you don't know you're never here, and that's a good thing! But if you must know, she is here for us, but this weird nanny is for you. Mother hired her, and since Louie is busy getting us food today, this weird one has to watch us. I like Louie better because she cares more about her looks, while this odd one is just as odd as you."

I wondered how so, and then I noticed she had a pin from the HIA. Maybe she was here to help me during the summer. She introduced herself. "Hi, you must be Ruby. I am Adena Grensworth. It is a pleasure to meet you, little one. I've heard all about you and your fun adventures, and I look forward to spending the summer with you."

I smiled at her. She was the nicest nanny I could have ever gotten. She handed me a piece of cake that hadn't fallen on the floor, and I questioned Clara and Charles about my life. "Do you guys know anything about where I was born?"

They both looked at me as if they didn't care, which they probably didn't, but at least they had the courtesy to respond. "You were born in London when we visited there in 1850."

It was astonishingly fascinating that they knew where I was born, but they hadn't told me until now. "Wait, both of you knew I was born in London, not Boston. Is there anything else?"

Clara added, "I don't know and don't care. But, worm, go and do your shyness. You disgust me."

Adena wanted to chime in, but I stopped her, "Clara, that doesn't even make any sense. You don't make any sense."

She stuck her tongue out at me and then shoved my face into a plate of cake. I wanted to retaliate, but I chose not to. She wasn't worth it. Also, the cake tasted incredibly divine. So, instead, I jumped off my stool and walked out of the room. On my way out, Clara shouted, "You know I wouldn't be surprised if you were adopted. You're a freak!"

She didn't know I was adopted. I mean, unlike me, who has a photographic memory, she doesn't, so I guess she doesn't remember that the person I once knew as Mother is not my mother and was never pregnant with me. Adena followed me out of the room as I went upstairs. Then she sat with me. "Don't listen to her, Ruby. She is cruel. I am only here to take care of you. I understand what it's like to be a special child in a family of normal people, and you don't have to worry. I'm here for you."

I was thrilled she was here! It was going to make this summer much less stressful than I presumed it was going to be. She picked the cake off my face and dress and ate a piece of it. I laughed at her, then picked some off of myself and did the same thing. By this point, we were laughing as she continued to help me fully clean up. She was charming. I wish she had been here before. "Adena, I can see that you are also part of the HIA. Are you an agent, or what do you do?"

She responded quickly, "Well, Ruby, I am not the same type of agent as you are. I am a caregiver agent. It means I help care for the agents' children when they go on missions. I am here with you because I wanted to meet the little girl who is the youngest agent, but also Florence instructed me to keep my eye on you so that you won't get into any trouble this summer."

I cackled, "Adena, do you know my parents? I mean, like my real parents?"

She went quiet for a minute and then replied, "Well, of course I do, Ruby. They are the best agents in the field, but I want to address something with you. What do you mean by 'real parents?"

I was confused why she asked me, "I mean my parents who birthed me and truly cared about me."

The small smile on her face faded a little, "Ruby, just because your biological parents made you doesn't necessarily mean they are your real parents. Even though your current parents don't believe in you, it doesn't make them your fake parents. Let me ask you this. Were they always there when you were sick or scared or at any of your first milestones, or was it the people who made you?"

I thought briefly, "Well, my non-biological parents were there, maybe not my biological mother, but," I paused, trying to process everything, "I guess you're right. I never really thought about it like that. Even though they aren't always the nicest people, and I don't necessarily like being around them, they always ensured I was properly cared for, felt safe, and had food to eat. I still don't appreciate how they treated me all my life, but they are my 'real' parents, aren't they?"

She nodded, "Yes, Ruby, they are. I'm sorry for how they treated you. The HIA has been keeping an eye on you since you were given to them, and even though they weren't always the friendliest, they do truly care about you. If they didn't, they wouldn't have taken you in."

She was right. They are my parents. I'm just furious because I never knew they weren't my biological ones. It explains why I look very different from most of my family. "Adena, I have to talk to my mother, don't I?"

She nodded again and enquired, "Do you want me to come with you?"

I shook my head, "Thank you, but I have to do this on my own."

I found myself at the door of my parents' room. I knocked on the door, and after a few seconds, Mother opened it. "Oh, hello, Ruby. What can we do for you?"

I responded, "I want to talk to you about what happened this morning."

She let me inside and then closed the door. When I entered, mother and father were lying around in bed. Mother picked me up and put me next to him, then Father questioned, "What can we help you with, Ruby?"

I was pretty nervous, but I had to know. "Why didn't you ever tell me about them? Also, what is my biological mother like? I know you explained a little bit about her in your story, but I would like to know. Also, why don't Clara and Charles know?"

Father faced Mother, then me, *"Ruby, your biological mother was a courageous but terrifying woman. I never understood her. She was the one who helped me start my railroad business. Without her, I wouldn't be where I am or nearly as wealthy. Just like you, she was very bright. She is one of the smartest people on the planet if you ask me. She even introduced me to your biological aunt—the person you had always known as 'Mother.'*

We never told you about Millie because we didn't want you sneaking away on some boat to go and find her alone. Additionally, we promised your biological parents to keep you safe and away from the agency they work for, but we knew it would be difficult when we first got you. We hoped that if we encouraged you to focus more on beauty than your talents, you would want to stay away from being a detective, that you could be a normal girl."

I didn't like the way he said "normal" because I am normal; I am just unique.

"When she first asked us to take you in, we said no, but as time passed, we agreed because we fell in love with you, even with all your differences. We swore to your biological parents that we would raise you as our own.

Your biological mother is courageous not only because she is one of the greatest detectives alive but also because it's difficult to let go of a child. Lastly, to answer your final question, Charles or Clara doesn't know because we knew they would treat you even worse than they do now. If you'd like, we can tell them."

As they went on and on about my biological mother, I was very intrigued, so I finally got the courage to ask, "Can I meet her, please? I mean, truly meet her and not just in snippets of time?"

They both glanced at each other and then yelped, "No!"

My heart sank when they exclaimed that. "Earlier, you mentioned I could visit her; she is my biological mother. So, why can't I see her?"

They just sent me out of the room and yelled, "We will not discuss this further."

I started to cry and began banging on their door. I wanted to meet this remarkable woman, but they wouldn't let me. After I left, I went to where I always go to cool off the ceiling of my room.

There was a little attic in the ceiling, which was supposed to be for storage, but I used it for a hideout. I decided to learn how to throw knives in my tool kit. I drew an archery target, started calculating the distance between my hand and the wall, and threw it. Every time, it was perfect. I just needed to work on my speed. Suddenly, as one was in the air, Mother opened the hatch. She nearly got hit, and I jumped, "I am very sorry, mother. I didn't mean to almost murder you."

She looked as if she wanted to yell but didn't. So, instead, she crawled into my space, and Father did, too. I gave them a grimy look. "I don't mean to be rude, but I don't think all three of us up here is a good idea. I don't want to fall through the ceiling boards."

They hushed me and uttered, "After thinking this through, we have decided to let you go with Mr. Henry. I understand that you must meet her, and we trust you will be okay."

I was shocked they had said that because of their reasoning earlier, "You will? But why wouldn't you let me go before? I don't understand. Why now?"

Both mother and father looked guilty and sighed, then whispered to each other, "Should we tell her the truth?."

I shouted, "You know I can hear you, right? Kids can hear frequencies adults can't because as you age, your hearing goes bad due to the aging hair cells dying in your ears. Also, your whisper isn't very much of a whisper."

Looking at me with the look of, *"Of course," you know that, Mother answered, "We are sorry we told you 'no' earlier. We don't want you to leave. Ruby, whether you believe us or not, we genuinely love you. We never told you that before because you never needed to hear it. You always were on your own, and so we respected it. We are scared that if you meet your biological mother, you'll want to stay with her. Ruby, your biological mother, has everything. She has a fantastic job, an amazing husband, and an incredible kid, you. She always got what she wanted when she wanted it because she was always perfect. I was always jealous.*

Then I got you. You are just as beautiful and perfect as she is. Although you remind me so much of her, you're our daughter, our baby girl. I don't want you to leave us. So, we figured that if you met her, we wouldn't be able to stop you, and you would stay there forever. But if you would like to go, you may. This is entirely your decision. We hope you will return if you go because you will always have a home here, even though you don't particularly like it here."

It took me a second to think. I never thought that I could stay with her. What if I could? This was great! I didn't know how to respond, so I whispered, "Yes, I want to go."

I felt terrible for saying that because their hearts sank. You could see it on their faces, especially because I didn't reassure them that I would come back, but I didn't know if I would. Was I a selfish person for thinking this?

They left to get me a ticket to London; as the next few days passed, my mother and father didn't want to leave me alone. It's as if they couldn't respect me enough to give me personal space. It was painful. Finally, the day I was leaving arrived. It was May 26, 1860, and we boarded the ship. It would take about a month to get there, enough time to live with Mr. Henry.

When we boarded the ship, it was very classy. I was technically in the same room as Mr. Henry, but it had a little den attached to it, specifically for children with a bunk bed, so I wasn't sleeping in the exact same room as him. In total, because of the bunk bed, there were three beds: one for me, one for Coco, and one for Mr. Henry, even though Coco always sleeps with me. It was a spacious room, which made sense, considering my parents were wealthy.

Once we settled in, Mr. Henry asked if he could tell me, "Ruby, how do you feel about everything you learned in the past few days? I'm sorry I never told you, but I couldn't."

I held my head down because I didn't want to look him in the eyes.

Then, I decided to build something while talking to him. "Well, for starters, it makes a lot more sense. Also, what do I call you now? You are technically my father, so do I call you Dad? Or do I still call you Mr. Henry?"

He laughed a little, "Well, you may call me what you feel comfortable with, but I would love it if you called me Dad only if you want to, though. There is no pressure there. Also, what are you building."

I respected his answer, but I think if I am going to call him dad, he needs to earn it, "Okay. I think it may take some time before I start calling you Dad. But, to answer your question, I am building an electrosphere telescope. I heard that the stars across the sea are beautiful, and I want to see them."

He chuckled once again, "Of course you are. You are my brilliant little girl. Do you need any help?"

I smiled but politely responded, "No, thank you. I can do it. It's not that complicated. I only need to finish adjusting this glass and wait for it. Whoopee! There it is!"

Over the following month at sea, we spent a lot of time together. I felt like a kid with a fantastic father who cared about me. At first, it felt odd, but then normal. It was brilliant! I had never felt this way before, so now that I had a dad who loved my uniqueness, this meant the world to me. The month couldn't have gone by faster. Finally, it got to the night before we arrived. I was incredibly nervous because I had never officially met my biological mother. Mr. Henry calmed me, though. He told me that she was just like me and that it would be effortless to connect with her. I don't have to worry. Then he kissed me on the head, tucked Coco and me in, and it was lights out.

The following morning couldn't have come slower. I swear that night, I was constantly tossing and turning in bed because of the nerves, but once the sun came up, my nerves died down. Finally, we got up and packed our stuff to leave. Before we left the boat, Mr. Henry stopped me and put a facial mask on Coco's face and mine. It wasn't until we got outside that I understood why.

Many people on the streets were lying with typhus, smallpox, yellow fever, etc... I was pretty disgusted, especially when one of them almost touched me. Mr. Henry didn't let that happen, though. He held Coco and me close and continued walking until we reached the horse carriage. I was anxious and scared, but not the same kind of fear that you get when you see a giant spider but terrified like I don't want to die. We arrived at a cute cottage after an hour of traveling in the horse carriage. It was pretty ginormous. It had a brown roof, white walls, two floors, a chimney, a lavatory, a well, and many flowers and ivy outside. It was gorgeous! This is what London looked like without disease.

Mr. Henry took me out of the cart, and the rest of the stuff, and we walked up to the house. Then he pulled out his key, and as he was unlocking the door, the lady with violet eyes opened it. She was ecstatic to see me. She got down to my level and cried, "Hi, Ruby. I know this isn't exactly how you should have found out, but I'm Millie Jones," she pushed some of my hair behind my ear, "your mother."

At first, I didn't feel anything toward her, which was odd, but then she hugged me harder than I had ever been. I froze in my tracks, had tears in my eyes, and hugged her back. She picked me up and kept kissing me. She welcomed us inside and greeted Coco like her second child. She knew how important Coco was to me. She even thanked Coco in sign language for being such a fantastic friend. She was like me, just as amazing and beautiful.

It felt like a dream! I was finally home. This is where I belonged.

Then, Millie took me to my room, where I would stay for the next month. It was such an adorable little room. There were many dolls and gadgets for me to build things. Each and every step that I took when I walked into the house made me feel more and more at home. I had never expected that a woman would allow their daughter to play with tools. I placed my stuff down and got on my bed when I entered the room. Then Millie asked, "Do you want to jump on the bed?"

My eyes widened. I was incredibly excited! Of course, I wanted to jump. "You're going to let me jump on the bed? I thought it wasn't proper for a girl to do."

Millie looked at me in a funny way, "Why, of course we will. In our house, we have fun, and since when do you care about the 'proper' thing a girl needs to do?"

Fair enough, she was right. So, I smiled, got on the bed, and started jumping. We must have jumped for about thirty minutes. Then Millie picked me up and jumped onto her back with me in her arms. This was the most fun I have ever had at home. Even at the academy, we couldn't jump on the beds. I'm glad that I am officially at home. After we stopped laughing, Mr. Henry went downstairs to make dinner. It was intensely funny to me because usually, the mother is the one making the food. Millie taught me about the earth's rotation during this time. I asked, "Well, how do people know the Earth is rotating?"

Millie always smiled and replied, "Well, we can try and build something to prove it."

I was suspicious about this. "What can we build? There isn't anything that has been invented yet."

Millie was very particular about this. She was an inventor just like me, it was great! "Hush, little one, we will build something with a spinning mass that will rotate along its axis. I want to see how you can do it before I help you."

I went to my toolbox and grabbed a gimbal, a small metal disk with a stick through it to create a spin axis, and a circular frame to put it together. I knew these pieces would work because if they measured the earth's rotation, they needed to spin as the world spins on a flat surface. After about ten minutes of constructing it, it was complete!

Millie picked it up and placed it on the flat surface of my room, a beautiful wooden dresser with engraved flowers and vines. Once she put it down, it started to spin. "Ahhh, see, Ruby, your machine works. What would you like to call it?"

I thought briefly, then blurted, "The gyrate metimur, which means...."

Millie cut me off and finished my sentence by saying, "The measurement of going around. It's perfect!"

I couldn't believe Millie could speak Latin, well I guess I could, but I couldn't! "You speak Latin?"

She chuckled, "Why, of course, I do; I speak many languages. Just like you do," and then booped me on the nose.

Every second became better and better. Finally, dinner was ready, and we headed downstairs. There was a giant duck cut into a dragon, as well as many fruits shaped like funny shapes, such as flowers, animals, etc...

"Wow, Mr. Henry, this looks amazing! I knew you could cook, but I didn't know you could cook this well."

He laughed, "Well, of course I can. Cooking isn't only a job for women. It's a job for all."

I had never seen him this happy before. He scooped me up and put me in the chair. Then we feasted on the fantastic meal. After that, we chatted for the next two hours about the theory of heat, mechanics, evolution, and many other theories about the earth and how it spins. Lastly, we talked about how people think Vulcan is the closest planet to the sun. But I say it doesn't exist because mercury has a very small precession that the sun's gravity cannot quite explain yet, so Vulcan couldn't exist. After all, it doesn't have enough space to rotate around the sun. But maybe I'm wrong.

By the end, Coco and I were going in and out of sleep. So, I went upstairs to get ready for bed. As I climbed into the bed, Mr. Henry entered and tucked me in. Then I said, "Mr. Henry, what was it like for you? I mean, you had to watch me grow up to the Ledgers. Also, why didn't you fight back? Is there anything else that I need to know about you? What about the—"

"Ruby, slow down. Would you like to know more about who I am? The real me?"

"Yes, I would love to! Please!"

He smiled and began his life story.

CHAPTER SEVENTEEN

Who is Henry Jones?

"*Ruby, to begin with the basics of some things you already know, my name is Henry Giles Jones, and I was born on August 29, 1817, in Sussex, Great Britain. I was born into a family that is part of a long generation of spies and detectives. It was inevitable that I would become one, and my children would also. I grew up in a small house, but not too small. It was a lovely cottage on the bay with three bedrooms, a living room, and a lavatory. My family had some money to their names, and we were considered part of the wealthy. As a child, I always found it fascinating to go on my own, create little missions, and invent my gadgets. I never understood people who didn't enjoy these things. Therefore, I tried to stay away from them. I was always considered the odd duckling of the bunch. It was always the*

perfect escape from the harsh reality of life that we were living in.

The streets were scattered with the disease, and people were dying daily. In my family, I had two brothers. One is Christopher, two years younger, and the other is Ambrose, five years younger. I was the oldest in my family and had to set a good example for my younger siblings."

"Wait! You have siblings? Why have you never mentioned them before? Also, did you have any sisters?" I charmingly asked as my eyes fluttered.

"Ruby, I didn't mention them before because it wasn't important. It would have been odd if I had told you more about my life since you were raised thinking I was your teacher, but now that you know who I am, I am able to tell you everything. However, it is getting late, and if you want me to continue the story, you have to be quiet."

"Sorry..." I grasped Coco tightly as she sat on my lap.

"I was always considered a role model; I would be punished if I did anything terrible. So, I learned to be quiet and diligent and stay to myself.

My mother always longed for a daughter, but she never got one. She always wished for at least one of her grandchildren to be a girl, which came true when you came along. It's probably one of the reasons why I have a different connection with you than I do with Theo. Unfortunately, my mother passed away when I was sixteen after getting shot by an opposing agency. This encouraged me to fight harder than ever before and become the best agent out there.

My father, however, is still alive today. He is currently in his sixties, which is incredible considering most people don't live past 40 due to disease, as you know. Luckily, my family knows how to avoid all the internal horrors that come when someone sneezes.

When I was eighteen years old, I was inaugurated into the HIA because, in 1834, I helped Lord Melbourne succeed Earl Grey as prime minister by proving that Grey illegally smuggled unique tea leaves into Great Britain. Unfortunately, he got the tea Earl Grey named after him, but I still stopped his conspiracies.

After joining the HIA, I failed one of my first missions when I was sent to the United States to stop a criminal from wreaking havoc on New York. The only problem was I was able to stop them and bring them to the HIA, but I accidentally caused what is now known today as the Great Fire of New York of 1835. After this occurred, I was put on probation for a few months until I could prove I was worthy of being in the HIA."

My mouth dropped open! "You caused the Great Fire of New York? But that was one of the greatest fires in American history!" Mr. Henry began to chuckle, "Sorry, I'll be quiet!"

"Most people don't realize I had made this major mistake because the HIA covered it up. As the years have gone by, I

have learned my lesson. Everyone makes mistakes, and now, I have become one of the best agents in the world.

But, to make up for my actions from the Great Fire of New York, I was sent to the Galapagos, where I met a lovely man named Charles Darwin. He was studying birds and noticed that the same species on different islands had different beak lengths, and their bodies were shaped differently. I had seen this before but never thought about the science behind it. So, I decided to help him.

For a few months, I collected many samples, and it was determined that these birds and specimens were different because of a theory called evolution. Evolution is the process of an organism that grows over many years to be different from earlier forms of the same species in history. This research was officially published after 23 years of work. I was only there initially, but it was not my primary focus. I was sent there because Darwin was a part of the organization and was sent there to determine a more logical way of learning about the earth, but it was as if he had left the organization because he hadn't responded for many months. He was known as an environmental agent.

There were many different types of HIA agents. Some field agents went out into the field and fought for justice. Some secretarial agents stayed behind the scenes and gave the assignments. The environmental agents that go out into the world to fight harsh wildfires or learn more about organisms. Then, they present their findings. The technologi-

cal agents that dealt with building the gadgets. The dressing agents made the clothes bulletproof and swordproof. The disguising agents were brilliant at disguising objects to make them look like something else than it was. And many more...

After this small expedition, I knew I had to prove myself before I could become a field agent again. So, I did this by helping build the settlement of Houston and separating the Mexicans from this territory, causing Texas to be declared an official state. This was necessary because the Americans wanted Texas, as did the Mexicans, causing the War of Texas Independence that I helped end, leading Texas to become its own colony, which later became the 28th state of the United States on December 29, 1845. I felt this was important because, at the time, this war would almost spread to the other states, and this became a problem as the Americans rightfully owned the States.

Shortly after I returned from New York, I met Violet, the woman you know as Miss Holmes. She was a beautiful woman who was wicked fast in her thoughts. She taught me patience and that I can't always jump into everything without looking into it first and learning the facts. At first, we didn't want children because we wanted to focus on our careers. After a few years had gone by, I was put on a mission to stop the Canadians from blowing up Michigan. Halfway through this mission, I met Millie Hartford, your mother, and we worked together.

Fortunately, we could stop the Canadians and reveal their complete plans, causing Michigan to become the 26th official state of the United States of America. As time passed, we became very close, but we didn't have a relationship yet.

My son Theodore was born on January 27, 1848. He was a unique, intelligent, witty little boy who loved exploring. He wanted to be an explorer. I had never met an explorer, so trying to raise him was quite the experience. Ever since Fabian Gottlieb von Bellingshausen and Mikhail Lazarev discovered Antarctica in 1820, every place has been studied.

Because of his birth, I spent much time at home, but he doesn't remember this. I was with Violet most of the time. However, one day, she went on this mission and was teamed up with Morland Holmes. He was a brilliant detective and gave me a run for my money.

Shortly after, in 1849, I discovered that Violet had an affair with a man named Morland, and I decided to leave her. I didn't want to leave my son, but I couldn't fathom that she would have an affair, so I also had one. Now, please keep in mind, Ruby, two wrongs don't make a right–"

"No, but three lefts do." I chuckled.

He shook his head and continued, " I went to Millie, which was very careless, but if I didn't, I wouldn't have gotten you."

"So, it was a win-win situation?"

He shook his head, lifted his eyebrows, and tensed his shoulders, "Ruby?"

"Sorry. I know just because someone does something wrong doesn't mean you should."

"Exactly; now, may I please continue?"

I smiled, and he went on, *"I knew Millie loved me back, considering there was always a spark between us. Even more than with Violet. Violet went off and married Morland and became Violet Holmes.*

I married Millie a short while later; we were compatible, and it was true love. About a year later, on May 18, 1850, you, Rebecca, were born. I had never truly understood what love felt like until the first time I got to hold you in my arms, you were a spitting image of Violet, and when you grabbed the tip of my thumb with your petite adorable little hand and smiled at me my heart melted.

I truly loved my son, but you were a whole different kind of love. I knew I needed to protect and keep you safe from the moment I held you. You are brilliant and beautiful. You were all I could have ever asked for. I grew very close to you and called you Ruby because you have the sweetest red cherry cheeks. You were our little Ruby, who never stopped shining a light on our lives.

A short while later, I went on another mission with Violet, and we kissed each other. I knew it was wrong, and I never wanted to hurt Millie, but she found out. "

"Mr. Henry! You cheated on her? How could you?" I shouted!

"Cheated? Ruby, your mother isn't a test."

"I know, but in tests, if you cheat, that means you did something disloyal, and that is exactly what you did! How could you be so clueless and reckless? That wasn't fair to her!"

"Maybe I should stop this story..."

"No! I was just saying. Is that why you aren't together with her anymore?"

"Patience, my child. I will answer all of your questions."

I huffed and leaned forward to tune into his story more.

"Even though she had an affair, I still cared for Violet because there was still some love there. Unfortunately, Millie wanted me to stay away from you after discovering this. She didn't trust me anymore, so her best motive was to send you to live with her sister, Margaret Ledger. Although Margaret was a lovely woman, she wasn't bright; she only cared about her appearance. I disagreed that you should grow up in an environment where your talents and intelligence would be discouraged. I fought Millie for multiple months before you were shipped off. I knew I had to follow you to America because you would have had a discouraging childhood if I didn't.

Shortly after you arrived in America, Millie and Violet became friends again. They apologized to each other for the times that I had an affair with them, and then they forgave me. It truly takes a lot of empathy to forgive someone like me who isn't proud of my actions. I never wanted to tell you this because I didn't want you to believe I was horrible, even though sometimes I feel I am.

Because of Violet and Millie's friendship, Millie asked Violet to help watch over you, and then she went on an extended mission over the past few years. Her mission was to try to help with the slavery problems in America. She constantly went back and forth, and during this time, she even got to watch you from a distance. It must have been difficult for Millie to protect her only child and grow up without her. I can imagine, but in a different way, because you only viewed me as your teacher.

When Violet went to America, she bought the previous academy from her relatives and turned it into Miss Holmes' Academy. She wanted to keep her true identity undercover and asked Margaret to send you to the academy when you were old enough, or at least almost old enough, you were nine, even though most students start at ten to grant Millie's wishes of watching over you.

Because of this, I could also spend time with my son and watch him grow. He never learned I was his biological father either because Morland raised him since he was about two. Morland and Violet had a few more children. We felt this was for the best, even though I still love Theodore.

Ultimately, I lost the relationship battle with my children because of my cheating. When I was younger, my father had an affair with a different woman than my mother, and I never wanted to end up like him, but I did. I wish I didn't because if I didn't, I could have spent your childhood with you. I'm glad that even though I never got to know Theodore that well, I learned you. I'm also grateful that you now know I am your biological father."

By the part of his story where he said I was getting shipped off, I had fallen asleep, so I didn't quite get to hear the end of it.

After he saw I was fully asleep, he tucked Coco and me in the covers.

CHAPTER EIGHTEEN

The Big Decision

Millie watched Mr. Henry slither down the stairs and into the kitchen, where he removed his jacket onto the chair. Millie smiled and asked, "Is she fast asleep?"

Mr. Henry went to grab a cup of tea before sitting down, "Yes, she is out like a light.

Millie grinned, then uttered, "Yes, she is. She is adorable. She is astonishingly little. I can't believe she is ours. You know, each and every year felt longer and longer without her after all of these years apart. She is just like you and me. So, brilliant, but I do have to thank you for that. I'm sorry for sending her away when she was a baby. I've regretted it every day, but I knew she would be in safe hands. I am truly sorry that she was stuck in that home, and my sister and brother-in-law never encouraged her talents. Instead, they discouraged them. I also forgive you for cheating on me many years ago because if you didn't follow her, she wouldn't be the amazing, brilliant, talented little girl she is today. I should have never tried to keep her away from you. But it's in the past, and it's not important now. What's important is that she is ours now."

Mr. Henry sat down and said, "You shouldn't be sorry. I would have done the same thing. But I will say that if we babied her, she wouldn't be who she is today. Living with your sister gave her strength; no matter how often her wall was broken down, she lifted herself back up again. She is our little fighter. Just as she always says, she may be tiny, but she is mighty."

Millie snuggled beside Mr. Henry, then vocalized, "She is a fighter. I can't imagine how hard it was for her to live in that house with my sister's stupidity. I don't know what I thought, but she is home now. She is in the organization. She is absolute brilliance!"

After talking for a few more hours, they went to sleep, and the following day, everyone had woken up; we decided to go on a beautiful walk near the bay. When we arrived at the destination of the bay, there was a cute little boat for us to sail on. We hopped on board and sailed. Around lunchtime, we put on our swimwear and went for a swim. Mr. Henry had a lovely swimsuit with a nice shade of blue shorts, while I had my pretty blue flower dress swimwear; Millie had a blue one-piece swimsuit with shorts. It was fascinating because I was always taught that girls must wear dresses and never shorts. Millie was so different; it was wonderful!

We played in the water, and Mr. Henry even started a game to determine the number of fish species in the water. I got ten, Mr. Henry got eight, and Millie got two. Naming fish species wasn't exactly her thing. It was okay because she was brilliant at many other things.

On the way back, we calculated how long it would take to get from the bay back to the house if we walked at four miles an hour for one point two kilometers and about point seven five miles on sand. You would think it would only take about eleven minutes, but it didn't because we didn't factor in the fact we were on the sand, so it took about twenty-five minutes. Before we got home, Eobard Brown was selling ice cream on the road. When they asked what flavor I wanted, he noticed I was American, while my parents were British. Then he grabbed me and said, "Little girl, how did you get here? Did these people kidnap you? Here, I'll take you back to the embassy to send you back to America and for these peasants to be sent to prison."

I shouted, "No! They are my parents; I was raised in America but am visiting now." Mr. Henry pulled me out of this skin-crawling person's arms, and the police were called. Luckily for us, the police officer knew my parents. When he arrived, he began to detain the street urchin; he stated, "You must be little Ruby. Your mother has spoken greatly of you, and it is a pleasure to meet you."

I was quiet because I was scared about being pulled. He then looked at Millie and exclaimed, "Millie, she does look like you. You weren't kidding."

Millie didn't want me to see what would happen to the man. I tried to help him, considering he technically didn't do anything wrong, by asking the police officer to leave him alone because he was doing what he felt was right. But the police officer didn't listen.

Little did I know when I got home, Mr. Henry explained to me, "Many people on the streets will see children and try to harm them because they are small. He was probably one of them, so Ruby, I very much appreciate what you were doing, but in the future, you must stay with us and let the police handle them."

It made sense to me. I never knew that people could be that dangerous. I always saw the good in people, well, for the most part, but I at least tried. I never realized that people would do things as foolish as kidnapping. Maybe they wanted to do it for money? I'm glad my parents were there to protect me. They were my heroes, and I loved them.

This was one of the first times I had been exposed to the real world. I never realized how harsh it could be. Later that evening, Millie and Mr. Henry took me out again, and we went to see *A Midsummer Night's Dream* in the theater. It was a charming love story about four people from Athenia who ran away to a forest only to have a fairy make the boys fall in love with the same girl. I have seen a Shakespeare play a few times before and read all of them. Hamlet is probably my favorite Shakespeare play. I have seen it multiple times in New York, but this was the first time I watched it. It was brilliant!

As the next week passed, we constantly did fun activities every day. This felt like life. It was great until Millie and Mr. Henry were called onto a mission.

"Millie, Mr. Henry, what's going on?"

Millie replied, "Ruby, we were called on a mission. British and French troops disappeared. We must find out who is doing this and stop them. We may need your help if you're up for the mission."

I nodded, and a smile crawled onto my face. We went to the nearest train station and were on one to France within two hours. After approximately two and a half hours of traveling, we arrived at the HIA's headquarters in Paris. We were greeted and entered this room, where they explained where these disappearances had been coming from. The very first one was Basford St. John, London. The most recent one was at Base Navale de Brest, France. This was one of the many army bases where people disappeared without a trace. "Well, they couldn't have disappeared without a trace. However, there is always something that will tell us where they went or how they went, which could then lead us to the true perpetrators." I humbly mentioned.

The head of this HIA laughed at me, which to me meant, "Whose child is this and why is she here?" So, I politely responded "Je m'appelle Ruby Ledger, et je suis votre plus jeune et nouvelle recrue, et je sais que je peux vous aider àrésoudre cette affaire."

Now, if you're wondering what this translates to, "My name is Ruby Ledger, and I am your newest and youngest recruit. I know I can help you solve this case."

His eyes widened after realizing who I was, and he returned to his conversation. He judged me because I was American, which is incredibly wrong on every level. So, finally, when I spoke French, he took me seriously; he was such a fussock.

After the meeting concluded, Millie, Mr. Henry, and I went to the most recent disappearance base because we knew if we were to find something, it would be there. Also, most likely, all of these cases were connected because it would be highly unusual if the same type of disappearance occurred and it wasn't the same person who did it.

When we arrived, we scoped out the whole area but found nothing. That was until Coco climbed up to the ceiling, and when she looked down, she saw a small piece of a Chinese candy bar. She pointed it out, and when we picked it up, it had Mandarin on it. We couldn't prove it was the Chinese, but who else could have done this?

We returned to the headquarters, and I took out my fingerprinting kit there. When we arrived, I went to the fingerprinting book. All soldiers must be fingerprinted just in case they die, and the HIA has records of every soldier from around the world. All of these are filled in a giant room in the back.

After entering the room, I headed straight for the Chinese database, and there were thousands of names. Luckily, each book was labeled with the type of fingerprint, and this guy had a scarce kind. Also, it didn't look like a swirl but a mountain. So, it didn't take long to find.

Once it was found, the base coordinates were located in the book. Thank goodness for the HIA. We determined they were obviously in a base in China, but it was located right next to Beijing in a desert. We took the first train out that night, which took almost 89 hours. We were all exhausted, but we knew we had to continue. Knowing this was in the desert, I knew there would be snakes, so I rubbed cinnamon all over my body to help repel them.

We planned to prove that our soldiers were there. Millie and Mr. Henry could speak Mandarin, so they went to the general while I went to find the soldiers. Luckily, I was small; therefore, if I was caught, I could speak, considering they were towards the end of the Second Opium War, in which the United States and China had a treaty. After crouching down and secretively searching their base, I found the soldiers. They were in the underground part of a large outhouse that was muddy and full of serpents and other creepy animals I had to stay away from. It was pretty revolting if you ask me, but the soldiers were captured, so it makes sense that they wouldn't be in the standard of luxury.

Once they were found, they gave me a funny look, and I told them they would be alright in English and French. They smiled at me and judged the fact that I was a child. Then, one of the British stated, "Little girl, it is not safe for you to be here right now. You will get hurt. Where are your parents?"

I hollered, "I won't! I am stronger than I look. Besides, I might be tiny, but I am mighty! And my parents do know I am here right now. They were the ones who brought me here. So, please don't fight me because I am here to help."

Then, a French soldier entered the conversation, asking in English with a powerful accent, "What is your name, little girl?"

I smiled and responded in French, "I'm Ruby Ledger, but you may call me Ruby."

He smiled back, and Coco jumped onto the British soldier's arm. He startled, began shaking, and yelled in a frightened voice, "Get this thing off of me. It's going to bite me!"

I laughed, as did Coco, then responded, "No, she won't. She is a trained monkey. She is my pet and won't hurt you; relax. You'll be fine," I shook my head. Soldiers are greatly dramatic. "You know, for being an all-mighty soldier, you aren't fearless against small but fierce creatures. I mean, if I am being completely honest, there are serpents surrounding this place, and the fact that you're scared of a monkey–a capuchin monkey at that–who is only 35.5 cm (14 inches) tall is sad."

The other soldiers started laughing at me, and another said, "I'm going to start calling you monkey girl."

I chuckled but got to the point, "Listen, I am here to help you, so don't move and let her pick your chain lock. While I help the others."

He gave me a disgusting look, "You know, little girl, you are very bright, but one day, that mouth of yours might get you in trouble."

I shrugged and brushed off his comment. Then we went to unlock all of their chains. Fortunately, we were successful and set them all free. Unfortunately, once free, they didn't use their brains and decided to run.

Because of this, the Chinese started firing bullets at the soldiers and us to make them accessible. Millie and Mr. Henry quickly found me. But what was shocking was that after she got to me, she got nervous and used me as a shield as a defense mechanism.

Fortunately, I wore my bulletproof dress, but I couldn't believe she would do that. Then Mr. Henry stood before me, grabbed me, and we ran. He protected me, even though he didn't have any bulletproof armor.

Fortunately, even though he was technically shot, it only scraped past his clothing and didn't fully penetrate the skin. After that, we tried to help the soldiers more with our weapons but weren't victorious. I think we made the efforts worse.

On the train back to France, I told Mr. Henry, "It was all my fault. I'm very sorry. I shouldn't have unlocked their chains. I was trying to help, and I didn't think they would fire bullets."

He held me in his arms, "Ruby, it's alright. It wasn't your fault. Not every mission you're going to succeed. At least we know where they are holding them for the time being. What matters to me right now is that you are okay! I love you so much, my sweet child."

Millie wanted to chime in, but I could tell she felt guilty. At this moment, I wanted to trust her, and I knew it was a fight-or-flight response, but maybe she wasn't suited to be a mother after all.

We had all our fun and games, but being a parent meant protecting your child, and she didn't do that. Instead, she did quite the opposite. I wish I hadn't gone on the mission so that I wouldn't have experienced that.

When we arrived at the base, I passed out of exhaustion as Mr. Henry and Millie spoke to the general. The general had exclaimed that we had succeeded in finding where the culprits were hiding our soldiers, but it was an extremely sloppy job. That I needed more training and practice. Mr. Henry agreed to teach me more when we got back home.

Millie and Mr. Henry sat down and discussed what had happened earlier that week. Mr. Henry stated, "I can't believe you used our daughter as a shield. She is just a little girl. It wasn't her fault she set the soldiers free. She was trying to help. She is only ten years old and still learning, but you have been in this industry for many years and used our daughter as a shield."

Millie held her head down, "I knew that she had a bulletproof dress on and that she was going to be fine."

Mr. Henry's face turned red and hot as his shoulders stiffened, "That is no excuse to use her as a shield. She is just a child. Might I remind you, our child! What matters is her safety, so this is what will happen now. In two days, I'm taking her back to America. I'm sorry that you couldn't be the mom you wanted to be, but I need to protect my child."

Millie started to cry and yell, "You can't do that! I haven't had her at all during her entire life. That little girl is everything to me. It was an honest mistake, but I can't let you take her away from me, not again. Please just let her choose if she wants to stay."

Mr. Henry marched out of the room.

The following morning, I woke up in my bed in London. Millie walked in quietly and asked, "How are you, Ruby?"

I exclaimed, "I am well, Millie. I also forgive you for what happened."

At the same time, I was still a little nervous. She smiled, and then Mr. Henry walked in. "Good morning, Ruby. I have to ask you an earnest question. I hope you make the right choice. We are leaving in one day, and I need you to decide if you want to stay here or go back to America."

I thought for a second. All parents make mistakes, don't they? I didn't want to lose her again. She was one of the most amicable parents in the world and even better than my own. However, she made a mistake that could have cost me my life. So, I replied, "I want to return to America, but I don't want to lose you. I want to visit you and spend even more time with you!" I hugged her as my eyes watered.

Mr. Henry packed up all of my stuff that night as I watched. Millie sat near me and embraced me in her arms. It was going to be very difficult leaving her. I didn't want to leave, but I knew I had to. We spent the last night going to the bay and having fun.

The following morning, we arrived at the docks to leave. Before we boarded the S.S. Rebellion, Millie hugged me tighter than a bear hug. I could feel her pain as she shed her tears. She didn't want me to leave, but it was the best thing for me. She put me down, got to my level, and then blurted, "Don't worry, little girl, I promised I would visit you very often. You are a special and talented child; don't let anyone tell you otherwise—especially my sister's family. I love you, my sweet one. Have safe travels!"

She kissed me on the head, and as I tried to hold her grasp, Mr. Henry took my hand with Coco on my shoulder, forcing me to let go, and we headed onto the boat. We found our cabin, and it was lovely. It was the same one we were in when we boarded a month ago. We put our stuff down and went to sit on the deck so that I could take in the scenery of Great Britain. It was a nice breath of fresh air. I knew this wasn't going to be my last time here, but I was still determining when the next time I would return.

CHAPTER NINETEEN

The S.S. Rebellion

The first few days on the boat were tough. I couldn't stop thinking about Millie. Mr. Henry could tell I wasn't enthusiastic each time he spoke to me. Each and every minute felt like an eternity. Mr. Henry felt horrible, but he knew it was for the best.

"Mr. Henry, when I get home, will I be living with you, or will I be living with my other family?"

He stopped and thought for a second. Then he answered, "I would love for you to live with me, but your parents have much more money than I do. They would give you a better life even though it would mean the world to me to live with my little girl. It's entirely your decision, Ruby."

I didn't know what to choose. I wanted to live with him, but at the same time, maybe he was right. Also, I knew my non-biological parents still loved me, and it wasn't fair to them if they couldn't see me. I wish I didn't have to make these decisions. My parents wanted me to be independent, but sometimes I wish to be the child.

By this time, we had done everything on the boat. My favorite thing to do was sit on a ledge on the top deck at night and read under the stars. I had to climb a pole to get there, but it was worth it. It was like a conservatory, considering there was no pollution in the air. It was beautiful.

One night, Coco came up to me with a bit of rolled parchment in her hand. "Ruby, I'm sorry I kept this from you before, but maybe it means something. Before we boarded, Millie handed this to me. I didn't show it to you because there aren't any words on it, and I thought you might feel bad about it. But you're a genius. So, it must mean something, right?"

I grabbed the parchment from her and tried to figure it out, but there wasn't anything on it. There wasn't even a header. It was a blank slate, and it smelled funny. "Why would Millie give this to me?"

Coco shrugged, and that's when Mr. Henry called us to dinner. We climbed down from the top deck and reached Mr. Henry. We sat down when we went to dinner, and the servers brought the first course. It was some weird-looking potato with other vegetables sticking out of it, making it look like a face. It was served to all children on board. It was pretty odd. Then the second course came out, and it was lobster. That thing freaked me out. Even though my parents were wealthy, we had never had lobster before. It looked like some demon sea bug that was staring into my soul. So, with wide eyes, I stared at it, "Mr. Henry, this sea scorpion is freaking me out."

He laughed, "Here, let me help you. It's not that difficult to open. It is scary at first, but it tastes delicious. If you don't want it, I can get you something else."

I stared at it and asked, "Can I please have something else? I can't bear to eat this sea demon. What if it comes back to kill me in my sleep?"

He laughed a little, "Oh, see, there is my humorous little girl. I'm glad you're back."

He then called for the server, "Waiter! Waiter! Can you please get my daughter something else? This lobster is making her nervous."

The server smiled, "You know, little girl, you are not the first child today to say that. How about some chicken?"

I nodded and felt that that was the best option. When it arrived, I stared at it for a few seconds to examine whether or not it was creepy. Mr. Henry questioned, "Ruby, are you alright? Is this one better?"

I fiercely answered, "Yes, it's alright. It just smells funny. I feel like I've smelled this but never seen it anywhere."

He came closer to me and smelled it, "Oh, that is vinegar."

I was questioning why there was vinegar on my chicken. I didn't even know it was edible because I had only ever heard of it being used to make invisible ink. Still, I could never get it because it wasn't ubiquitous, and Mother or Father would never agree to pay for it, "Vinegar?"

He smiled, "Yes, vinegar; vinegar helps remove the gooey and fatty substances from the chicken, so the skin of the chicken holds better to the chicken itself."

Wait a second. I pulled out the letter from my pocket and smelled it. It reeked of vinegar. That was it. The ingredients in invisible ink were vinegar and fire. I got up and ran to the top deck. There was a lovely little fit pit there. As I ran away, Mr. Henry yelled, "Ruby, where are you going? You haven't finished your dinner yet! Ruby?"

He knew I was onto something and decided to let me go. It was best for both of us for him to do that. While he was eating alone at the table, a man came up and asked, "You're going to let your seven-year-old daughter venture off on her own? What if she gets hurt or falls off the ship?"

Mr. Henry wasn't too pleased with his remark and replied, "My daughter isn't seven years old; she is ten, and I am not nervous because she is the smartest child you will ever meet. If not one of the smartest people. She won't fall off the ship; wherever she goes, she probably just needs some space alone. Besides, she has her pet to help protect her. So, she will be fine."

The other guy laughed, "Please, she is not ten years old. Do you see how much of a munchkin she is? You know, you are a terrible parent for letting her go on her own. I never let my kids go on their own because it's unsafe. Maybe you should take a page out of my book. Besides, at that age, they don't even know how to get dressed alone, let alone explore without an adult present. You're probably just delusional that your daughter is that bright. No girls are, so don't overestimate your daughter's abilities."

Mr. Henry wanted to fight him but didn't. He didn't want to get kicked off the boat, so he faced him and screeched, "My little girl is ten years old. Not seven. Also, She may be tiny, but she is mighty and bloody brilliant! That little girl can solve anything; I wouldn't be surprised if something happened on this trip because of her. I would watch your mouth because maybe your daughter is a wanker, but mine isn't. Remember this: don't ever underestimate the ability of a girl or woman because they can do anything a man can do, if not better!"

The other guy laughed it off, "You're a blithering idiot!"

After replying, he walked away with tears of laughter in his eyes. Mr. Henry was infuriated but got up to check on me. By this point, I had found the fire pit and was burning my letter. Typically, I'm not supposed to play with fire, but I was being safe using a safety claw I had built. I didn't want to get burned.

After a few seconds of it burning, the message appeared. I blew out the small fire on the edge of my paper. This was when Mr. Henry arrived. He watched me from a distance as I climbed up to my little area on the deck. I made myself comfortable and started to read. Mr. Henry knew I was safe and threw me some bread to ensure I would eat; then, he sat on one of the deck chairs and waited for me to come down.

The note read,

Dear my beautiful Ruby,

I knew you would find my message. I know you are probably still on the ship back to America, but I wanted to tell you how much I enjoyed seeing you and spending time with you this summer. I never wanted it to end, especially the way it did. I wasn't trying to use you as a shield. Your father doesn't know this, but that morning when I helped you get ready, the dress I put you in was the type of dress that was not only bulletproof but absorbed the bullets and spat them back out. I was trying to use you as a weapon to take them down and not to kill you. I should have told you that was my motive instead of scaring you, and now, once again, I have pushed you away.

I did this as a safety measure, as I could only fit the technology in your clothing since you are petite. I couldn't fit it in my clothing because I didn't have enough of the material. Since I can pick you up, I could use you like a little gun. I am terribly sorry for all the trouble I caused you. I want you to know how much I love you and that you are the most important thing in the universe to me. I want you to know I never wanted you to leave, and I hope one day you can forgive me because I would love to spend time with you again and get to raise you. You are the sweetest, most lovable, brilliant, and most amazing little girl, and don't ever let anybody take that away from you! I love you, my sweet Ruby!

Love,

Mummy

I began to tear up out of frustration. Now I really couldn't stop thinking about her. I was still deciding what I wanted to do. I wanted to go back to my biological mother. It is astonishing that she tried to use me as a gun. I wish Mr. Henry saw it that way. I knew one thing. I had to stop this ship for a few days to think about this because if I didn't, we were going to keep going, and I needed to be sure that I wanted to go back to America since we were only a few days by ship away from England, and very close to Spain. I could tell this by how fast we were going. I read in a book once that if I tie a rope to an object, I have to count how many seconds it takes before it passes its stern. It was known as the Dutchman's log. I also had to see the distance from where I was standing to the ocean below, which I did because I asked a sailor on the first day. I calculated that we were going at approximately eight knots per hour, meaning we were only mere miles away from Spain. So, I had to redirect the ship's navigation there.

When I climbed down from the pole, Mr. Henry was standing there. I lied to him by saying I was sleepy, so we went back to the room, got ready for bed, and then I waited for him to pass out. It took a little bit of time.

Once he did, I snuck out of the room and tried to find my way to the ship wheel near the captain's quarters. When I got there, many prominent men were helping steer the ship, so I pretended I was lost to ask them when any of them were sleeping. I began to fake cry, but I made it believable. I did it loud enough for the captain to come over. He said, "Aww, sweetie, are you lost? Do you need me to help you find your parents?"

I nodded, and we started walking. I was taking him to a different room so Mr. Henry wouldn't get in trouble for me wandering. On my way there, I questioned, "Are there always people in the captain's quarter room? Also, how would one go about that if someone were to change the ship's direction?"

He was shocked that I was interested and had a brain. Then he sat me down and replied, "Well, little girl, for starters, what's your name?"

"Ruby," I answered.

He continued, "Well, Ruby, normally, we don't have little girls ask about these topics, but there are always people in that room steering the ship. Unless there is an accident somewhere else, the ship can steer itself for a few moments without any presence. To answer your second question, you must move the steering wheel, which is too heavy for a little girl like yourself. I'm sorry, but why do you ask these questions?"

I needed to move this ship, so I had to figure something out to get the strength to move the boat. I also needed a diversion. But for now, I had to reply, "I was just wondering. My father always teaches me about these things, but he is not a captain like you. So, I just wanted to learn more!"

The captain laughed and then knocked on what he thought was my door. A woman opened it, and I hugged her, pretending she was my mother. When the captain saw this, he said, "It was a pleasure meeting you, Ruby," and walked off.

The woman tried to get the captain's attention to say I wasn't her child, but I stopped her. "Thank you, madam. Sorry for the inconvenience."

I decided I was going to make a smokey area without a fire. I went to one of my cases and got my masks for Coco and me. Then, I pulled out the chemicals ammonia and hydrochloric acid. I needed to do this in a controlled environment so nobody would get hurt. I had made this smoke in the past. It would only last about ninety seconds. I decided to use a pulley system and simple physics to move the steering wheel. I gathered all my pieces together, put them in the pocket sewed into my under-dress garment, and headed to the other side of the ship in a little cabin area closed on three sides with wood and one with glass to start my diversion.

I made the little smoke bomb go off, and the captain was immediately notified. He didn't worry about any passengers, and all crew members went to the opposite side of the ship while I went to the captain's headquarters. I set up my pulley system and knew we needed to go far west. I read the map and was able to change the ship's direction in about thirty seconds. Then, I took down my pulley system and tried to run to my room, but the captain walked in. I hid under the floorboard and heard him speaking to someone else.

His friend asked, "How did this smoke go off, and where did it come from?"

The captain voiced, "I don't know, but until we find out, I think we should head to Spain for a quick stop to determine the true cause before we head on the open seas."

He approached the steering wheel and realized, "The wheel is already facing towards Spain, meaning someone did this. I was talking to a little girl named Ruby earlier, but she couldn't have done this. I mean, she is a little girl."

His accomplice laughed, "It couldn't have been the girl; girls aren't smart enough, and I saw her. She was, what, seven years old. If that. She couldn't have moved the wheel at this time. It would have been too heavy for her."

The captain agreed, and I wanted to come out, but I couldn't; otherwise, I would have gotten in trouble. I needed to find my way out. So, I went further into the cabin down below. I trekked along the long hallway and finally saw the light. It leads to the vents of each cabin. It was creepy to think that anybody in this hall could hear conversations. I used my key to unlock one; fortunately, it was small enough to fit through. Unfortunately, it leads to someone else's room. It was pretty embarrassing for me as I entered because a man was in there with a woman resting next to each other. It made it more awkward when the woman got up and asked, "Sweetie, where did you just come from?"

So, I pretended I couldn't speak English and began speaking Russian to her. She let me go, and I ventured to my cabin. When I entered, Mr. Henry was sitting on the bed when the captain used an oversized-sounding cone to say, "We will be stopping in Spain for a day or two. The ship had a slight complication, but everything is alright; we want to be certain."

Mr. Henry shook his head back and forth and said, "Ruby, how much should I bet that you had something to do with this?"

I held my head down and faked a smile, replying, "You can't prove this was me. There is no evidence that I did this."

Then he asked, "So if it wasn't you, what were you doing at this time, not in the cabin?"

I scrunched my face and responded, "Okay, fine, it was me, but the diversion wasn't big. It was just a small smoke bomb on the top deck that dissipated in about ninety seconds. So, it's not that big of a deal. Besides, everything is alright."

He was visibly upset. "Ruby, before I tell you off for doing this, why did you do it? I will forgive you if there is a reasonable reason, and we can forget this. Also, did you get caught at all?"

I stared at the floor. It took a few minutes to say anything because I didn't want to lie. "Alright, I did it because Millie wrote me a letter explaining why she did what she did, and I just don't know if going back to America is the right decision. I knew there was no going back for a while once we left Europe. I just wanted another day to think about it because tomorrow would be too late if I didn't do this now. I'm sorry, Mr. Henry. I used a pulley system to steer the ships toward Spain, and then they said they would go there anyway. I just wanted another day to think about my mom. And no, I didn't get caught, for the most part... I ended up in some old lady's room and pretended I couldn't speak English."

He chuckled at that last part, "Ruby, come here. I forgive you, and I don't blame you. I know it cannot be easy to choose where you want to live, but instead of going on your own, I wish you had just talked to me about it. My little one, I will always be here for you, no matter the circumstance. I love you, my sweet child. Also, you're not in trouble, alright. Everything is okay."

I smiled, and then he continued, "Nice job with the smoke bomb. I was talking to this crass man before, and I was telling him how I wouldn't be surprised if you pulled something off. Did I think you were going to do it? No. But, here we are."

I started to laugh as well; I could be pretty naughty at times. It would take approximately nine hours before arriving at the docks in Spain. I fell asleep and woke up with two hours remaining. Mr. Henry and I went to breakfast, and the guy Mr. Henry talked about went up to us and jokingly chirped, "I suppose your seven-year-old is the reason for going to Spain. Please, she is just a small wanker of a child; she couldn't have done this."

I wanted to fight this unlicked cub and put his money where his mouth was, but instead, I had a better idea. I noticed the key to his room was sticking out of his pocket, and it read 221B. So, I decided I was going to outsmart the bastard. After he finished his glass, I offered to put it away for him. Only for him to respond, "Oh, you are such a well-natured little girl who is going to grow up to be the best housewife."

That only infuriated me the most; I didn't want to be a housewife. If anything, I was going to be the boss in my family! But I couldn't let him figure out what I would do, so I just said, "Well, I don't know about being a housewife, but I will make an impression on whichever lucky man I marry." The revolting guy smiled and then left.

Instead of taking the cup to the disposal, I returned to my room to remove the fingerprints with some dust and paper. After that, I wiped down the chemical canisters that I used. This was because I hadn't hit puberty yet, so there were higher levels of cholesterol and branch chain free fatty acids that were unstable, which made the fingerprint break down more quickly, which is why it's challenging to fingerprint a child. In adults, it's quite the contrary because they have a higher concentration of stable lipids like wax and squalene, which don't vaporize as quickly, so I could get my fingerprints off the bottle but not his.

Then I planted the chemicals in his room and told the captain, "Excuse me, sir, I think I know what started the smoke. As I was walking by room 221B, I noticed some crazy chemicals in there, and I think maybe it had to do with the smoke."

The captain looked at me and immediately directed people to his room while I followed. They found the chemicals and blamed them on him. Then, I left quickly before he could return. The captain had announced that the culprit was found and would no longer be able to stay on the ship.

I went back to the main hall to find Mr. Henry. He smiled, "You caused him to get kicked off the ship, didn't you?"

I smirked evilly, "Was it that obvious? Of course, I did. Nobody calls me a wanker without having me retaliate against them. I figured it was better not to beat him up physically but mentally. Anyways, I'm smarter than that fussock was anyway."

Mr. Henry smiled, "Ruby, you are growing into a very well-nurtured and mature young lady. I am extremely proud of you!"

A few moments later, the captain approached me and said, "Thank you for helping me find the culprit. Unfortunately, as you know, he will no longer be sailing with us. However, because of your heroic actions, we grant you the ability to come into the captain's quarters and steer the ship with us if you'd like!"

My eyes widened. Mr. Henry and I went to the quarters, and the captain picked me up and put me on the stool. Then he helped me steer, and I steered until we hit the port of Algeciras, Spain. It was mightily surreal! Then the captain pulled out the sounding cone and announced to the ship, "We will be leaving the port in approximately two days. You may leave the ship if you wish, but remember, if you do not return by 9:00 am in 48 hours, we will leave without you."

CHAPTER TWENTY

The Twyndyllyngs of Algeciras, Spain

Shortly after the announcement, many people decided to leave the ship. "Mr. Henry, may we please explore Spain as well? I promise Coco and I'll stay near you since We've never been here."

Mr. Henry continued to smile, "Well, of course!"

He set his stopwatch for exactly forty-five hours and thirty-seven minutes to be sure we would be on the ship in time, considering we had about forty-eight hours until we had to be aboard the boat again.

When we exited the ship, it was a wonderfully beautiful place. Mr. Henry explained that Algeciras was one of the earliest remains that had belonged to the Neanderthal populations in the Paleolithic era. It was pretty interesting. Walking out of the port, we saw thousands of palm trees and beautiful buildings that could be passed as sculptures. The first place Mr. Henry took me to was the Aqueduct of Algeciras. It looked like a bridge that trains could go over. Well, it was an aqueduct, so that made sense, but still, it was a fantastic site to see. "Mr. Henry, I feel like I've seen this place before, even though I know I've never been here."

He laughed a little and then replied, "Well, Ruby, that is probably because this is one of the most common paintings in the world."

After exploring the area, it was lunchtime, and Mr. Henry decided to take me into the city. We went to this lovely little shop, but the workers didn't speak much English, which is alright because I speak Spanish fluently. Even though they had a slightly different dialect of Spanish called Andalusian, it was fascinating and easy to pick up.

The man who came over to be our waiter had a large bow tie and a nice-looking suit. He asked us in broken English, "Good afternoon, my name is Martin, and I will serve you today."

I turned towards Mr. Henry and decided to speak in Andalusian for the remainder of our time here: "It is incredibly nice to meet you, Mr. Martin. I'm Ruby, and this is my father, Henry. What do you recommend is a good option?"

He had a shocked look because I could speak so well. "I am very sorry. I assumed you couldn't speak Andalusian;

you seem like you're British, and most British people I have met can't or don't want to learn."

I faced Mr. Henry as I tapped on the table, and then Mr. Henry continued, "Well, we are in your country, so it is only right that we learn your language. Now, may you please answer my daughter's question?"

Martin smiled, "Why yes, of course, we have a special. It is a fresh tuna filet seared in scorching olive oil and served with chips. I strongly recommend it."

My eyes widened! That genuinely sounds delicious. So, we ordered two of those and the server left.

While waiting, I noticed these three boys chasing some type of creature down the street. They were yelling their heads off and cursing at the poor animal. "Mr. Henry, look! Can I please go find out what they are doing? I have to help the poor creature."

Mr. Henry chuckled, "Ruby, we are in a foreign country. I don't know if letting you go off on your own is such a good idea."

"Please! What if they hurt the animal," my eyes widened, and my shoulders stiffened, "or worse, they kill it!"

Mr. Henry sighed, "Okay. You may go, but please return here before the food arrives."

My face lit up, "Of course.

I pushed the seat back as it scratched the floor so I could leave. I convinced Coco to stay with Mr. Henry, just in case the creature would want to hurt her. Once I was out of the chair's grasp, I ran as quickly as possible after the stupid boys. I ran about a block before I found them hovering over the poor raggedy-looking creature. It was a brown and white dog. They had tied things to its paws, and it was clearly tangled. There were these two girls who stood next to it.

Both girls looked about the same age, probably twyndyllyngs or good friends. Their facial structure was similar, but their eye and hair colors differed. One was blonde with blue eyes, which was unusual as everyone I had seen here had dark hair and eyes. The other had brunette hair with blue eyes. They both had similar facial features and body types, which were slim. I recognized them from the restaurant. They probably followed after seeing the commotion as well.

"Leave him alone! What did the poor dog ever do to you?" I shouted in Andalusian.

The boys dropped the creature on its side as it slowly managed to crawl behind the garbage bin. Then, they surrounded me. "Or what? Who are you anyway? Is this stupid dog yours?"

I paused for a moment, "Yes. As a matter of fact, it is mine!" I didn't take my eyes off them, even though they towered over me.

"Well, since it is yours, I guess you are a piece of trash just like this stupid dog is."

I managed to give a hard punch to the biggest boy's right eye, causing him to fall over and me to grasp my hand and shake it from the pain that comes with the pack of a punch.

I held my fists out and let them know I was willing to fight the others, but they backed up. After a few minutes, the boy with the black eye ran at me and picked me up, and I fought. "Put me down, you filthy, vazey scoundrel!"

He ignored me as I tried to kick and scream in his arms. The other girls who were standing there looked fearful but ultimately chose to stand by my side. "Put her down, Ramon! She didn't do anything." The merely taller one announced.

He smiled and said, "Okay!" As he reached the dirtiest trash bin filled with fish skulls and dropped me in it. The girls looked at him disgusted as the barbarian boy continued, "What, you said drop her." Then he turned towards me, "You belong with the trash, as does this stupid dog." They shouted as they ran off, screaming in hysteria.

I gagged, and the other girls helped me get out as fast as I could, "Are you okay?"

I wiped the fish guts out of my hair, "Yes. I'm fine now. Let's help this poor dog."

The girls managed to get the dog's trust and helped clean him up. The one who was a little shorter said, "Sorry about him. That was Ramon. He is in our class. He is a bully."

The merely taller one agreed, "Nobody has ever stood up to him like that before. How did you do it?"

"Well, I don't like bullies," I continued, untying the knots of the garbage that were tied to the dog.

The other girls laughed, "Neither do we! We should probably head back to the restaurant now. Don't you think?"

I agreed, "Shoo! Shoo, dog. You should be okay now."

When we returned to the restaurant, we realized the dog had followed us the entire way. I returned to Mr. Henry's table as they went back to theirs. The dog approached, and Mr. Henry laughed a little. "Who is this? I see you made a friend, Ruby."

"This was the creature that was being chased. Can we keep him?"

Mr. Henry shook his head, "I'm sorry, kid, but we can't take a stray back into America. It is illegal."

I sighed, and after the meal ended, the girls approached me with their parents.

When they arrived, they saw Coco and asked, "Is the monkey in a cute little outfit real?"

Honestly, I would have wondered the same thing if I hadn't known Coco my entire life. Coco jumped on my arm, and I screeched, "Yes, she is. Her name is Coconut, but I call her Coco for short. She is my little partner in crime. I don't think we actually introduced ourselves yet. I'm Ruby, by the way, Ruby Ledger. Who are you?"

They smiled, and the blonde expressed, "I'm Zeva, and this is my sister Miranda. We are the Phluberg sisters. We aren't natives of the city. We were born in Greece but moved here when we were small."

I stared at them, "Zeva, your name is quite interesting. What does it mean?"

She faced me and mentioned, "It means sword in Greek because when I was in my mother's womb, I supposedly kicked her a lot. Now, in real life, I enjoy excavating. It's tremendously fun!"

I stated, "Um, not trying to be rude, but don't you mean brawling?"

She started laughing at me. "Brawling, that's a funny word. You're a funny girl and very interesting. You know so many big words for being so small."

I had a questionable look, "Anyone can use big words. It doesn't matter how big or small you are."

Miranda chimed in, "Really, but how? How does that work?"

Wow, they were pretty vazey, but that was alright. They seemed fun. "Well, I read a lot, and you just learn and speak the words, just like I am now with these simple ones. Some other words that are synonyms include fight, altercation, clash, confrontation, brawl, riot, feud, conflict, melee, rivalry, and many more."

Miranda asked, "What's cinnamon? Do you mean like the spice?"

I chuckled a little, "No, not cinnamon, synonym. It means a similar but different word with the same or at least similar meaning to the original word you used."

A few seconds later, Mr. Henry called me to eat, but before I left, the girls screamed, "Wait, you should hang out with us later!"

I veered my head towards Mr. Henry and asked, "May I please go? I will be conscientious and be sure to meet you back here tonight, and then we can spend all of tomorrow together?"

I couldn't tell if he was a little disappointed that I didn't want to spend time with him, but he smiled, "Yes, of course, you may go," he turned towards the parents if it was alright with you."

Mr. Henry scanned the parents. They seemed to have known each other from the past. It was highly odd. It felt like he knew everybody everywhere we went. It was wild. "Mr. Henry, how do you know these people? It seems like you know everyone."

The Phlubergs responded, "Well, when we were little, your father came to Greece to visit. While there, he met us, and we have never forgotten him. He was the smartest, bravest, and toughest man out there. So, it doesn't surprise me that he has such a remarkable, smart, and beautiful little girl as yourself. It is a pleasure to meet you, Ruby! We happily invite both of you to our humble home."

"Mr. Henry, can we please go? This way, you can reconnect with them, and I can get to know the twins. Please!"

Of course, Mr. Henry agreed. So, we left a lot of money on the table and headed out. The dog still followed us for the fifteen-minute walk to their house; it was lovely. It was near the ocean, and you could see dolphins flipping their fins at many exotic birds and me. This felt like one of those dreams people have about a dream country that they never really get to go to in their lifetime, but instead, it's reality. I never thought I wanted to go to Spain because I needed to learn more about it, so being here, I can learn a lot! I've always believed that visiting a place is only when you truly learn about its culture and history. Otherwise, it's just a figment of imagination like a unicorn. You know they exist, but you've never actually seen one in reality before.

When we arrived at their home, it was enormous. Miranda asked, "Mom, can we please keep this dog since Ruby can't?"

The twyndyllyngs parents were named Iris and Atticus. "I'm not sure yet. Let us talk about it, okay?"

The twyndyllyngs shrugged. The parents were in the architecture business and built houses for people who couldn't. "We even let the buyer choose the price based on what they could afford, and sometimes we will give a home for free. We want to ensure everyone wasn't homeless and that it was okay to ask for help to get a better life that they would enjoy."

I appreciated that they did this. After all, statistically, 12% of children are homeless, leading to adulthood in which they couldn't get out of being homeless because these people weren't educated and couldn't afford one.

I never really thought of it like that until now. Fortunately for my family, my parents were incredibly wealthy; therefore, we could afford everything. That's one of the reasons why I'm very educated. Well, also because of Mr. Henry. I have always taken him for granted, but I am a privileged child. Even with my privileges, though, I still have had difficulties. The first lesson I took away from meeting these people is that you don't know everyone's story, and you can't assume it.

When we entered their home, I went to the twyndyllyngs' room while Mr. Henry stayed with the parents. Mr. Henry asked them, "How have you been over the years? I see you have built a nice life for yourselves, and I am very happy for you!"

Iris was the first to respond, "Well, after you left Greece twenty years ago, you made us realize the important things in life. As you might remember, we were careless and didn't care about the people around us. We wanted everything for ourselves, and you taught us the true meaning of value and what is important to us. We decided to stay in Greece for a few more years until we had twins twelve years ago. We dedicated our lives to teaching them the importance of selflessness, and it's all in gratitude to you. I can see that you do the same with your daughter, Ruby. She is an incredibly precious child. You are fortunate to have a daughter as intelligent as she is. So, how have you been? What was your experience like with your partners in crime?"

Mr. Henry smiled at them, "Well, I would first like to say that I am very proud to have Ruby as my daughter. But my experience over the years has been difficult. I got married and divorced twice. Ruby's mother ended up becoming my second wife. Shortly after we married, Ruby was born. She was unexpected, as my ex-wife Millie had a cryptic pregnancy. We didn't learn she was with the child until about six months later. At first, I didn't know what to expect, but I have always wanted a daughter, and the day she was born was the happiest day of my life. I also have a son with my first ex-wife. He isn't quite like Ruby, though. Even though I love him deeply, it is a different relationship. So, my life has had its ups and downs, but overall, I am happy with how it turned out."

While they were conversing, Miranda, Zeva, and I went to their room. It was lovely! When I entered the room, it was colored pink, with portraits on the wall, a nice little painting area in the right corner, and quite a few books. "Do you guys ever read any of your books?"

Zeva laughed and stated, "No, not really. I wouldn't say I like to read. I paint for fun or play outside. Reading is boring to me."

I gave her a dirty look but didn't make it too obvious. No wonder she wasn't that bright, but she was fun, and that's what mattered. Attached to their room was a balcony. We walked outside, and it was hovering over the land; it was magnificent and magical. It reminded me of what it was like to imagine what Atlantis would be. Many colors, white buildings, and the sea. It felt very calm and relaxing to live there. "Miranda, do you like living here or prefer it in Greece?"

She quickly responded, "I love it here, and this is my home. We sometimes visit Greece, but not often, as it's expensive, and our father can't get away from work."

That was the second lesson I learned from them. You can't travel whenever you want because it's expensive. "You know reading is fascinating! It's like stepping into a fairytale or an adventure. It's kind of like a vacation in your head. I love to read! It also encourages my thinking about the world and learning about what's in it. I read all the time; it's how I'm astonishingly knowledgeable. I also have my dad, who teaches me a lot! It's why I speak mightily well for my age. Reading also helps me discover the types of spies there are. Have either of you ever met a spy or wanted to go on a mission?"

They gave me a funny look and then laughed. "Girls can't be spies. Only boys can."

I wasn't too surprised they said that, but it was disappointing. "Yes, they can. I go on missions all the time. Here, why don't I try to take you on one? Is there anything you have always wondered about but can't figure out?"

Zeva replied, "Well, there is always the mystery of the plants that grow here."

Trying to get it out of them would be more complicated than I thought. "No, that's not a mystery. That's just science. I'm talking about things that might have been stolen or lost or anything like that."

I noticed Miranda was a little more intelligent than Zeva. Then Miranda continued, "Well, at night, the townspeople tell us we are required to stay inside our houses as something dangerous always lurks in the shadows."

Now, that's what I'm talking about! "That's perfect, so why not tonight? We stay up and wait for this dangerous shadow."

Zeva and Miranda looked a little nervous, "Um, I don't know how comfortable I am with that. What if we die?"

Coco and I chuckled, "I promise you won't die. Let's not be dramatic. Tell me more about this mysterious creature."

We all sat down, and Zeva continued, "It's called 'Lo Bueno de la luz versus lo malo de la oscuridad,' meaning *the good of light versus the evil of dark. It's the story of this little girl named Luciana, who reminds me of you. She was different; she was a god; she had violet eyes like you, brunette hair, and always wore this gold bracelet. Her family's kingdom had a huge celebration when she was first born.*

Now, the kingdom was split into two: the good side of light and the evil side of darkness. The family was a part of the light side. The little girl had special gifts; she could speak to animals like you and Coco and make anything shine bright, be healed, and be happy. The problem was she was very curious and wanted to explore the world around her.

One night, she got a little message through her window telling her to follow the golden flowers on the road. So, she did. When she arrived at her destination, it was in front of the gates of the evil of the dark. She was supposedly kidnapped by this creature, a monster with glowing eyes, sharp teeth, and big claws.

She fought for her life, and the next morning, when her parents went to find her, all they found was the bracelet that their daughter wore. It is rumored that if a townsperson leaves their home at night, this creature will come, find, and kill them. Luciana's parents set this curse to ensure that nobody ever has to die again."

That was a nice story, but it couldn't be true. I wanted to learn the real reason, "Tonight, we will go out and discover what truly happens at night. Did your parents tell you that story?"

They were still nervous, "Um… yes, they did. All the children who live here know the story. That's why if you look out the window to your left, you can see the town of more darkness. Supposedly, we are in the town of light, and I don't know if I want to mess with the gods."

I shook my head, "We will be fine, I promise; just follow me, and you won't die. You have to trust me."

They took a deep breath, stared at each other, and in unison, mumbled, "Okay…"

When we went to the kitchen, the family offered for us to stay the night, and we accepted. After nightfall had awoken and the adults were asleep, we decided to go. The dog, of course, followed us. We snuck out and went into the city. It was tranquil, dark, and gloomy. Then we heard a loud banging sound. It was the clock tower; it had struck midnight, and suddenly, the streets started to fill with a "dark" presence, but not townspeople. There were a few strangers.

One of them walked up to us and had an evil-like laugh. It was creepy, but it was okay. The dog began to bark as a pedestrian said, "Hello, children. What are you doing out at this time? You are supposed to be in your beds."

I rolled my eyes, "We wanted to go on a midnight walk."

The lady grinned, "A midnight walk? Haven't you heard of the story of Lo Bueno de la luz versus lo malo de la oscuridad?"

I sighed, "Yes, and I know it isn't true, so what is going on out here? Why don't they want children outside?"

A few seconds after I asked, I heard howling. Of course, wolves. That would explain the glowing eyes, teeth, claws, and fur!

The lady then grabbed us and took us into her home. The dog guarded us and kept its eye on us at all times as the kind lady exclaimed, "Children, you're not supposed to be out here because it's too dangerous. At night, all of the nocturnal creatures fill the streets. I need you all to go home and go to bed."

"Why are you out here then?" I hummed.

She squished her nose, "IT is safer for adults because we know how to deal with dangerous creatures. They usually only bother smaller creatures, but children panic, freeze, and then die."

I rolled my eyes and pretended to listen. However, I wanted to help, so when we returned to the Phluberg's house, I opened my little case of "medicine," took out the little pills, crushed them, mixed them, and added some water. Each capsule contains phenothiazines, thioxanthenes, butyrophenones, clozapine, and rauwolfia alkaloids.

Then, I injected my unique mixture into the pen dart gun I had created on the ship before I left. You might be wondering why I brought these with me. It is because I know they block the neurotransmitter known as dopamine from going into the brain. Its purpose is to knock someone or something out just in case someone tried to mess with me. After all, I'm small. I mean, you never know what might happen.

I snuck out again, but this time alone. Some people were trying to capture these animals, so I walked up to one and handed them the darts I had created. At first, they were skeptical, but as they eyed me down, they realized I resembled Luciana, so they used them. Then I went back to the Phlubergs' home and went to sleep.

The following morning, when I awoke, we went to the town's square. The townspeople revealed, "Our problem of the dangerous creatures that lurk and kill in the night has been destroyed. The real Luciana has returned and helped us solve the problems. She is our hero!" Then they pointed to me.

Mr. Henry sighed and shook his head back and forth, "You gave them one of your sleeping darts, didn't you."

I smirked, "How could I not? They told me this odd story about a girl, and I just wanted to help."

Mr. Henry sighed, "Alright, Ruby, We came here to clear your head, not fight off some mythical folklore. Ruby, I need you to stop going on these crazy missions alone, especially without me, because you could have died. I am only saying this to you to protect and keep you safe. You are my daughter, and I don't know what I would do if I lost you. So, this is what we will do; we will head back to the ship now and not turn back, do you understand?"

That wasn't fair! All I did was try to help. This was lesson number three: no good deed goes unpunished. "Fine, let's go!"

Before I left, I heard the parents say, "You may keep the dog since it helped keep you safe last night."

The sisters jumped up and down, "It needs a name, doesn't it?" Zeva exclaimed.

Miranda said, "How about we name it Bravo after the bravery that Ruby taught us."

I smiled and hugged them before I said my final good-byes, "Don't worry, I'll be back one day!"

They smiled.

As we were leaving, the town leader tried to stop us and shower us with gifts because I was apparently Luciana. We respectfully declined them and tried to return to the boat, but they forced me to take the all-mighty, sacred bracelet that was once Luciana's thousands of years ago. I graciously accepted it, and then we went back on the ship. Unfortunately, Mr. Henry is forcing me to stay on the boat until we depart tomorrow.

After dinner, Mr. Henry told me, "Your bracelet is beautiful. But, Ruby, why didn't you believe that story? Most children would have."

I laughed hysterically until I realized he wasn't joking. "Well, Mr. Henry, I knew it was just a story. It wasn't real and couldn't have happened. It's a theoretical folklore, and I wanted to help. So, I did, and I got this fascinating and beautiful free bracelet. Also, it helped me think about who I truly wanted to live with. I've decided I want to go back to America because, in my story, my biological mom is the wolf. After all, she was never there.

How could I pick her if my mother at home raised me? Even though I don't particularly like being around her, she has always been there for me: when I was sick, when I was upset, when I couldn't do my hair, which I technically still can't do on my own, but that's not the point.

The point is, she has always been there for me, and even though she wasn't always the nicest person to me, which is a bit of an understatement of the century, she is my mom, and I couldn't replace her." He nodded and smiled, knowing I had made a good decision. The following morning, we departed for Boston at 9:00 AM sharp.

CHAPTER TWENTY-ONE

My Way Back Home

A little over two and a half weeks later, we finally arrived in Boston. It was a very long and tiring journey, but it was gorgeous. When we arrived, I first wanted to go to Mr. Morrison's ice cream shop. Mr. Morrison was a lovely man who loved hearing the stories I would tell. Sometimes, to preoccupy myself with something to do at home, I would create stories about many different beasts and fairy tales, which was lovely!

When we arrived, two giraffe-sized men in black were robbing his store. I rolled my eyes and slowly crept inside. I instructed Coco to get the police while I hid to think of a plan. I overheard Mr. Morrison exclaim, "You can take all the money you want. Just please don't hurt me!"

They chuckled, "Please, how could we not? You support that revolting Lincoln guy. How could we not hurt you if you not only supported him but probably paid him as well? I'm sorry, Mr. Morrison, but your time has come to an end–"

I began to breathe heavily as I could feel the fear emanating from Mr. Morrison, "STOP! You can't hurt him!"

One of the masked man's guns shot to the left because he was distracted and smashed Mr. Morrison's prized glass ice cream cups that were on the delicate see-through shelf. My hands raced to my ears to cover them from the sound.

"Ruby, run!" Mr. Morrison kept exclaiming over and over again.

Then, the bigger one turned his gun towards me. "Get over here, you little twirp."

I grabbed two marshmallows that had crashed to the ground and put them at the edge of my ears as cushions to prevent my hearing from dying.

As I got closer, they picked me up and put me on the counter right next to Mr. Morrison. "You know, if you wanted to shoot us, you should probably hold that gun properly because right now, you are not only going to knock yourselves in the head, but you will shoot your foot."

The bigger masked man scoffed, "Please, kid. You don't know what you are talking about."

I gulped, "Okay, then try your shot."

I breathed a little heavier and tried to think about not dying today. "Go on, shoot it if you don't believe me."

He took it up on the offer, and the second the gun went off at the same time as I rolled behind the counter to hide unharmed. The smaller one yelled, "You just shot a kid! That wasn't the plan, you vazey idiot!"

Luckily, he didn't know he didn't shoot me. I just needed to distract him enough. The small robber continued to yell at the bigger guy as they placed the guns on the counter, thinking they killed us. I slithered quietly around with lace and tied their boots together with licorice and wire from my little tool kit. By the time they stopped fighting, their laces were tied, as were their legs. Then, I grabbed their guns with a towel and crawled to the front of the door.

When I was ready, I shouted, "Missing something?"

Their eyes widened so fast they still didn't realize their legs were tied together, so they tried to run. They both face-planted into the hard floor and were stuck there like bugs on their backs.

After a few minutes, the police showed up. Luckily, Coco found the policeman, Mr. Dunky, who didn't fear Coco because he was deaf and spoke sign language to communicate; he recognized her as mine.

Mr. Dunky, a medium-sized, dark-haired man, stood in front of the doorway, took the guns from my hands, and then placed them in his car away from the robbers' reach. Then came back inside to take the robber to prison.

I ran to grab a broom to help Mr. Morrison, but he shoved it away. "Thank you, Ruby, but you risked your life today. I hope you know never to do that again."

I smiled, "It was worth it. I knew I was going to be fine anyway," I said as I removed the marshmallows from my ears.

He laughed a little, "Smart. Using them as protection."

I shrugged, and then saw the icy blonde hair and hazel eyed man with a large smile that stretched from ear to ear, he excitedly exclaimed, "Oh my, you are truly the little fearless Ruby? You know, kid, I've waited for you to come through my door for three months, but you never appeared. Why is that? Did you go on a little mission?"

I laughed, "No, I didn't go on a mission. I did something better. I learned more about my ancestry. This part of my family is British, and they live in London, Great Britain. I have visited there for the past three months. Also, I am happy to say I have a new story for you."

He smiled, "Is that so? Well, why don't you sit up here and tell me!"

He picked me up, put me on the only table that wasn't covered in glass like it was a stage, and asked, "What is it about?"

I smiled, "Before the first humans were documented, there was a group of magical beings known as the Elementum Tribe. These people had the ability to control the four elements. Unfortunately, they went "extinct" due to an asteroid. Flash forward to the present day, a little girl named Violet with the markings of the tribe is born. Since she is the most powerful person on the planet due to the Elementum genetic mutation, the government kidnaps her due to fear. Their goal is to raise her to become a super soldier. She must fight for her freedom and find a way to escape. So, what do you think? Would you like to hear it?"

Mr. Morrison smiled instantly, "Of course!"

"Once upon a time, many years from now, there was this little girl. Her name was Violet Hailstone, and she was the last remaining living member of the Elementum tribe. Now, this element of the tribe was always talked about in myths, and many people didn't know if it truly existed.

Only a few people knew of her existence, one of whom kidnapped her as a mere infant to be experimented on, and her "father," Victor Hailstone. The one who kidnapped her wanted to use her abilities for himself. To unlock most people of this tribe, she was the most powerful because she had all four elements: earth, air, water, and fire. The person who raised her always told her the outside world was too dangerous and she must never leave her cabin, but one day, she decided to. It was her time to explore the outside world.

So, she escapes when her supposed father goes to sleep. When she makes an alarm sound, the father wakes up immediately to get her back. He pulls her back into the laboratory. What she doesn't know is the true reason why she is here. Shortly after this alarm goes off, her biological father sees her in this box with moving pictures. Because of this, he goes to the laboratory and finds her.

At first, she doesn't trust him but soon realizes she is trapped in prison and uses all her strength to escape. The father finally takes her back to her family, and she is raised to be a hero who goes out and fights for justice! I could tell you the full story, but that is not the point. Now, Mr. Morrison, why do you think I am telling you this story?"

He was excited, "What? Ruby, where is the full story? You always tell the best stories while you're here. I just don't understand why you told this one since, typically, you tell a story about mythical creatures versus these abilities?"

I glanced at him, "No, the reason I told you this story is because of the meaning behind it. Over the past summer, I've learned you can't always trust people because they aren't always who they say they are. People will try to use you for your special talents. The most important people to trust and listen to are those who truly care about you, such as your family or friends. You can't trust everyone because someone pretending to be your friend or family might stab you in the back."

He was shocked that I had said that, but it was true. Before leaving, I told him, "I'm sorry, Mr. Morrison, but this may be the last time I will see you for a very long time. I am returning to school in two weeks, and I wanted to wish you a formal goodbye." So, I hugged him, and before

I left, he handed me a flavor of ice cream I had never tasted before. My eyes lit up so much; it was the best flavor in the world, "Mr. Morrison, what is this?"

He chuckled, "I was looking for a new flavor to make, and I accidentally heated up sugar the other day as it fell into a revolver. I made this stringy-like candy, and I put it in this ice cream. Do you like it?"

"Yes! I love it! Wait, what is the candy? Can I try that, too?"

He chuckled a little, then went to his closet when his wife appeared, "Hello, Mrs. Morrison, how do you do?"

She smiled with a very small baby in her arms as I noticed a small child. "You had a baby?"

She chuckled, "Yes, he is only a few weeks old. We were in Nashville when he came, but we returned a while ago. I'm surprised you didn't show up at all this summer. You love it here, and we love your stories!"

Coco jumped onto my shoulder, "I told Mr. Morrison one recently, but congratulations. I'm sorry about your shop."

She laughed again as Mr. Morrison said, "It is alright, Ruby, we will fix it. Thank you for your bravery. What you did was very dangerous, but I appreciate it!"

"I am dangerous, too. I will always be here to protect people." I exclaimed as Mr. Morrison approached me with a little bundle of whitish string candy. It was delicious. "We flavored it with vanilla, Ruby."

A smile beamed across my face, "I can tell; it is the most scrumptious candy I have ever tasted! What is your baby's name?"

"William."

I nodded, "My best friend has that name. I like it!"

They both thanked me, "Have a lovely rest of your summer and good luck in school! We look forward to hearing how it goes!"

"Thank you!" I replied hastily as I grabbed Coco and my ice cream and headed home.

A reason why I went there and spent so long there was that I didn't want to see my family immediately. But I knew I had to. I wouldn't say I like to procrastinate, but I sometimes do if it's family-related. When I arrived home and rang the door, Mother went to open it. She looked down at me, grabbed me, and bear-hugged me to the point where I couldn't breathe. "Ruby, you chose to come back, but why would you do that?"

A small part of me still asked that question, but that was alright. "I came back because I realized that no matter how different you treat me from Clara and Charles, you were always the person who raised me, and my biological mother wasn't. I wish she did, but I got you instead. It made me realize that you are my family," then whispered to myself, "even though I have shed countless tears here."

A small tear ran down her face from excitement; I rarely saw her this way. Then she turned towards Mr. Henry and smiled, "Thank you for returning her to me. As always, you're welcome anytime!"

He smiled and kissed me on the head. I didn't want him to leave, but I knew he couldn't stay. Mother took me to the kitchen, where Clara and Charles ate breakfast. "Hello, chumps. How was your summer?" I cheerfully asked.

Clara stared at me with absolute disgust. "You're back. Wow, I thought you were gone forever. That's horrible. Where did you even go anyways?"

I wondered why Mother and Father didn't tell them where I went. I rolled my eyes, "I'm delighted you missed me, Clara. I went to Great Britain, and it was lovely. I even got to see a little bit of Algeciras, Spain."

Their mouths dropped open, "Wait, you got to go to the country of Europe? That's not fair! Mother, why does she get to go to Europe?"

Clearly, there is such a huge difference in our intellectual abilities, but that is okay. I didn't want to yell at her or say much because I'd like to think I'd grown a little. "I'm surprised you knew where Great Britain was, but Europe isn't a country. It's a continent."

She didn't believe me but was also one of those flat-earthers. She fears water because she thinks she will fall off the earth if she goes far enough. Isn't that hilarious?

Mother stared at me and stated, "Now, Ruby, play nice."

I shrugged. How was I not playing nice? I didn't want to apologize because I was in the right, but Mother kept pushing me to. "Fine, I'm sorry; I didn't mean to insult your geographical knowledge."

She smiled, then sneered at me, "You just apologized?"

"Indeed. I have the ability to recognize when I am wrong." I rebutted as I lifted my eyebrows.

She shook her head, "Why did you get to go to Europe and we didn't?"

She was awfully irritating! I always had to dumb everything down for her. For example, I didn't want to tell her I was adopted because Mother told me not to, to which I agreed. "I got to go to Europe because Mr. Henry invited me on one of his intellectual trips. He was teaching me about the history and science of the world by showing me around Great Britain, and we figured you didn't want to do that."

She responded with a disgusted look, "Oh, you're right. That is boring, as all history is. No, thank you!"

Once again, I stared into her eyes like I was eating out her soul. "History isn't boring if you are taught it correctly. If you like hearing stories, then you must like learning about history because that's all it is, so don't be daft."

At this point, I decided to leave. Before I could do so, Mother handed me a letter from Lulu. She had come to drop it off a few days prior. I was sad that I didn't see her, but I was excited to open it because even though she needed to regain my trust, she was still a friend of mine who I hadn't seen in about three months.

I ran to my room and climbed on my bed. On the front, it said my name, and when I opened it, there were water stains. I wondered why. Then I read:

Dear Ruby,

Before I begin, how are you? How was your summer? Last year was such a fantastic year, and you have been such an amazing friend to me, especially after everything that happened! I'm sorry about trying to betray you. However, it did work out very well in the end.

I am writing this letter to you today because I will not attend Miss Holmes' Academy next year. Now, I know you may be saddened, as am I, which is why there are teardrops on the letter. I wish I could be there, but my parents say they don't want me at that school anymore because they don't want me to be around you. They think you are too dangerous to be around, considering we were at the place of what could have been a major assassination. Additionally, since you are in an agency opposing ours, they are nervous that you are a bad influence. I know I still have to work on regaining your trust, Ruby, but I will try to write to you very often. I hope you find new friends next year, but you also have Willie. I wish it could be different.

Love your best friend,

Lulu Hughes

I started to cry. I wanted to see her next year. After she explained everything to me, I wish I could fully trust her. I forgive her for protecting her family, but she lied, which could have cost Mr. Lincoln his life. On the other hand, she was the first person I connected with. What if I get a lousy roommate like the Acker sisters next year? I wish it were different, but there wasn't anything I could do. Coco comforted me, "Don't worry, Ruby, maybe you can visit or write to her."

My eyes were filled with tears, "Coco, if her parents went as far as to take her out of the Academy to not be around me anymore, then I'm certain they don't want me to be around her outside of school. Thanks for the idea, though." I paused for a short period, "Coco, do you think that I made the right decision in not fully trusting or forgiving her?"

Coco held her head low, "I don't know, but she could have created some serious casualties. You should trust everyone you meet the second you think they are nice because, just like Lulu did, she stabbed you in the back. You have to be careful around the people you meet. As my previous feelings revealed, I knew she wasn't someone to trust. Ruby, as long as you have me, I will always be there to protect you, so maybe still not being able to trust her is the best thing right now. I'm sorry it didn't end the way you wanted it to with her, but you will make other friends, and besides, you still have me and Willie."

I smiled but continued to tear up for about thirty minutes in my room before deciding to get fresh air. I tried to hide my tears so nobody would ask if I was alright if I passed anyone in the hall.

As I passed my father's office, he saw me and stopped me. He called me inside and asked, "How was Great Britain? I'm glad you decided to come back to us."

My head veered towards the ground so he wouldn't be able to tell I was crying. "Um.. it was good, I guess."

He smiled, "Oh, that reminds me, your special organization you joined wants you for a meeting later tonight. I don't know where to go, but Adena will take you."

I smiled and went outside. I climbed into a tree and sat there for a few hours until lunch was ready. Then, Adena came out, "There you are. I figured you'd be back here. Your parents have been looking everywhere for you."

I looked down at her, "Why did you figure I'd be back here?"

She grinned, "Well, I would be out here with the breeze of fresh air if I found out my best friend wasn't allowed to be around me anymore, as well."

I had a questionable look, "How did you know that, Adena?"

As I climbed down the tree, she took the letter from under her dress, "I found this on your bed. I'm very sorry, Ruby, but I promise you will make new friends next year. Don't think too hard about it. I always believe things happen for a reason, even if you don't know it now." Then she hugged me and directed me inside to get lunch before we left.

When lunch was over, we headed to the horse carriages and rode into the heart of Boston. The largest HIA headquarters in America was located in Boston. When we arrived, they were about four times the size of the place I stayed in Chicago. It was built similarly, though, so it wasn't much of a surprise. The only difference other than size was the name. This one was known as the Hexing International Auberge, while the other one was different. It was probably a chain for the HIA since the initials were "HIA."

The entrance to the HIA is behind the front desk, with a rotating bookshelf, and upstairs to the headquarters. The outside and upstairs were supposed to be hotels, and when you fully entered, as long as you had your unique key, you could enter the heart of the base.

We headed downstairs and straight to the head agent's office when we arrived. His name was Jeffrey Skabara. He started as a brilliant scientist, but halfway through his work, he found pleasure and peace in joining the HIA. Although he is still at the HIA, he does critical research daily. He is a drug discoverer who tries to find cures for all the dreadful diseases we have, such as enteric fever, pneumonia, and Roman fever. It's pretty exciting but revolting because he has to work with the deadly diseases daily.

When we entered the room, five other agents joined us. Before we began, one of the other agents approached me and asked, "Aww, sweetie, are you lost? Do your parents work here?"

I just stared at her while the other agents laughed. One even had the decency to put her in her place, "No, Matilda, that is Ruby Ledger. She is Jones' kid and is the youngest member here. Don't you remember? She will be one of the best spies because no one would ever suspect an adorable little girl to have power. Also, it was inevitable that she would join, considering her parents are legends."

She had a blank look on her face and apologized. Then we began the meeting.

We started by discussing the election results as Abraham Lincoln was elected president of this upcoming election. Then, we began discussing harsher topics, such as slavery. This was a significant concern for many at the company. The North was against slavery and wanted to abolish it immediately, while the South had other ideas. I was delighted that I lived in the North. I believe slavery is horrific, and nobody should be considered enslaved.

If people work, then they should be fairly compensated. It's the only right thing to do. This was an escalating problem in America because the government wanted nothing to do with it. They didn't seem to try to make a compromise between both parts of the country and were worried it would end in battle.

If I'm being candid, I don't want there to be a battle here. It is just not worth it. Mainly because America has a scarcity of resources. However, I want a compromise because slavery is one of the worst forms of punishment. We must have discussed this complex topic for about an hour before concluding with the mission assignments. People were split into groups except for me. I was the first to be given an assignment. Mr. Skabara told me, "Ruby, you are up first since you are our newest recruit. You will return to Miss Holmes Academy this fall, am I correct?"

I nodded and answered, "Yes, in less than two weeks."

He smiled and continued, "Well, Ruby, this coming school year in the Spring, I want you to go to the South. Please go to the state known as South Carolina because this state has one of the enslaved populations. While there, you will go to Fort Sumter in Charleston to explore and gather as much information about them as possible. We are worried they are going to be the cause of the war.

But, first, during your fall break, you will go and meet with a man named George S. James. I caution you as he is not a nice man, but he is very reputable as a lawyer. Don't let him fool you. You will go to his office and tell him you are interested in his field of law and are a huge supporter of him. Then, we will send one of our agents with you to pretend to be your father from the army and that you are an army child. We have already informed Miss Holmes about this. Ruby, when you are there, you must write in a journal to document as much as you can about your surroundings. Do you understand?"

I stared at him and replied, "Yes, I won't disappoint you."

As for the rest of you, men, you will go straight to Fort Sumter and become soldiers of the United States Army. You will train with them, and just like Ruby, you will gather as much information as possible. Now, Ladies, unfortunately, I don't quite have a mission for you yet, but I just needed you to be aware. The meeting is now adjourned."

Before we left back home, Mr. Skabara gave me a unique journal. It was engraved with a little blue, purple, and silver rose with many plants on corners surrounding the center; the only way to open it was once again by my key. This was to be used for my future missions. When I opened it, there was a secret code in it. I closed it so that I could reopen it later for memorization.

On the way out, as we were walking, I looked up at Adena as she squealed, "I am so proud of you! Are you excited about your first official HIA mission?"

I was ecstatic! "Of course, but I feel bad for the other woman since they can't do anything."

Adena stopped me and got down to my level, "Ruby, while there are many missions for the woman, they are the more subtle and secretive ones. Sometimes, women must not go on our missions to help keep anyone from accusing us of suspicion. The only reason you are going is that you are a child genius, and even if George S. James knew about the HIA, he wouldn't know that we have a child working for us. I'm sorry, Ruby, but that is, unfortunately, how life works."

I was disappointed, but it was the time I was growing up. I hope that in the future, people will respect girls as much as they should be respected. She got off the floor, and we continued walking to the carriages to go home. Over the next two weeks of summer vacation, I had to get all the materials to prepare and pack for this coming school year. I had to get a new uniform, books for Mr. Henry's lessons, makeup tools, culinary arts weapons, sewing materials, new ballet shoes, and many other items. It wasn't until the day before I left that we finished gathering all my school supplies for this year.

Instead of spending the night with my family, I visited Mr. Henry's American house for the first time. It was fascinating. It was similar to the one in London, with a few differences. While this one did have a white structure and a brown roof, its windows were shaped like a semi-circle rectangle, and there were fewer flowers but a large tree to climb in the backyard. The interior was furnished with typical Victorian furniture. What surprised me, though, was that there were multiple paintings of me from over the years. He must have done them when I wasn't paying attention. It was charming because it showed he truly cared about me. His house is two stories, and upstairs, there is an adorable room with dolls, art supplies, MANY gadgets, and a piano. This one was supposedly mine. I loved playing the piano! Creating music always felt especially magical, and I was very good at it, considering music and math are correlated.

Looking back, this past year was quite eventful. If I told myself a year ago what I had accomplished, I would have been overjoyed with happiness. Instead, looking back, I started to tear up a little as I knew my next year was about to begin, and I was looking forward to what significant journeys lay ahead.

I couldn't have gotten to where I am today without my true friends and family. So, I will be forever grateful for what I have, and I hope that even though Lulu isn't here anymore this year, Coco is right: I will make new friends.

This coming school year doesn't start for another two weeks, but I am ready for my first official HIA mission. For all people in the future who may or may not find this journal, this was how I began my detective career, in which I hope one day I will be even better than my biological parents at their jobs—no offense to them, of course. I can't wait to see what happens next year!

About the Author

Children's fiction author Ari Skolnick has a personal connection for her inspiration in writing her debut middle-grade novel, *Ruby Ledger and the Assassination of Abraham Lincoln*, a historical fiction mystery about a science-savvy girl looking to solve a mystery involving the president.

As a mechanical engineer who loves solving complex problems, building, and inventing things, Ari noticed the lack of females in her field. While writing her novel, she wanted to empower young girls, showing them that they can pursue any dream, including roles in the STEAM field, just like her story's protagonist, a burgeoning inventor. It was also a goal for Ari to present history, the Civil War in this case, in an accurate yet entertaining way while sharing the importance of understanding how history affects all of us. She hopes her young readers connect with these tenets and that they stay with them long after the book is closed.

When she isn't writing fascinating detective stories for young readers, Ari enjoys doing culinary arts and photography, designing things on CAD—computer-aided design used to build and invent things—and 3D print them, playing sports, building with LEGOs, and spending time with friends, family, and her pets. *Ruby Ledger and the Assassination of Abraham Lincoln* is her debut installment in the series.

Instagram: @Ari.Skolnick
TikTok: @rubyledger

www.ingramcontent.com/pod-product-compliance
Lightning Source LLC
Chambersburg PA
CBHW071217300726
48975CB00002B/255